NORMAN SPINRAD ON AMERICA:

"By any rational criteria, it's Science Fiction Time in America right now . . . we have seen the future and it is us, I said just a moment ago, but of course we all know that there's no such thing as *the* future at all. There are many multiple futures struggling to be born at any given moment, nowhere more so than in America. Some of them are worthy of our aspiration while others are trying to crawl out from under wet rocks, and in the multiplex American reality none of them exactly precludes any of the others.

"Where does science fiction end and the "real world" begin? Figure it out for yourself if you can. Lotsa luck! But don't expect to come up with a simple answer while you read

★ NORMAN SPINRAD ★

ace books
A Division of Charter Communications Inc.
A GROSSET & DUNLAP COMPANY
360 Park Avenue South
New York, New York 10010

THE STAR-SPANGLED FUTURE

An ACE Book

Cover art by Vincent de Fate

First Ace printing: July 1979

2 4 6 8 0 9 7 5 3 1
Printed in U.S.A.

ACKNOWLEDGEMENTS

"Carcinoma Angels" was first published in *Dangerous Visions*, copyright © 1967 by Harlan Ellison, reprinted in *The Last Hurrah of the Golden Horde*, copyright © 1970 by Norman Spinrad.

"All the Sounds of the Rainbow" was first published in *Vertex*, copyright © 1973 by Mankind Publishing, Inc., reprinted in *No Direction Home*, copyright © 1975 by Norman Spinrad.

"The Last Hurrah of the Golden Horde" was first published in *New Worlds*, copyright © 1969 by *New Worlds*, reprinted in *The Last Hurrah of the Golden Horde*, copyright © 1970 by Norman Spinrad.

"The National Pastime" was first published in *Nova 3*, copyright © 1973 by Harry Harrison, reprinted in *No Direction Home*, copyright © 1975 by Norman Spinrad.

"It's a Bird! It's a Plane" was first published in *Gent*, copyright © 1967 by Dugent Publishing Company, reprinted in *The Last Hurrah of the Golden Horde*, copyright © 1970 by Norman Spinrad.

"The Entropic Gang Bang Caper" was first published in *New Worlds*, copyright © 1969 by *New Worlds*, reprinted in *The Last Hurrah of the Golden Horde*, copyright © 1970 by Norman Spinrad.

"The Big Flash" was first published in *Orbit 5*, copyright © 1969 by Damon Knight, reprinted in *No Direction Home*, copyright © 1975 by Norman Spinrad.

"No Direction Home" was first published in *New Worlds 2*, copyright © 1971 by Michael Moorcock, reprinted in *No Direction Home*, copyright © 1975 by Norman Spinrad.

"Sierra Maestra" was first published in *Analog*, copyright © 1975 by the Condé Nast Publications, Inc. Reprinted by permission of the author.

CONTENTS

Dedicated to my parents
MORRIS AND RAY SPINRAD
. . . by way of explanation.

THE STAR★SPANGLED FUTURE

Introduction:
The Star-Spangled Future

I've always been resistant to the notion of writing a series of short stories around a theme or a "future history" and doing them up in a book as if they were some kind of "episodic novel." To me, that would be like sitting down to write 26 episodes of the same television series, one right after the other. Durance vile!

Good Lord, I've never been able to write short stories to order one at a time for *other* people's theme anthologies! I never know when I'm going to come up with an idea that moves me to write a story. It comes to me, or it doesn't, and I have no control over the process. The panoply of hack devices for generating a "story idea" in an empty brain strikes me as pure-blind lunacy. You know, open a book at random, type the first paragraph you come to and "springboard" from there . . . or put down a random word, then a second, and a third, and keep typing this jabberwocky until it starts to make sense or they take you to the funny farm . . . or as a last resort start typing the telephone book to flagellate yourself into creativity.

Seems to me, you simply *can't* make yourself experience the magic moment that gives a story life by intellectual process or ex-lax generated logorrhea. It's like trying to will yourself in or out of love. Stories written without genuine inspiration will be golems, literary television, Velveeta for the mind. And usually unsalable.

When I in my total naivete began writing science fiction, I was determined to write at least three stories a month to maximize my mathematical chances for breaking into print. Some of the stories I wrote under this regime came to me with that burst of creative insight that emotionally involved the writer, and hence the reader, with the story. Without exception, these eventually sold and were anthologized many times. The stuff I churned out in between based upon the mandatory "sf notion" of the week never sold and is now mercifully lost to posterity. This taught me a lesson in the monetary practicality of esthetic morality which I try to remember.

Once, however, I was tempted. I had just finished "The Lost Continent," and, upon evening contemplation of the title and all that it meant to me, I thought about writing a series of stories taking the reader on a grand tour of the future ruins of America, and calling the book *The Lost Continent.* I had the title novella already, "A Thing of Beauty" fitted perfectly, and the basic image that was to become "Sierra Maestra" was already rattling around in my brain, lessee, that's 28,000 words maybe, two more novellas would make—

Fortunately, that's as far as it got, and with the dawn I came to my senses. You don't write stories that way, kiddo. You couldn't even if you wanted to.

So I never churned out those two other novellas and this book isn't called *The Lost Continent*.

And yet . . .

And yet it didn't start out as *The Star Spangled Future* either. James Baen, the esteemed editor of Ace science fiction, simply wanted to do a collection of my best science fiction stories. We had no title or theme in mind or even the idea of looking for one.

And yet what we came up with was a book called *The Star Spangled Future*, a definitive collection of all my short science fiction about America. Fourteen stories, northward of 90,000 words of fiction, a rather weighty tome.

For when I sat down to ponder all my short stories, written over a period of fifteen years, in New York, Los Angeles, San Francisco and London, there this book was.

With few exceptions, all the stories that Jim and I considered were my best were set in America—somewhere, somewhen, some transmutation. Truth be told, maybe two-thirds of *all* the short stories I had written had to do with some kind of transmogrified American reality. A collection of my best short stories had organized themselves into a book of science fiction about America called *The Star Spangled Future* as if possessed of independent will.

Maybe this is true on some level. All these stories were written by the same process I've not described. Which is to say a creative inspiration came to me from somewhere and I then applied intellectual processes to its development. These stories were written at diverse times in diverse environments and equally diverse headspaces. The one time I had the conscious notion of doing anything like writing a book of short stories about America, I shitcanned the idea.

And yet here it is.

You will notice that all of the terms in this literary equation are defined except one: creative inspiration. But of course that's the key to the whole process and very little about it seems to operate on a conscious intellectual level at all.

What is creative inspiration anyway? This Faustian question has long obsessed me. After all, if one knew how creativity worked, one might be able to make oneself creative on demand, reason oneself into the fulltime possession of the illusive magic, and banish the very concept of writers' block. One might be able to teach creativity. All people of a sufficient intellectual level might be able to be creative whenever they wanted to, and then we'd *really* be mind-mutants with transcendant powers.

Unfortunately, the only answer I've found to this question is too Zen to be taught by the Famous Writers School or even a Clarion Workshop. Which is that creativity, like science fiction, like human consciousness itself, is a product of the interface between the human psyche as created by genes and memory, and the ever-changing external environment, which is far beyond our will to control.

Each of us is the product of genetic endowment and the story of our lives. We have no control over our heredity at this writing, and since the story of our lives is also the story of other people's lives, even the most egomaniacal and charismatic among us can never really write his own scenario.

So this flood of data from a mutating external environment pours in on us and interacts with what we've become at any given moment to form our consciousness. When the interaction is synergetic, an inspiration, a leap of consciousness takes place, a magical something is called into being that is not implicit in the data, and this is what we mean by creativity.

This is why creativity is a will o' the wisp, why it can neither be taught nor analyzed. For it is the dynamic between what we are and the flood of data impinging on our consciousness as we move and mutate through time.

But is this data random? Maybe it only seems so at the time. Take the stories in *The Star Spangled Future*. Most of them didn't seem to be connected to anything else or to each other when I wrote them. And yet through hindsight, a pattern emerges, and not one that I consciously created.

For me, the impulse to write science fiction is somehow deeply involved with some long-standing gestalt of perceptions and feelings about American realities.

But what *is* the central gestalt that caused this book to be written. What is America?

It's like asking what creativity is or trying to define science fiction.

Definition of America: a certain nation-state, a political entity with clear, legally-defined geographical borders.

Or is it? Europe is becoming infested with Holiday Inns and McDonald's golden arches.The Japanese play baseball. Every rock musician in

Europe wants to be a star in the United States. And during the nadir of the Viet Nam War yet, a New Guinea cargo-cult tribe inquired as to whether they had enough cowrie shells to purchase Lyndon Johnson from the United States to come and be their god.

I was in Europe during a piece of the Viet Nam War, in London when America put the first men on the Moon. The war had created a lot of European anti-Americanism, which of course was to be expected. But the tenor of it was peculiar. The real gut-feeling had little to do with the plight of the Vietnamese. It was a feeling of sorrow, of loss, of betrayal. Europeans felt diminished by what America was doing, abandoned by the "leader of the Free World," let down by something they had believed in.

Well there might have been a certain ho-hum attitude in the States when America landed the first men on the Moon, but let me tell you they went bugfuck over it in England. They were proud of America. They were relieved that America had once more given them something to be proud of. America for the moment had once more taken up the mantle of its own myth.

A myth of America that exists in countries all over the world. America, the demon of dehumanized technology. America, the hope of the underdog. America, the gobbler of the planet. America, where you go to become a star. The land of opportunity and the belly of the beast.

Mythic America extends far beyond the borders of the United States. America is not just another nation. America first impinged on world consciousness as a fabulous new world where the streets were paved with gold, a self-created new Atlantis. The myth has mutated many times, but its power still holds. Out there, America is an object of love, hate, admiration, loathing, envy, and longing wish-fulfillment. What is in short supply is indifference.

So no outside viewpoint is going to give you a definitive definition of America. It's an image implanted too deep in the collective unconscious of the species for anyone to be cool and objective about it.

And can Americans define themselves any better? It doesn't look that way. How many Americans even define themselves as Americans? We've got Irish-Americans and Polish-Americans and Jewish-Americans and Italian-Americans and Greek-Americans. We're blacks and Nisei and Amerinds and Latinos. The only Americans that don't self-hyphenate themselves are white Anglo-Saxon Protestants, and the rest of us call them WASPS. And even WASPS subdivide themselves in Easterners and Westerners, Yankees and Southerners, hillbillies, Hoosiers, rednecks, and Southern Californians.

Frenchmen, Englishmen, Italians, Germans, Swedes, Indians—most of the other great nations of the world speak a national language, eat a characteristic cuisine, have national music, one or two characteristic religions, and an indigenous literature and culture.

The same parameters define a sense of "national identity" for most of the nations on Earth. We all know what they are. Nationalism is the style, the very look of a people. Who would mistake a Swede for your average Turk? A street scene in Moscow looks nothing like a street scene in Marakesh. France, Germany, Spain, Italy—most of the western nations are the recognizable brand-names of a people.

But . . . *the United States?* What other country in the world has a name that's pure political definition, devoid of ethnic image? Only the "Union of Soviet Socialist Republics," with whose national karma we seem inextricably entwined, and there you have an ideological nationalism in words of one syllable.

In a certain sense, there is no real America. Not the way there's a France or Sweden or Poland.

When the mutant hordes of Europe overran the native American Indian culture, this continent's continuity with a millennial past was broken, and what emerged after the dust had settled was a huge empty new world populated by religious refugees and zealots, political utopians, losers in Europe's many wars, land-hungry ex-serfs, exiled troublemakers, wheelers and dealers, impoverished minor noblemen, and just plain pirates. Weirdos and malcontents from all over Europe in a magic new land of endless bounty, theirs for the taking.

For which they showed great enthusiasm. Taking Manhattan for 24 bucks, buying the vast Louisiana Territory for a song from a Napoleon who didn't exactly own it, and finally forthrightly ripping off great big chunks of Mexico. And dragooning slave labor from Africa all the while. Finally, mass waves of immigrants swept in to populate the empty golden continent.

And here we are today, a quarter of a billion of us, the descendants of the footloose, freebooting, utopian hippies of the eighteenth century and refugees from most of the nations of the Earth, and nobody is in the majority. With the exception of a few pitiful American Indian enclaves, everything that makes America America was brought here from somewhere else. Or mutated under the skies of the New World in the past three hundred years. We have no common past stretching back into the dim millennial mists. We are bits and fragments of the rest of the world thrown together here in dynamic instability to interact in quicksilver new combinations.

We're not just a new nation, we're a new *kind* of nation. By the traditional parameters of nationhood, America does not exist. The genes of the species intermingle freely here, and so do national styles. We are the test tube baby of the human species, the mutant child of the nations of the world, the homeland not of the time-honored past but of the transnational future.

In America, men first learned to fly. Here was the awesome power of the atom first placed in men's hands for good or ill. Here the first transnational mass culture was created by American rock music. Here the secular democracy was invented. Here western science and eastern mysticism are engaging in their first meaningful dialectic. And from America the human species launched its first expedition to another planet.

All a chain of coincidences or some deep mythic truth buried in the pre-cog collective unconscious of the human race?

Trying to define America is like trying to define creativity . . . or science fiction.

They all tend to merge into the same illusive

indefinable. America is a nation which fits no conventional definition of nationality. Science fiction is the only branch (mode? genre? form?) of literature which cannot be definied by parameters of form, style, or content. Both "science fiction" and "America" are multiple states of mind; indeed the only way to define either of them is by their very multiplicity.

Inevitable then that both science fiction and America embody humanity's dreams of its future, and its nightmares as well.

The essence of science fiction is the speculative element. Something new under the human sun must be generated by the interaction between the psyche of the writer and his environment. Which brings us back to creativity. Because creative mental mutation *is* science fiction.

GIGO, garbage in, garbage out—a maxim of computer programmers. The quality of the input data determines the quality of the output no matter how good the data processor. But when it comes to the magic human data processing program called creativity, you can look at it more positively, since humans *are* able to synergize mutations not implicit in the data.

Nevertheless the data does determine the quality and frequency of creative mutation, statistically speaking. The more of it there is, the denser it is, the more varied and complex, the higher the incidence of creative synergy. Of mutation. Of invention. Of science fiction. Of a sense of self-creating our futures.

And if we look at America as the input data, as a dynamic data bank, the external information system of internal creation, we begin to see why America is such a science fiction reality, indeed why science fiction may now be emerging as a characteristic American literature while it emerges as a transnational literature at the same time.

America was set up as a laboratory and a model for a future which the world has not yet attained. A transnational future. A future in which the peoples of the world mingle and interbreed genetically and psychically.

Not a melting pot, but a fusion plasma where all the cultures, wisdoms, and evils of all the peoples in the world are jammed together in a high energy state all the time. In everyone's head. The peoples of the Earth flooded into the emptiness of America, filling it with their genes and their cultures and their ways of looking at the world. Almost immediately, this forced transnationalism began to mutate because of its very complex and compacted mix. Only in America are the elements of scores of national realities so thoroughly mingled, geographically and culturally.

This American fusion plasma is so complex and dense that it keeps generating new complexity and increased density, so that it never stabilizes into a fixed cultural matrix, an American national style. Bits and pieces of the cultures of the world forever fuse into new American elements and with the flood of American mutations.

America is something new under this sun. Not so much a nation at all as a precog flash of the future of the species, the leading edge of the evolution of world man. Which, of course, is also what science fiction is all about.

And that's how *The Star Spangled Future* ended up writing itself.

One of the things that had historically limited

science fiction to its peculiar ghettoized state was the tendency of science fiction writers to live in the pocket reality of the world of science fiction, a cozy familiar Ruritania where you have a secure patent of nobility, and where the input of the real world comes third hand and creates mutations not of realities but of previous science fiction. Indeed, it is common for citizens of the Grand Duchy of SF to speak disdainfully of the "mundane" world outside the borders of the magic kingdom.

But I grew up outside this realm. I didn't even know it existed until I had published a first novel. What ever gestalt of input made me a science fiction writer, it came from general American reality, not the subculture of science fiction. At a stage when other new science fiction writers were doing their extracurricular bullshitting in fanzines, I was doing mine in the underground press. Sure, I read a lot of science fiction, but American realities seemed far more science fictional to me than spaceships and alien planets.

Mundane? Oh really?

You be the judge. In *The Star Spangled Future*, you will find fourteen stories written over the span of a decade in many places and many headspaces, and all of them about "mundane" America, not spaceships and other worlds. I wrote them believing that I was simply writing disconnected science fiction stories from whatever came into my head. Most of them were first published in the usual science fiction markets. And they all turn out to be about America, the leading edge of the possible futures unfolding around us right here where we live.

After all, that *was* what was coming into my head, that's the mother lode of science fiction realities—the American fusion plasma of which we are creatures—and all we have to do is keep ourselves open to it. That's where I get my crazy ideas, Charley, and that's my definition of science fiction.

We have seen the future and it is us.

PHASE ONE

Science Fiction Time

Introduction

By any rational criteria, it's Science Fiction Time in America right now; hence the title of this section of *The Star Spangled Future*. We have seen the future and it is us, I said just a moment ago, but of course we all know that there's no such thing as *the* future at all. There are many multiple futures struggling to be born at any given moment, nowhere more so than in America. Some of them are worthy of our aspiration while others are trying to crawl out from under wet rocks, and in the multiplex American reality none of them exactly precludes any of the others.

So for all any of us know, any of the stories in this section could be happening right now. The present and the future have a very fuzzy boundary in these times. Consider that in America, right now, we know that:

Mass media has impressed comic book heroes like Superman into the Jungian unconscious. Death, sex, and power dance to the beat of an electric guitar. Cancer has become such a dreaded metaphor for bad karma that there are those who seriously believe it is the result of bad karma itself. Religion, psychotherapy, and marketing have created scores of specimens of new *kinds* of cults vying with mutated Eastern imports for landlordship of the New Jerusalem. Sports events have replaced tribal warfare as the mythic area for local chauvinism. History is molded on national television. Men are seriously launching a political movement to build cities in space.

Science Fiction Times indeed! Who knows how close fiction is to unfolding realities? I saw the "Holy War on 34th Street" nearly break out on more than one occasion. There is now a doctor in Texas using a kind of cancer therapy based on the transmogrification of disease into inner myth, a treatment based literally on fantasy itself which has shown some positive results. And there are people learning to consciously craft their dreams.

Where does science fiction end and the "real world" begin? Figure it out for yourself if you can. Lotsa luck! But don't expect to come up with a simple answer while you read these stories.

Introduction to Carcinoma Angels

In a funny kind of way, this story is sort of true; the disease, character, and mythic imagery have been changed, though not necessarily to protect the innocent.

I once contracted a fatal disease called toxic hepatitis in a hospital. Ran a temperature of 106° for days. Supposedly fatal, and certainly the moral equivalent of about 1000 mikes an hour of acid on intravenous drip. Convinced I was being tortured for secret information by Russian spies, supposedly near death, and weighing in at 115 pounds, I became possessed of strange powers indeed.

I leapt out of bed, snatched up a bedpan, and used it as a weapon to fend off two burly aides, gained control of the room telephone, and while defending it by force, scammed and bullshitted my way through telephone operators and underlings using an imperious voice and a series of made-up priority codes I was convinced were real and got a Pentagon general woken up by his home red phone in the middle of the night. I started to gibber at this dazed and disoriented general about spies and plots. Then the orderlies grabbed me, shot me full of thorazine, and hung up what they thought was a dead phone on the sucker.

By the time the Pentagon had satisfied itself that the hospital was not a KGB front—and everyone did speak with middle European accents, come to think of it—my fog had cleared, my fever broke, and I was recovering with a rapidity that was pretty eerie to the doctors. . . .

Carcinoma Angels

At the age of nine, Harrison Wintergreen first discovered that the world was his oyster when he looked at it sidewise. That was the year when baseball cards were *in*. The kid with the biggest collection of baseball cards was *it*. Harry Wintergreen decided to become *it*.

Harry saved up a dollar and bought one hundred random baseball cards. He was in luck—one of them was the very rare Yogi Berra. In three separate transactions, he traded his other ninety-nine cards for the only other three Yogi Berras in the neighborhood. Harry had reduced his holdings to four cards, but he had cornered the market in Yogi Berra. He forced the price of Yogi Berra up to an exorbitant eighty cards. With the slush fund thus accumulated, he successively cornered the market in Mickey Mantle, Willie Mays and Pee Wee Reese and became the J. P. Morgan of baseball cards.

Harry breezed through high school by the simple expedient of mastering only one subject—the art of taking tests. By his senior year, he could outthink any testwriter with his gypsheet tied behind his back and won seven scholarships with foolish ease.

In college, Harry discovered Girls. Being

reasonably goodlooking and reasonably facile, he no doubt would've garnered his fair share of conquests in the normal course of events. But this was not the way the mind of Harrison Wintergreen worked.

Harry carefully cultivated a stutter, which he could turn on or off at will. Few girls could resist the lure of a good-looking, well-adjusted guy with a slick line who nevertheless carried with him some secret inner hurt that made him stutter. Many were the girls that tried to delve Harry's secret, while Harry delved *them.*

In his sophomore year, Harry grew bored with college and reasoned that the thing to do was to become Filthy Rich. He assiduously studied sex novels for one month, wrote three of them in the next two which he immediately sold at a thousand a throw.

With the $3,000 thus garnered, he bought a shiny new convertible. He drove the new car to the Mexican border and across into a notorious bordertown. He immediately contacted a disreputable shoeshine boy and bought a pound of marijuana. The shoeshine boy of course tipped off the border guards, and when Harry attempted to walk across the bridge to the states, they stripped him naked. They found nothing and Harry crossed the border. He had smuggled nothing out of Mexico, and in fact had thrown the marijuana away as soon as he bought it.

However, he had taken advantage of the Mexican embargo on American cars and illegally sold the convertible in Mexico for $15,000.

Harry took his $15,000 to Las Vegas and spent the next six weeks buying people drinks, lending broke gamblers money, acting in general like a fuzzy-cheeked Santa Claus, gaining the confidence of the right drunks and blowing $5,000.

At the end of six weeks he had three hot market tips which turned his remaining $10,000 into $40,000 in the next two months.

Harry bought 400 crated government surplus jeeps in four one-hundred-jeep lots at $10,000 a lot and immediately sold them to a highly disreputable Central American Government for $100,000.

He took the $100,000 and bought a tiny island in the Pacific, so worthless that no government had ever bothered to claim it. He set himself up as an independent government with no taxes and sold twenty one-acre plots to twenty millionaires seeking a tax haven at $100,000 a plot. He unloaded the last plot three weeks before the United States, with U.N. backing, claimed the island and brought it under the sway of the Internal Revenue Department.

Harry invested a small part of his $2,000,000 and rented a large computer for twelve hours. The computer constructed a betting schema by which Harry parlayed his $2,000,000 into $20,000,000 by taking various British soccer pools to the tune of $18,000,000.

For five million dollars, he bought a monstrous chunk of useless desert from an impoverished Arabian sultanate. With another two million, he created a huge rumor campaign to the effect that this patch of desert was literally floating on oil. With another three million, he set up a dummy corporation which made like a big oil company and publicly offered to buy his desert for seventy-five million dollars. After some spirited bargaining, a large American oil company was allowed to outbid the dummy and bought a thousand square miles of sand for $100,000,000.

Harrison Wintergreen was, at the age of twenty-five, Filthy Rich by his own standards. He lost his interest in money.

He now decided that he wanted to Do Good. He Did Good. He toppled seven unpleasant Latin American governments and replaced them with six Social Democracies and a Benevolent Dictatorship. He converted a tribe of Borneo headhunters to Rosicrucianism. He set up twelve rest homes for over-age whores and organized a birth control program which sterilized twelve million fecund Indian women. He contrived to make another $100,000,000 on the above enterprises.

At the age of thirty, Harrison Wintergreen had had it with Do-Gooding. He decided to Leave His Footprints in the Sands of Time. He Left His Footprints in the Sands of Time. He wrote an internationally acclaimed novel about King Farouk. He invented the Wintergreen Filter, a membrane through which fresh water passed freely, but which barred salts. Once set up, a Wintergreen Desalinization Plant could desalinate an unlimited supply of water at a per-gallon cost approaching absolute zero. He painted one painting and was instantly offered $200,000 for it. He donated it to the Museum of Modern Art, gratis. He developed a mutated virus which destroyed syphilis bacteria. Like syphilis, it spread by sexual contact. It was also a mild aphrodisiac. Syphilis was wiped out in eighteen months. He bought an island off the coast of California, a five-hundred-foot crag jutting out into the Pacific. He caused it to be carved into a five-hundred-foot statue of Harrison Wintergreen.

At the age of thirty-eight, Harrison Wintergreen had Left sufficient Footprints in the Sands of Time. He was bored. He looked around greedily for new worlds to conquer.

This then, was the man who, at the age of forty, was informed that he had an advanced, well-spread and incurable case of cancer and that he had one year to live.

Wintergreen spent the first month of his last year searching for an existing cure for terminal cancer. He visited laboratories, medical schools, hospitals, clinics, Great Doctors, quacks, people who had miraculously recovered from cancer, faithhealers and Little Old Ladies in Tennis Shoes. There was no known cure for terminal cancer, reputable or otherwise. It was as he suspected, as he more or less even hoped. He would have to do it himself.

He proceeded to spend the next month setting things up to do it himself. He caused to be erected in the middle of the Arizona desert an air-conditioned walled villa. The villa had a completely automatic kitchen and enough food for a year. It had a five-million-dollar biological and biochemical laboratory. It had a three-million-dollar microfilmed library which contained every word ever written on the subject of cancer. It had the pharmacy to end all pharmacies: a liberal supply of quite literally every drug that existed—poisons, pain-killers, hallucinogens, dandricides, antiseptics, antibiotics, viricides, headache remedies, heroin, quinine, curare, snake oil—everything. The pharmacy cost twenty million dollars.

The villa also contained a one-way radiotelephone, a large stock of basic chemicals, including radioactives, copies of the Koran, the Bible, the Torah, the Book of the Dead, *Science and Health with Key to the Scriptures*, the *I Ching* and the complete works of Wilhelm Reich and Aldous Huxley. It also contained a very large and ultra-expensive computer. By the time the villa was ready, Wintergreen's petty cash fund was nearly exhausted.

With ten months to do that which the medical world considered impossible, Harrison Wintergreen entered his citadel.

During the first two months, he devoured the library, sleeping three hours out of each twenty-four and dosing himself regularly with benzedrene. The library offered nothing but data. He digested the data and went on to the pharmacy.

During the next month, he tried Aureomycin, bacitracin, stannous fluoride, hexylresercinol, cortisone, penicillin, hexachlorophene, shark-liver extract and seven thousand three hundred and twelve assorted other miracles of modern medical science, all to no avail. He began to feel pain, which he immediately blotted out and continued to blot out with morphine. Morphine addiction was merely an annoyance.

He tried chemicals, radioactives, viricides, Christian Science, Yoga, prayer, enemas, patent medicines, herb tea, witchcraft and yogurt diets. This consumed another month, during which

Wintergreen continued to waste away, sleeping less and less and taking more and more benzedrene and morphine. Nothing worked. He had six months left.

He was on the verge of becoming desperate. He tried a different tack. He sat in a comfortable chair and contemplated his navel for forty-eight consecutive hours.

His meditations produced a severe case of eyestrain and two significant words: "spontaneous remission."

In his two months of research, Wintergreen had come upon numbers of cases where a terminal cancer abruptly reversed itself and the patient, for whom all hope had been abandoned, had been cured. No one ever knew how or why. It could not be predicted, it could not be artificially produced, but it happened nevertheless. For want of an explanation, they called it spontaneous remission. "Remission," meaning cure. "Spontaneous," meaning no one knew what caused it.

Which was not to say that it did not have a cause.

Wintergreen was buoyed; he was even ebullient. He knew that some terminal cancer patients had been cured. Therefore terminal cancer could be cured. Therefore, the problem was removed from the realm of the impossible and was now merely the domain of the highly improbable.

And doing the highly improbable was Wintergreen's specialty.

With six months of estimated life left, Wintergreen set jubilantly to work. From his complete cancer library, he culled every known case of spontaneous remission. He coded every one of them into the computer—data on the medical histories of the patients, on the treatments employed, on their ages, sexes, religions, races, creeds, colors, national origins, temperaments, marital status, Dun and Bradstreet ratings, neuroses, psychoses and favorite beers. Complete profiles of every human being ever known to have survived terminal cancer were fed into Harrison Wintergreen's computer.

Wintergreen programmed the computer to run a complete series of correlations between 10,000 separate and distinct factors and spontaneous remission. If even one factor—age, credit rating, favorite food, *anything*—correlated with spontaneous remission, the spontaneity factor would be removed.

Wintergreen had shelled out $100,000,000 for the computer. It was the best damn computer in the world. In two minutes and 7.894 seconds it had performed its task. In one succinct word it gave Wintergreen his answer:

"Negative."

Spontaneous remission did not correlate with *any* external factor. It was still spontaneous; the cause was unknown.

A lesser man would've been crushed. A more conventional man would've been dumbfounded. Harrison Wintergreen was elated.

He had eliminated the entire external universe as a factor in spontaneous remission in one fell swoop. Therefore, in some mysterious way, the human body and/or psyche was capable of curing itself.

Wintergreen set out to explore and conquer his own internal universe. He repaired to the pharmacy and prepared a formidable potation. Into his largest syringe he decanted the following:

Novocaine; morphine; curare; *vlut*, a rare Central Asian poison which induced temporary blindness; olfactorcaine, a top-secret smell-deadener used by skunk farmers; tympanoline, a drug which temporarily deadened the auditory nerves (used primarily by filibustering Senators); a large dose of benzedrene; lysergic acid; pscilicibin; mescaline; peyote extract; seven other highly experimental and most illegal hallucinogens; eye of newt and toe of dog.

Wintergreen laid himself out on his most comfortable couch. He swabbed the vein in the pit of his left elbow with alcohol and injected himself with the witches' brew.

His heart pumped. His blood surged, carrying the arcane chemicals to every part of his body. The Novocaine blanked out every sensory nerve in his body. The morphine eliminated all sensations of pain. The *vlut* blacked out his vision. The olfactorcaine cut off all sense of smell. The tympanoline made him deaf as a traffic court judge. The curare paralyzed him.

Wintergreen was alone in his own body. No external stimuli reached him. He was in a state of total sensory deprivation. The urge to lapse into blessed unconsciousness was irresistible. Wintergreen, strong-willed though he was, could not have remained conscious unaided. But the massive dose of benzedrene would not let him sleep.

He was awake, aware, alone in the universe of his own body with no external stimuli to occupy himself with.

Then, one and two, and then in combinations like the fists of a good fast lightweight, the hallucinogens hit.

Wintergreen's sensory organs were blanked

out, but the brain centers which received sensory data were still active. It was on these cerebral centers that the tremendous charge of assorted hallucinogens acted. He began to see phantom colors, shapes, things without name or form. He heard eldritch symphonies, ghost echoes, mad howling noises. A million impossible smells roiled through his brain. A thousand false pains and pressures tore at him, as if his whole body had been amputated. The sensory centers of Wintergreen's brain were like a mighty radio receiver tuned to an empty band—filled with meaningless visual, auditory, olfactory and sensual static.

The drugs kept his senses blank. The benzedrene kept him conscious. Forty years of being Harrison Wintergreen kept him cold and sane.

For an indeterminate period of time, he rolled with the punches, groping for the feel of this strange new non-environment. Then gradually, hesitantly at first but with ever-growing confidence, Wintergreen reached for control. His mind constructed untrue but useful analogies for actions that were not actions, states of being that were not states of being, sensory data unlike any sensory data ever received by the human brain. The analogies, constructed in a kind of calculated madness by his subconscious for the brute task of making the incomprehensible palpable, also enabled him to deal with his non-environment as if it were an environment, translating mental changes into analogs of action.

He reached out an analogical hand and tuned a figurative radio, inward, away from the blank waveband of the outside side universe and towards the as-yet-unused waveband of his own body, the internal universe that was his mind's only possible escape from chaos.

He tuned, adjusted, forced, struggled, felt his mind pressing against an atom-thin interface. He battered against the interface, an analogical translucent membrane between his mind and his internal universe, a membrane that stretched, flexed, bulged inward, thinned . . . and finally broke. Like Alice through the Looking Glass, his analogical body stepped through and stood on the other side.

Harrison Wintergreen was inside his own body.

It was a world of wonder and loathsomeness, of the majestic and the ludicrous. Wintergreen's point of view, which his mind analogized as a body within his true body, was inside a vast network of pulsing arteries, like some monstrous freeway system. The analogy crystalized. It *was* a freeway and Wintergreen was driving down it. Bloated sacs dumped things into the teeming traffic: hormones, wastes, nutrients. White blood cells careened by him like mad taxicabs. Red corpuscles drove steadily along like stolid burghers. The traffic ebbed and congested like a crosstown rush-hour. Wintergreen drove on, searching, searching.

He made a left, cut across three lanes and made a right down toward a lymph node. And then he saw it—a pile of white cells like a twelve-car collision, and speeding towards him a leering motorcyclist.

Black, the cycle. Black, the riding leathers. Black, dull black, the face of the rider save for two glowing blood-red eyes. And emblazoned across the front and back of the black motorcycle jacket in shining scarlet studs the legend: "Carcinoma Angels."

With a savage whoop, Wintergreen gunned his analogical car down the hypothetical freeway straight for the imaginary cyclist, the cancer cell.

Splat! Pop! Cuush! Wintergreen's car smashed the cycle and the rider exploded in a cloud of fine black dust.

Up and down the freeways of his circulatory system Wintergreen ranged, barreling along arteries, careening down veins, inching through narrow capillaries, seeking the black-clad cyclists, the Carcinoma Angels, grinding them to dust beneath his wheels. . . .

And he found himself in the dark moist wood of his lungs, riding a snow-white analogical horse, an imaginary lance of pure light in his hand. Savage black dragons with blood-red eyes and flickering red tongues slithered from behind the gnarled boles of great airsac trees. St. Wintergreen spurred his horse, lowered his lance and impaled monster after hissing monster till at last the holy lung-wood was free of dragons. . . .

He was flying in some vast moist cavern, above him the vague bulks of gigantic organs, below a limitless expanse of shining slimy peritoneal plain.

From behind the cover of his huge beating heart, a formation of black fighter planes, bearing the insignia of a scarlet "C" on their wings and fuselages, roared down at him.

Wintergreen gunned his engine and rose to the fray, flying up and over the bandits, blasting them with his machine-guns, and one by one and then in bunches they crashed in flames to the peritoneum below. . . .

In a thousand shapes and guises, the black and red things attacked. Black, the color of oblivion, red, the color of blood. Dragons, cyclists, planes, sea-things, soldiers, tanks and tigers in blood vessels and lungs and spleen and thorax and bladder—Carcinoma Angels, all.

And Wintergreen fought his analogical battles in an equal number of incarnations, as driver, knight, pilot, diver, soldier, mahout, with a grim and savage glee, littering the battlefields of his body with the black dust of the fallen Carcinoma Angels.

Fought and fought and killed and killed and finally. . . .

Finally found himself knee-deep in the sea of his digestive juices lapping against the walls of the dank, moist cave that was his stomach. And scuttling towards him on chitinous legs, a monstrous black crab with blood-red eyes, gross, squat, primeval.

Clicking, chittering, the crab scurried across his stomach towards him. Wintergreen paused, grinned wolfishly, and leapt high in the air, landing with both feet squarely on the hard black carapace.

Like a sun-dried gourd, brittle, dry, hollow, the crab crunched beneath his weight and splintered into a million dusty fragments.

And Wintergreen was alone, at last alone and victorious, the first and last of the Carcinoma Angels now banished and gone and finally defeated.

Harrison Wintergreen, alone in his own body, victorious and once again looking for new worlds to conquer, waiting for the drugs to wear off, waiting to return to the world that always was his oyster.

Waiting and waiting and waiting. . . .

Go to the finest sanitarium in the world, and there you will find Harrison Wintergreen, who made himself Filthy Rich, Harrison Wintergreen who Did Good, Harrison Wintergreen, who Left his Footprints in the Sands of Time, Harrison Wintergreen, catatonic vegetable.

Harrison Wintergreen, who stepped inside his own body to do battle with Carcinoma's Angels, and won.

And can't get out.

Introduction to All the Sounds of The Rainbow

Harlan Ellison had gotten me a story assignment on a TV show called The Sixth Sense where he was one of three story editors. The format had this team of investigators dealing with supernatural or esp occurrences. Anthony Spinner, the creator of the show, and now associate producer, or maybe story consultant, or co-co-story-editor (the staff structure of this production was worthy of a Borgia), wanted a story done around a Russian study of synesthesia which he threw at me.

Well this material on synethesiacs was fascinating, but it wasn't a story, so I got to make one up. Phony gurus, real gurus, and their followers have long been a subject of fascination to me. Now what if there was this scam-artist who really did *have supernormal powers. . . .?*

Well that idea was axed at about the time the show was expiring, and for the same reason. The network guidelines *required that each week's* paranormal *occurrence must be explained away by the end of the show. This made it very hard to get coherent scripts, which was why there were so many story editors, all twisting slowly in the wind.*

And I was left with this story, to do with what I would, all by myself with no formats and no network guidelines. . . .

All the Sounds of The Rainbow

Harry Krell sprawled in a black vinyl beanbag chair near the railing of the rough-hewn porch. Five yards below, the sea crashed and rumbled against convoluted black rocks that looked like a fallen shower of meteors half-buried in the warm Pacific sand. He was naked from the waist up; a white sarong fell to his shins, and he wore custom-made horsehide sandals. He was well-muscled in a fortyish way, deeply tanned, and had the long, neat, straight yellow hair of a beach bum. His blue eyes almost went with the beach bum image: clear, empty, but shattered-looking like marbles that had been carefully cracked with a ball-peen hammer.

As phony as a Southern California guru, Bill Marvin thought as he stepped out onto the sunlit porch. Which he is. Nevertheless, Marvin shuddered as those strange eyes swept across him like radar antennae, cold, expressionless instruments gathering their private spectrum of data. "Sit down," Krell said. "You sound awful over there."

Marvin gingerly lowered the seat of his brown suede pants to the edge of an aluminum-and-plastic beach chair, and stared at Krell with cold gray eyes set in a smooth angular face perfectly framed by medium-length, razor-cut, artfully styled brown hair. He had no intention of wasting any more time on this oily con-man than was absolutely necessary. "I'll come right to the point, Krell," he said. "You detach yourself from Karen your way, or I'll get it done my way."

"Karen's her own chick," Krell said. "She's not even your wife anymore." A jet from Vandenburg suddenly roared overhead; Krell winced and rubbed at his eyes.

"But I'm still paying her a thousand a month in alimony, and I'll play pretty dirty before I'll stand by and watch half of that go into your pockets."

Krell smiled, and a piece of chalk seemed to scratch down a blackboard in Marvin's mind. "You can't do a thing about it," he said.

"I can stop paying."

"And get dragged into court."

"And tell the judge I'm putting the money in escrow pending the outcome of a sanity hearing, seeing as how I believe that Karen is now mentally incompetent."

"It won't work. Karen's at least as sane as you are."

"But I'll drag you into court in the process, Krell. I'll expose you for the phony you are."

Harry Krell laughed a strange bitter laugh and multicolored diamonds of stained glass seemed to flash and shimmer in the sum. "Shall I show you what a phony I am, Marvin?" he said. "Shall I really show you?"

Waves of thick velvet poured over Bill Marvin's body. In Krell's direction, he felt a radiant fire in a bitter cold night. He heard a chord that seemed to be composed of the chiming of a million microscopic bells. Far away, he saw a streak of hard blue metal against a field of loamy brown.

All in an instant, and then it passed. He saw the sunlight, heard the breakers, then the sound of a high-performance engine accelerating up in the hills that loomed above the beach house. Krell was smiling and staring emptily off into space.

A tremor went through Marvin's body. I've been a little tense lately, he thought. Can this be the beginning of a breakdown? "What the hell was that?" he muttered.

"What was what?" said Krell. "I'm a phony, so nothing could've happened, now could it, Marvin?" His voice seemed both bitter and smug.

Marvin blotted out the whole thing by forcing his attention back to the matter at hand. "I don't care what little tricks you can pull; I'm not going to let you suck up my money through Karen."

"You've got a one-track mind, Mr. Marvin, what we call a frozen sensorium here at Golden Groves. You're super-uptight. You know, I could help you. I could open up your head and let in all the sounds of the rainbow."

"You're not selling *me* any used car, Krell!"

"Well, maybe Karen can," Krell said. Marvin followed Krell's line of sight, and there she was, walking through the glass doors in a paisley muumuu that the sea breeze pressed and fluttered against the soft firmness of her body.

A ball of nausea instantly formed in Marvin's gut, compounded of empty nights, cat-fights in court, soured love, dead hopes, and the treachery of his body which still sent ghosts of lust coursing to his loins at the sight of the dyed coppery hair that fell a foot past her shoulders, that elfin face with carbon-steel behind it, that perfect body which she pampered and honed like the weapon it was.

"Hello, Bill," she said in a neutral voice. "How's the smut business?"

"I haven't had to do any porn for four months," Marvin lied. "I'm into commercials." And then hating himself for trying to justify his existence to her again, even now, when there was nothing to gain or lose.

Karen walked slowly to the railing of the porch, turned, leaned her back against it, seemed to quiver in some kind of ecstasy. Her green eyes, always so bright with shrewdness, seemed vague and uncharacteristically soft, as if she were good and stoned.

"Your voice feels so ugly when you're trying not to whine," she said.

"Bill's threatening to cut off your alimony unless you leave Golden Groves," Krell said. "He wants to force a sanity hearing and prove that you're a nut and I'm a crook."

"Go ahead and pull your greasy little legal stunts, Bill," Karen said. "I'm sane and Harry is exactly what he claims to be, and we'd both be delighted to prove it in court, wouldn't we, Harry?"

"I don't want to get involved in any legal hassles," Krell said coldly. "It's not worth it, especially since you won't have a dime to pay toward your residency fee with all your alimony in escrow."

"Harry!"

Her eyes snapped back into hard focus like steel

shutters, and the desperation turned her face into the kind of ugly mask you see around swimming pools in Las Vegas. Marvin smiled, easily choking back his pity. "How do you like your little tin guru now?" he said.

"Harry, you can't do this to me, you can't just turn me off like a lamp over a few hundred dollars!"

Harry Krell climbed out of his beanbag chair. There was no expression on his face at all; except for those strange, shattered-looking eyes, he could've been any aging beach bum telling the facts of life to an old divorcée whose money had run out, "I'm no saint," he said, "I had an accident that scrambled my brains and gave me a power to give people something they want and fixed it so that's the only way I can make a living—a good living."

He smiled, and broken glass seemed to jangle inside Bill Marvin's skull. "I'm in it for the money," said Harry Krell. "So you better clean up your own mess, Karen."

"You're such a rotten swine!" Karen snarled, her face suddenly looking ten years older, every subtle wrinkle a prophet of disaster to come.

"But I'm the real thing," said Harry Krell. "I deliver." Slowly and haltingly he began walking toward the doors that led to his living room, like someone moving underwater.

"Bill—"

It was all there in his name on her lips two octaves lower than her normal tone of voice, the slight hunch forward of her shoulders, the lost, scared look in her eyes. It was a trick, and it was where she really lived, both at the same time. He wanted to punch her in the guts and cradle her in his arms.

"If you're crazy enough to think you're going to talk to me—"

"Just let me walk you to your car. Please."

Marvin got up, brushed off his pants, sighed, and, suddenly drained of anything like emotion, said tiredly, "If you think you need the exercise that bad, lady."

They walked silently through a slick California-rustic living room, where Krell sat on a green synthetic-fur-covered couch stroking a Siamese cat as if it were a musical instrument. On either side of him were a young male hippie in carefully cut shoulder-length hair and a well-tailored embroidered jeans suit, and a minor middle-aged television actor whose name Marvin could not recall.

Marvin kept walking across the black rug without exchanging a look or a word with Krell, but he noticed that there was quick eye contact between Krell and Karen, and at that moment he felt the fleeting taste of cinnamon in his mouth.

Krell's private house fronted on a rich, rolling green plateau across the highway from the Pacific end of the Santa Monica Mountains. Rustic bungalows were scattered randomly about the property, along with clumps of trees, paths, benches, a tennis court, a large swimming pool, a sauna, a stable, the usual sensitivity-resort paraphernalia. The parking lot was tucked nicely away behind a screen of trees at the edge of the highway, so as not to spoil the bucolic scene. But the whole business was surrounded by a ten-foot chain-link fence topped by three strands of barbed wire, and the only entrance was a remotely controlled electric gate. As far as Marvin was concerned, that pretty well summed up Golden Groves. This area north of Los Angeles was full of this kind of guru-farm; the only thing that varied was the basic gimmick.

"All right Karen, what's Krell's number?" he said as they walked toward the parking lot. "Let me guess . . . organic mescaline combined with acupuncture . . . tantric yoga and yak-butter massage. . . . Ye gods, what else *is* there that you haven't been hung up on already?"

"Synesthesia," she said in deadly earnest, "and it works. You've felt it yourself; I could tell."

Uneasily, Marvin remembered the strange moments of sensory hallucination he had been getting ever since he met Krell, like short LSD flashbacks. Was Krell really responsible? he wondered. Better than turning out to be the results of too much acid, or the beginning of a nervous breakdown. . . .

"Harry had some kind of serious head injury three years ago—"

"Probably fell off his surfboard."

"He was in a coma for three weeks, and when he came out of it, the lines between his senses and his brain were all crossed. He saw sound, heard color, tasted temperature . . . synesthesia, they call it."

"Yeah . . . now I remember. I read about that kind of thing in *Time* or somewhere. . . ."

"Not like Harry, you didn't. Because with Harry the connections *keep* changing from minute to minute. His world is always fresh and new . . .

like being high all the time . . . like . . . it's like nothing else in the world."

She brought him up short with a touch of her hand, and a flash from her eyes, perhaps deliberate, reminded him of what she had been, what they had been, when they first drove across the San Fernando Valley in the old Dodge, with the Hollywood Hills spread out before them, a golden world they were sure to conquer.

"I feel alive again, Bill," she said. "Please don't take it away from me."

"I don't see—"

Overwhelming warmth enveloped his body. He tasted the wine of her hand on his arm. He heard the symphony of the spheres, tone within tone within tone, without end. He saw the dark of inky night punctuated with fountains of green, red, violet, yellow, fantastic flowers of light, celestial fireworks. He felt his knees go weak, his head reel; he was falling. The fountains of light exploded faster, became larger. He put out his hands to break his fall, smelled burning pine, heard the whisper of an unfelt wind.

He was crouched on the grass supporting his bodyweight on his hands, staring down at the green blades. "Are you okay? Are you all right?" Karen shouted.

He looked up at her, blinked, nodded.

"What Harry never let the doctors find out was that he could project it," she said.

Marvin got shakily to his feet. "All right," he said. "So I believe that that greasy creep Krell can get inside your brain and scramble it around! But what the hell for? What dumb spiel does he throw you to make you want it, that you're experiencing the essense of Buddha's rectum or something?"

"Harry's no mental giant," she said. "He doesn't know why it opens you up—oh, he's got some stupid line for the real idiots—all he really knows is how to do it, and how to make money at it. But, Bill, all I can tell you is that this seems to be opening me up at last. It's the answer I've been looking for for five years."

"What the hell's the *question?*" Marvin said, an old line that brought back a whole marriage's worth of bad memories, like a foul-tasting burp recalling an undigested bad meal. Acid trips that went nowhere, two months of the Synanon game learning how to stick the knife in better, swinging, threesomes both ways, trial separations and trial reconciliations, savage sex, battle sex, dull sex, and no sex. Always searching for something that had been lost somewhere between crossing the continent together in that old Dodge and the skin-flick way of life that meant survival in Los Angeles after it became apparent that he wasn't the next Orson Welles and she wasn't the next Marilyn Monroe.

"What I think is that this synesthesia must be the natural way people are supposed to experience the world. Somewhere along the way our senses got separated from each other, and that's why the human race is such a mess. We can't get our heads together because we experience reality through a lot of narrow windows, like prisoners in a cell. That's why we're all twisted inside."

"Whereas Harry Krell is the picture of mental health and karmic perfection!"

They were nearing the parking lot now; Marvin could see his Targa, and he longed to be in it, roaring along the freeway away from Golden Groves and Karen, away from one more expensive last hope.

Once again, she presented him with her flesh, touching both hands to his shoulders, staring full face at him until something inside him ached with yearning. Her face was as soft as it had been when they had been lovers instead of sparring partners, but her eyes were full of an aging woman's terrors.

"All I know is what I feel," she said. "When I'm living in a synesthetic flash, I feel really alive. Everything else is just waiting."

"Why don't you just try smack?" Marvin said. "It may not be cheaper than Krell, but at least it's portable."

"Harry claims that eventually we can learn to do it on our own, that he can retrain our minds, given enough time—"

"And enough money."

"Oh, Bill, don't make me lose this! Don't let me drown!"

Her hands dug into his shoulders, her body slumped toward him, wrinkles formed in the corners of her mouth, the stench of pathetic desperation—

He saw huge woman's hands knotted in fear raise themselves in prayerful supplication toward him from a forest of sharp metallic edges. He felt her flesh moving over every inch of his body in long-forgotten personal rhythms, and how it had felt to snuggle toasty beside her in bed. He tasted bitter gall and the nausea of panic, smelled musky perfume.

He heard his own tears pealing like church bells

as they rolled down his cheeks; he drew the giant hands to him, and they dissolved into an armful of yellow light. Wordless singing filled his ears, and he smelled a long night by the fireside, felt the freshly warm glow of nostalgia's sad contentment.

He was holding Karen in his arms; her cheek was nestled against his neck. She was crooning his name, and he felt five years and more younger. And suddenly scared silly and burning mad.

He thrust her away from him. "It won't work," he snarled. "You're not going to play me for a sucker again, and neither is Krell!"

"You felt—"

"What you and Harry Krell wanted me to feel! Forget it, it won't work again! See you in court."

He sprinted the rest of the way to his car, tearing little divots out of the moist turf of Golden Groves.

With four underground films totaling less than ninety minutes to Bill's credit and with Karen having "starred" in the last two of them, the Marvins had left New York to seek fame and fortune in the Golden West. What they found in Hollywood was that beautiful women with minor acting talent were a dime a dozen (or at best fifty dollars a trick) and that Bill's "credits" might as well have been Cuban Superman flicks.

What they also found out after four months of starving and scrounging was that Los Angeles was the pornography capital of the world. For every foot of feature film shot in Hollywood, there were miles of split beaver, S&M, and just plain stag films churned out. The town was swarming with "film makers" living off porn while waiting for The Big Break and "actresses" whose footage could be seen to best advantage in Rotary smokers or the string of skin-flick houses along Santa Monica Boulevard known as Beaver Valley. Porn was such a booming industry that most of the film makers knew less about handling a camera than Bill. So when the inevitable occurred, he had plenty of work and the Marvins had an abundance of money.

Seven years later, Bill Marvin was left with his excellent connections in the porn industry, a three-year-old Porshe Targa, a six-room house in Laurel Canyon which he would own outright in another fifteen years, enough cameras and equipment to live well off pornography forever, and no more illusions about Making It Big.

He was set for life. Sex, both instant and long-term, was certainly no problem in his line of work; four months of screwing around between serious relationships that averaged about six months in duration seemed to be his natural pattern. In the porn business, you connect up with a good lawyer and a tricky accountant early if you know what's good for you, so he had come out of the divorce pretty damn well: fifteen grand in lieu of her share of the house and one thousand dollars a month, which he could pay without feeling too much pain.

He had felt that he could breeze along like this forever, happy as a clam, until that scene last week at Golden Groves. Now he was rattling around the house as if it were the dead shell of some enormous creature that he was inhabiting like an overambitious hermit crab. He couldn't get his head into a new project, sex didn't turn him on, drugs bored him. He could think of only one thing: Harry Krell's head on a silver platter. And the fact that his lawyer had told him that the sanity-hearing ploy probably wouldn't work certainly hadn't improved his disposition.

What possible difference can it make to me that Karen is throwing my money away on Krell, he wondered as he paced the flagstone walk of his deeply shadowed overgrown garden. If it wasn't Krell, it'd be some other transcendental con-man. The hills are full of them.

If this were a Universal TV movie, I'd still be carrying a subconscious torch for Karen, which is why Krell would be getting under my skin—guru-envy, a shrink might call it. But I wouldn't have Karen back on her hands and knees. No, it's got to be something about that crazy creep, Krell—

That crazy Krell!

Bill Marvin did a classic slow-take. Then he double-timed through the ferns and cacti of his hillside garden, trotted around the edge of his pool, through his living room, and two stairs at a time up to his second-floor office, where he called Wally Bruner, his hotshot lawyer.

"Look, Wally, about this con-artist my wife is—"

"I told you, you miss one alimony payment, and she'll have *you* in court as defendant, and unless you succeed in getting her committed—"

"Yeah, yeah, I know I probably can't have her declared incompetent. But what about Krell?"

"Krell?" Wally's voice had slowed down about twenty miles per hour. Marvin could picture him leaning back in his chair, raising his eyebrows, rolling the word around in his mouth, tasting it out. "*Krell?*"

"Sure. This guy had a head injury so serious he was in a coma for weeks, and when he came out of it, he claimed he could see sound, hear light, feel taste, and then he goes into business claiming he can scramble other people's brains the same way. What would that sound like in court?"

"Who swears out the complaint?" Bruner said slowly.

"Huh?"

"The only way to get Krell into court is on a fraud charge, claiming that he can't really project this synesthesia effect, and that he's swindling the marks. That puts him in the position of having to defend himself against criminal fraud by proving he's got this strange psychic power, which, let me tell you, is not a position *I'd* care to defend. If I was his lawyer, I think I'd have to plead insanity to try to beat the felony rap. If he wins, he spends a few months in the booby hatch and this Golden Groves thing is broken up, which is what you want. If he loses he goes to jail, which you'd like even better. If he tries to convince a Los Angeles judge that he's got psychic powers, he won't get to first base, and, if he tries it before a jury, I'll get him *and* his lawyer thrown in the funny-farm."

"Well, hey, that's great!" Marvin shouted. "We got him coming and going!"

"Like I say, Bill," Bruner said tiredly, "who's the complainant?"

"In English, please, Wally."

"In order to get Krell into court on a fraud charge, someone has to file a complaint. Someone who can claim that Krell has defrauded him.

Therefore, it must be someone who has paid Krell money for his hypothetical services. Who's that, Bill? Certainly not Karen—"

"What about me?" Marvin blurted.

"You?"

"Sure. I go up there, pay Krell for a month's worth, stay a few days, then come out screaming fraud."

"But according to you, he really delivers what he claims to. . . ."

"As of now, I never told you that, right?"

"You'd have to testify under oath. . . ."

"I'll keep my fingers crossed."

"You really think Krell will take a chance on letting you in?"

Bill Marvin smiled. "He's a greedy pig and an egomaniac," he said. "He tried to get Karen to help convince me he was Malibu's answer to Buddha, and he's more than jerk enough to convince himself that he succeeded. Will it work, Wally?"

"Will what work?" Bruner said ingenuously. "As of now, this phone conversation never took place. Do you read me loud and clear?"

"Five by five," Marvin said. He hung up on Bruner and dialed the number of Golden Groves.

Sprawled across his green couch, Harry Krell's body contradicted the lines of tense shrewdness in his face as his eyes for once focused sharply on Marvin. "Maybe I'm making a mistake trusting you," he said. "You made it pretty clear what you think of me."

Marvin leaned back in his chair, emulating Krell's casualness. "Trust's got nothing to do with it," he said. "You don't have to trust me and I don't have to trust you. You show me that you can give *me* my money's worth; that should convince me that Karen is getting my money's worth, too. Turn me down, and it's one thousand dollars a month you stand to lose."

Harry Krell laughed and microscopic pinpricks seemed to tickle every inch of Marvin's body. Beside Krell on the sofa, Karen's body quivered once. "We don't like each other," Krell said, "but we understand each other." There was something patronizing in his tone that grated on Marvin, an arrogant overconfidence that was somehow insulting. Well, the greedy swine would soon get his!

"Then it's a deal?"

"Sure," Krell said, "Come back tomorrow with your clothes and a five hundred dollar check that won't bounce. You get a cabin, three meals a day here in the house, free use of the sauna, the tennis courts, and the pool, at least two synesthesia groups a day, and whatever special events might go on. The horses are five dollars an hour extra."

"I'm paying for the two of us," Marvin said. "I should get some kind of discount."

Krell grinned. "If you want to share a cabin with Karen, I'll knock two hundred and fifty dollars a month off the bill," he said. There was something teasing in his voice.

Involuntarily, Marvin's eyes were drawn to Karen's. There was an emotional flash between them that brought back long-dead memories of what that kind of eye-contact had once meant, of what they had been together before it all fell apart. He found himself almost wishing he was what he pretended to be: a pilgrim seeking to clean the stale cobwebs out of his soul. He had the feeling that she just might agree to shack up with him. But the glow in her eyes was forced by desperate need. Los Angeles was full of faces like that, and the Harry Krells sucked them dry and let them shrivel like old prunes when the money ran out. He had to admit that his body still felt something for Karen's, but he was long past the point where he'd let sex drag him where his head did not want to be; the going up was just not worth the coming down.

"Pass," he said. Karen's expression did not change at all.

Krell shrugged, got up, and walked out onto the porch in that strange uncertain gait of his, inhaling sharply as he crossed the shadow-line into sunlight.

"I know you're up to something cheap and tricky," Karen said.

"Then why did you agree to warm Krell up for me?"

"You wouldn't believe me."

"Try me."

She sighed. "Because I still care a little for you, Bill," she said. "You're so frozen, so tied up in knots inside, and who should know what that's like better than me? Harry has what you need. Once you've been here a while, you'll see that, and it won't matter why you originally came."

"Saving your alimony had nothing to do with it, of course."

"Not really," she said. And as the words emerged from her mouth, they became brightly colored tropical butterflies, and she became a lush greenness from which they flew. There was a soft musical trilling, and the smell of lilacs and orchids filled the air. In that moment, he felt a pang of regret for what he had said, saw the feeling she still bore for him, heard the simply clarity of her body's animal love.

In the next moment, they were staring at each other, and tension hung in the air between them. Karen broke it with a small, smug madonna-smile. Marvin found himself sweating at the palms, and somewhat leary of what he was getting himself into.

The cabin was sure a dump for five hundred dollars a month: a bed, a dresser, a couch, a bathroom, two electric heaters, and a noisy old motel-type air conditioner. Breakfast had been granola (sixty-nine cents a pound), milk, and coffee, and Marvin figured that Krell would use the same health-food excuse to dish out cheap lunches and dinners. The only thing that required expensive upkeep was the riding stable, and that ran at a profit as a separate operation. Krell must be pocketing something like half the residency fee as clear profit. Fifteen cabins, some of them double-occupancy . . . that would be seven grand a month at least!

There's no business like the guru business, Marvin thought as he followed Krell and three of his fellow residents out onto the porch above the rumbling sea.

Four large, plush cushions had been placed on the bare wood in a circle around an even larger zebra-striped pillow. Krell, in his white sarong, lowered himself to the central position in a semblance of the lotus position, looking like the Maharishi as played by a decaying Tab Hunter. Marvin and the other three residents dropped to their cushions in imitation of Krell. On Marvin's left was Tish Connally, a well-preserved thirty-fiveish ex-Las Vegas "showgirl" who had managed to hold on to a decent portion of the drunk money that had swirled around her for ten years, and who had eyed him a couple of times over the granola. On his right, Mike Warren, the longhair he had seen the first day, who turned out to be an ex-speedfreak guitarist, and, on the far cushion, a balding TV producer named Marty Klein, whose last two series had been canceled after thirteen weeks each.

"Okay," said Krell, "you all know Bill Marvin, so I guess we're ready to charge up for the morning. Bill, what this is all about is that I unfreeze everybody's senses together for a bit, and then you'll have synesthetic flashes on your own off it for a few hours. The more of these sessions you have, the longer your own free-flashing will last, and finally your senses will be reeducated enough so you won't need me."

"How many people have . . . uh, graduated so far?" Marvin asked sweetly.

To his credit, Krell managed not to crack a scowl. "No one's felt they've gotten all I've got to give them yet," he said. "But some are far along the way. Okay, are we ready now?"

The morning sun had just about burned away most of the early coastal fog, but traces of mist lingered around the porch, freshened by the spray churned up by the ocean as it broke against the rocks below. "Here we go," said Harry Krell.

There was light: a soft, all-enveloping radiance that pulsed from sunshine yellow to sea green with the tidal rhythm of breakers crashing against a rocky shore. Marvin tasted a salty tang, now minty-cool, now chowder-hot. To his right, he heard a thin, throbbing, blues-like chord, something like a keening amplified guitar stretching and clawing for some spiritual stratosphere, higher, higher, higher, but never quite getting there, never resolving the dynamic discord into a bearable harmony. To his left, a sound like the easy ricky-tick of a funky old piano that had been out of tune for ten years, and had mellowed into that strange old groove. Across from him, a frantic syncopated ticking, like a time-bomb running down as it was running out, a toss-up as to whether entropy would outrace the explosion.

And dominating it all, the central theme: a surging, blaring, brassy wailing that seemed a shell of plastic around a central motif of sadness —a gypsy violinist playing hot jazz on a tuba— that Marvin knew was Harry Krell.

Marvin was knocked back on his mental heels by the flood of transmogrified emotions pouring in on him from unexpected sensual directions. He sensed that in some way, Mike Warren *was* that screaming non-chord that was the aural transformation of his visual persona, that Tish Connally was the funky ricky-tick, and Klein's running-down rhythm, a has-been wondering whether he would fall apart or freak out first. And Krell, phony brass within sad confusion within cheap pseudo-sincerity within mournful regret within inner emptiness like a Muzak version of himself—a man whose existence was in the unresolvable tension between his grubby phoniness and the overwhelming, rich strangeness of the unique consciousness a random hit on the head had given him, grandeur poured by fate into the tawdriest available vessel.

Marvin had never felt pressed so close to human beings in his life. He was both fascinated and repelled by the intimacy. And wondered what they were experiencing as him.

Then the universe of his senses went through another transformation. His mouth was filled with a spectrum of tastes that somehow spread themselves out along spatial dimensions: acrid spiciness like smoked chili peppers to the right, soft furriness of flat highballs to the left, off aways something like garlic and peptic gall, and everywhere the overwhelming taste of peppermint and melancholy red wine. He could hear the pounding of the surf now, but what he saw was a field of orange-red across which drifted occasional wisps of cool blue.

"Now join hands in a circle and feel outsides with your insides," said the plastic peppermint and musky red wine.

Marvin reached out with both hands. The right half of his body immediately became knotted with severe muscular tension, every nerve twanging to the breaking point like snarled and taut wire. But the left half of his body went slack, soft, and quietly burned-out as four A.M. in bed beside someone you picked up a little after midnight at a heavy boozing and doping party.

"Okay, now relax and drift back through the changes," said peppermint and red wine.

Sight became a flickering sequence: blue mists

drifting across a field of orange-red, sunshine yellow pulsing through sea green in a tidal rhythm, four people seated in a circle around Harry Krell on a sunlit porch. Back and forth, in and out, the visions chased each other through every possible variation of the sequence, while Marvin heard the pounding of the surf, the symphony for four souls; tasted minty-cool, chowder-hot, smoked chili peppers, flat highballs, peppermint, and red wine. The sensual images crossed and recrossed, blending, clashing, melding, bouncing off each other, until concepts like taste, sight, hearing, smell, feel, became totally meaningless.

Finally (time had no referents in this state) Marvin's sensorium stabilized. He saw Tish Connally, Mike Warren, Marty Klein, and himself seated on cushions in a circle around Harry Krell on a sunlit wooden porch. He heard the crashing of the surf on the rocks below, felt the softness of the cushion on which he sat, smelled a mixture of sea breeze and his own sweat.

Krell was bathed in sweat, looked drained, but managed to smile smugly in his direction. The others appeared not quite as dazed as Marvin felt. His mind was completely empty in that moment, whited-out, overwhelmed, nothing more than the brain center where his sensory input merged to form his sensorium, that constellation of sight, smell, sound, taste, touch, and feel which is the essential and basic ground of human consciousness.

"I hope you weren't disappointed, Mr. Marvin," Krell said. "Or would you like your money back?"

Bill Marvin had nothing to say; he felt that he

hardly had enough self-consciousness to perceive words as more than abstract sequences of sound.

The bright afternoon sun turned the surface of the pool into a rippling sheet of glare which seemed to dissolve into glass chiming and smashing for a moment as Marvin stared at the incandescent waters. Even his normal senses seemed unusually acute—he could clearly smell the sea and the stables, even here at poolside, feel the grainy texture of the plastic cloth of the beach chair against his bare back—perhaps because he could no longer take any sensory dimension for granted, with the synesthetic flashes he was getting every few minutes. There was no getting around the fact that what he had experienced that morning had been a profound experience, and one that still sent echoes rippling through his brain.

Karen pulled herself out of the pool with a shake and a shudder that flashed droplets in the sun, threw a towel around herself, and plopped down in the beach chair next to his. She was wearing a minimal blue bikini, but Marvin found himself noticing the full curves of her body only as an abstract design, glistening arcs of water-sheened skin.

"I can see you've really had a moving session," she said.

"Huh?"

He saw that her eyes were looking straight at him, but in a glazed, unfocused manner. "I'm flashing right now," she said. "I hear you as a low hum, without the usual grinding noises in the way you sit, and . . ."

She ran her hand along his chest. "Cool green and blue, no hard silvers and grays. . . ." She sighed, removed her hand, refocused her eyes. "It's gone now," she said. "All I get unless Harry is really projecting is little bits and pieces I can't hold onto. . . . But someday . . ."

"Someday you'll be able to stay high all the time, or so Krell claims."

"You know Harry's no fraud now."

Marvin winced inwardly at the word "fraud," thinking what it could be like testifying against Krell. Lord, he might drop me into a synesthetic trance in the middle of the courtroom! But . . . but I could fake my way through if I was really ready for it, if I have enough experience functioning in that state. *Krell* seems to be able to function, and he's like that all the time. . . .

"What's the matter, Bill?"

"Does my body sound funny or something?" he snapped.

"No, you just had a plain, old-fashioned frightened look on your face for a minute there."

"I was just thinking what it would be like if Krell really could condition you to be like him all the time," Marvin said. "Walking around in a fog like that, sure I can see how it might make things interesting, but how could you function, even keep from walking into trees? . . ."

"Harry *is* like that all the time, and he's functioning. You don't exactly see him starving in the street."

"I'll bet you don't see him in the street, period," Marvin said. "I'll bet Krell never leaves this place. The way you see him walking around like a zombie, he probably goes on memory half the time, like a blind man in his house." Yeah, he thought, people, food, money—he makes it all come to him. He probably couldn't drive a mile on the freeway or even walk across a street without getting killed. Suddenly Marvin found himself considering Harry Krell's inner reality, the strange parameters of his life, with a certain sympathy. What would it really be like to be Krell? To be wide open to all that fantastic experience, but unable to function in the real world except by somehow making it come to you?

Making it come to you through a greasy con-game, he told himself angrily, annoyed at the softness toward Krell that had snuck into his consciousness, at the momentary blunting of the keen edge of his determination.

Rising, he said, "I'm going to take a dip and wash some of these cobwebs out of my head."

He took four running steps and dove off the concrete lip of the pool.

When he hit the water, the world exploded for a moment in a dazzling auroral rainbow of light.

"How long have you been here?"

"Six weeks," said Tish Connally, lighting a cigarette with a match that momentarily split the darkness of her cabin with a ringing gong in Bill Marvin's head. Another synesthetic flash! He had been at Golden Groves for only three days now, and the last session with Krell had been at least five hours ago, yet he was still getting two or three flashes an hour.

He leaned back against the headboard of the bed, felt Tish's body exhale against him, saw the glow of her cigarette flare brightly, then subside.

"How long do you think you'll stay?" he asked.

"Till I have to go make some money somehow," she said. "This isn't the cheapest joint I've ever seen."

"Not until you graduate, become another Harry Krell?"

She laughed; he could feel her loose flesh ripple, almost see pink gelatin shaking in the dark. A flash—or just overactive imagination?

"That's a con," she said. "Take it from an expert. For one thing, there are people who have been in and out of here for months, and they still need their boosters from Harry to keep on flashing. For another, Krell wouldn't turn you on permanently if he could. We wouldn't need him anymore then; where would his money come from?"

"Knowing that, you still stick around?"

"Billy-boy, I've kicked around for ten years, I've been taken every way there is to be taken, took men every way there was for me to take 'em. Before I came here, I'd felt everything there was to feel fifty thousand times, so no matter what I did to get off, I was just going through the motions. At least here I feel alive in bits and pieces. So I'm paying Krell a pretty penny for getting me off once in a while. I've made most of my money on the other end of the same game, so what the hell, it keeps the money in circulation, right?"

"You're a mean old broad," Marvin said, with a certain affection.

She snubbed out her cigarette, kissed him lightly on the lips, rolled toward him.

"One more for the road, Billy-boy?"

Diffidently, he took her tired flesh in his arms.

"Oh, you're golden!" she sighed as she moved against him. And he realized that she had been hoping for a synesthetic flash to give her a bit of the sharp pleasure that he alone could not.

But he could hardly feel anger or disgust, since he too had been looking for something more spectacular than a soft human body in the darkness.

Strolling toward his cabin near the sea cliffs in the full moonlight, Bill Marvin saw Harry Krell emerge from Lisa Scott's cabin and walk down the path toward him, more rapidly and surely than he usually seemed to move in broad daylight. They met in a small grove of trees, where the moonlight filtered through the branches in tiger-stripes of silver and black that shattered visual images into jigsaw patterns.

"Hello, Marvin," Krell said. "Been doing some visiting?"

"Just walking," Marvin said neutrally, surprising himself with his own desire to have a civil conversation with Krell. But, after all, strictly as a curiosity, Krell had to be one of the most interesting men on earth.

Krell must have sensed something of this, because he stopped, leaned up against a tree, and said. "You've been here a week now, Marvin. Tell me the truth, do you still hate my guts? Are you still out to get me?"

Glad to have his reaction masked by the camouflage-pattern of moonlight and darkness, Marvin caught his breath and said, "What makes you think I'm out to get you?"

Krell laughed, and for a moment Marvin saw a

bright blue cataract smashing off a sheet of glass in brilliant sunlight. "I heard the look on your face," Krell said. "Besides, what makes you think you're the first person that's come here trying to nail me?"

"So why'd you let me come here?"

"Because half the Golden Groves regulars come here the first time to get the goods on that phony Harry Krell. If I worried about that, I'd lose half my trade."

"I just can't figure where you head's at, Krell. What do you think you're doing here?"

"What am I doing?" Krell said, an edge of whining bitterness coming into his voice. "What do you think I'm doing? I'm surviving as best I can, same as you. You think I asked for this? Sure, a lot of nuts come through here and convince themselves they're getting religious visions off of me, a big ecstasy trip. Great for them! But for Harry Krell, synesthesia's no ecstasy trip, let me tell you! I can't drive a car or walk across a street or go anywhere or do anything. All I can do is hear the pretty colors, smell the music, see the taste of whatever crap I'm eating. After three years, I got enough experience to guess pretty well what's happening around me most of the time as long as I stay on familiar ground, but I'm just guessing, man! I'm trapped inside my own head. Like now, I see something blue-green off to the left—probably the sea I'm smelling—and pink-violet stuff around us—trees, probably eucalyptus. And I hear some kind of gong. There's a moon out, right? If you're saying something now, I can't make it out until I start hearing sound again. Man, I'm so alone here inside this light-show!"

Bill Marvin fought against his own feelings, and lost. He couldn't stop from feeling sympathy for Harry Krell, locked inside his weird private reality, an ordinary slob cut off from an ordinary life. Yet Krell was entirely willing to put other people into the same place.

"Feeling like that, you still don't mind making your bread by sucking other people in with you. . . ." he said.

"Jesus, Marvin, you're a pornographer! You give people a kick they want, and you make your living off of it. But does it turn *you* on? How'd you like your whole life to be a pornographic movie?"

Bill Marvin choked on a wisecrack which never came out, because the deadening quality of what his life had become slammed him in the gut. What *is* the difference between me and Krell? he thought. He gives the suckers synesthetic flashes and I give 'em porn. What he's putting out doesn't turn him on any more than what I put out turns me on. We're both alone inside our heads and faking it. He got hit on the head by a surfboard and got stuck in the synesthesia trip, and I got hit on the head by Hollywood and got stuck in the porn trip.

"Sorry to put you on such a bummer, Marvin," Krell said. "I can smell it on you. Now I can hear your face. What? . . ."

"We're both alike, Krell," Marvin said. "And we both stink."

"We're just doing what we gotta do. You gotta play the cards you've been dealt, because you're not going to get any others."

"Sometimes you deal yourself your own lousy hand," Marvin said.

"I'll show you lousy!" said Krell. "I'll show you how lousy it can be to walk just from here to your cabin—the way I have to do it. You got the guts?"

"That's what I'm paying my money for," Marvin said quietly. He began walking back up the path. Krell turned and walked beside him.

Abruptly, the darkness dissolved into a glowing gingerbread fairyland of light. To Marvin's left, where he knew the sea was crashing against the base of the cliffs, he saw a bright green-yellow bank of brilliance that sent out pulses of radiance which struck invisible objects all around him, haloing them in all the subtle shades of the spectrum, forming an infinitely complex lattice-work of ever-changing, intersecting wavefronts that transformed itself with every pulse from the aural sun that was the sea. Beside him, Harry Krell was a shape of darkness outlined in a shimmering aurora. He heard a faraway gong chiming pleasantly in the velvet quiet. He tasted salt and smelled a rapidly changing sequence of floral odors that might have been Krell speaking. The beauty of it all drenched his soul through every pore.

He walked slowly along, orienting himself by the supposition that the green-yellow brilliance was the breaking surf, that the areas of darkness outlined by the living lattice-work of colored wavefronts were solid objects to be avoided. It wasn't easy, but it was somehow enchanting, picking his way through a familiar scene that had transformed itself into a universe of wonder.

Then the world changed again. He could hear the crashing of the sea. On his left, he saw a thick blue-green spongy mass, huge and towering; on the ground, the path was a ribbon of blackness through a field of pinkish-gray; here and there fountains grew out of the pinkish-gray, with grayish stems and vivid maroon crests, tree-high. He smelled clear coldness. Krell was a doughy mass of colors, dominantly washed-out brown. Marvin guessed that he was seeing smell.

It was easy enough to follow the path of dead earth through the fragrant grass. After a while there was another, subtler transformation. He could see that he and Krell were walking up the path toward his cabin, no more than twenty yards away in the silvery moonlight. But his mouth was filled with a now-winey, now-nutty flavor that ebbed and flowed with an oceanic rhythm, here and there broken by quick wisps of spiciness as bird-shapes flapped from tree to darkened tree. The only sound was a soft, almost subliminal hiss.

Dazed, transported, Marvin covered the last few yards to his cabin open-mouthed and wide-eyed. When they reached the door, the strange tastes in his mouth evaporated, and he could hear the muffled grumble of the pounding surf. He laughed, exhilarated, refreshed in every atom of his being, alive to every subtle sensory nuance of the night.

"How do you like living where I live?" Krell said sourly.

"It's beautiful . . . it's . . ."

Krell scowled, snickered, smiled ruefully. "So the big wise-guy turns out to be a sucker just like everyone else," he said, almost regretfully.

Marvin laughed again. In fact, he realized, he had been laughing for the first time in over a week. "Who knows, Krell," he said, "you might enjoy living in one of my pornographic movies."

He laughed one more time, then went into his

cabin, leaving Krell standing there in the night with a dumb expression on his face.

Later, when he got into bed, the cool sheets and the soft pillow were a clear night full of pinpoint-bright multicolored stars, and the darkness smelled like a woman's perfume.

The world went livid red, and the wooden slats beneath his naked body became a smoky tang in his mouth. Marvin felt himself glowing in the center of his being like a roaring winter fireplace, heard Dave Andrews' voice say, "Really sweats the tension out of you."

The flash passed, and he was lying on the wooden bench of the sauna shack, bathed in his own luxuriant sweat, baking in the heat given off by the hot stones on their cast-iron rack. The fat towel-wrapped man on the bench across from him stared sightlessly at the ceiling and sighed.

"Phew!" Andrews said as his eyes came back into focus. "I could really hear my muscles uncoil. *Twooong!*"

Marvin just lay there sucking up the heat, going with it, and entirely ignoring Andrews, who was some kind of land speculator and a crashing bore. He closed his eyes and concentrated on the waves of heat which he could all but feel breaking against his body, the relief of the grain of the wood against his skin, the subtle odor of hot stone. He had learned to bask in the world of his senses and let everything else drift by.

"I tell you, old Krell may be charging a pretty penny, but it sure cleans out the old tubes and charges up the old batteries. . . ." Andrews babbled on and on like a radio commercial, but Marvin found little trouble in pushing the idiot voice far into the sensory background; it was easy, when each sense could become a universe entire, when your sensorium was no longer conditioned to sight-sound dominance.

Suddenly Andrews' voice was gone, and Marvin heard a whistling hurricane wind. Opening his eyes, he saw wispy white billows of etherial steam punctuated by the multicolored static of Andrews' words. He tasted something like curry and smelled a piney, convoluted odor.

When the flash passed, he got up, slipped on a bathing suit, dashed out of the sauna, ran across the rich green grass in the high blue sunlight, and dove straight into the swimming pool. The cool water hit his superheated body with an orgasmic shock. He floated to the surface and let the little wavelets cradle him on his back as he paddled over to the lip of the pool, where Karen sat dangling her feet in the water.

"You're sure a different man than when you came here," she said.

Looking up, Marvin saw her bikinied form as a fuzzy vagueness against a blinding blue sky. "Well, okay, so Krell's got something going for him," he said. "But at these prices, he's still a crook, and, the funny thing is, *he* thinks he's even a *bigger* crook than he really is. . . ."

She didn't answer for a long moment, but stared into the depths of the pool to one side of him, lost in the universe of her own synesthetic flash.

When she finally spoke, it came out as a gusher of glistening green-black oil emerging from soft lavender clouds, while Marvin tasted icy cotton-candy. Judging from the discord of her face jarring the soothing melody of the sunlit sky, it was probably just as well.

Marvin luxuriated in a shower of blood-warm rain, saw a sheen of light that pulsed from sunshine-yellow to sea-green; then the flash passed. He was sitting on his cushion on Harry Krell's sunny porch, in a circle around Krell, along with Tish, Andrews . . . and Karen.

Strange, he thought, I've been here nearly three weeks, and I haven't had a booster group with Karen yet. Stranger still was the realization that this hadn't seemed peculiar or even significant until this moment. Like the rest of the outside world, his former relationship with Karen seemed so long ago and far away. The woman to his right seemed no closer to him emotionally than any of the other residents of Golden Groves, who drifted through each other's private universes like phantom ships passing in the night.

Harry Krell took a deep breath, and the vault of the sky became a sheet of gleaming brass; below, the sea was a rolling cauldron of ebony. The porch itself was outlined in dull blue, and the people around him were throbbing shapes of yellowish pink. To his left, the odor of fading incense; across the way, rich Havana smoke, and the powerful tinge of ozone pervaded all. But the smell that riveted Marvin's attention was the one on his right: an overwhelming feminine musk that seemed compounded of (or partially masked by) unsubtle perfume, drying nail polish, beauty cream, shampoo, deodorants—the full spectrum of chemical enhancers which he now realized had been the characteristic odors of living with Karen.

Waves of nostalgia and disgust formed inside him, crested, broke, and merged in a single emotional tone for which there was no word. It simply *was* the space that Karen occupied in his mind, the total image through which he experienced her.

Another change, and he saw light pulsing from yellow to green once more, tasted a salty tang. From his left, he heard the ricky-tick of a funky old piano; across the way, a staccato metallic blatting; over it all, the brassy, hollow, melancholy wailing of Harry Krell. But once again, it was the theme on his right that vibrated a nerve that went straight from his senses through his brain and into the pit of his gut. It was as if a gong were striking within an enclosure that rudely dampened its vibrations, slamming the echoing notes back on each other, abruptly amputating the long, slow vibrations, creating a sound that was a hysterical hammering at invisible walls, the sound of an animal caught in some invisible trap. Ironically, the smell of a woodland field in high summer was heavy in Marvin's nostrils.

After a few more slow changes, Krell brought them flickering back through the sequences: blood-warm rain, a sheet of gleaming brass over an ebony sea, the smell of feminine musk and body chemicals, light pulsing from yellow to green, rich Havana smoke, peppermint and red wine, high summer in a woodland field, flat highballs, melancholy wailing, ricky-tick. . . .

Then Marvin was seated on his cushion next to Karen's, while the sea grumbled to itself below, and Harry Krell breathed heavily and wiped sweat out of his eyes.

Marvin and Karen simultaneously turned to look at each other. Their eyes met, or at least their focal planes intersected. For Marvin, it was like staring straight at two cold green marbles set in the alabaster face of a statue, for all the emotion that the eye-contact contained. Judging from the ghost of a grimace that quivered across her lips, she was seeing no less of a stranger. For an instant, he was blinded by yellow light, sickened by the odor of her chemical musk.

When the flash passed, he saw that she was in the throes of one of her own; her eyes staring sightlessly out to sea, her lips twitching, her nostrils flaring. For a moment, he was overcome with curiosity as to how she was experiencing him; then, with a small effort, he put this distasteful thought from his mind, knowing that this was the moment of true divorce, that the alimony was now the only bond that remained between them.

A moment later, without a word to each other, they both got up and went their separate ways. As Karen walked through the glass doors into the house, Marvin saw a billowing spongy green mass, and heard her hysterical trapped hammering beat time for her march out of his life forever.

And time became the flickering procession of sheets of flashing images. The sun set over the cliffs into the Pacific, now a globe of orange fire dipping into the glassy waters and painting the sky with smears of purple and scarlet, now the smoky tang of autumn fading into the sharply crystal bite of winter night, now a slow-motion clap of enormous thunder dying slowly into the velvet stillness. The morning light on the porch of the beach house was a shower of blood-warm rain, a field of orange radiance shot with mists of cool blue, a humming symphony of vibrating energy.

For Bill Marvin, these had become the natural poles of existence, the only time-referents in a world in which night might be the toasty woman-smell of his bedroom darkness, the brilliant starry night of cool sheets against his body, or the golden light of anonymous female flesh against his, in which day was the coruscating fireworks of food crunching between his teeth, the celestial chime of his hot body hitting the cool water of the pool after the curry flavor of the sauna, the billowing green clouds of the surf breaking against the foot of the cliffs.

People floated through this quicksilver wonderland as shifting, illusive constellations of sensory images. Ricky-tick piano. Chemical female musk. Cloud of Havana smoke. The wail of an electric guitar. Peppermint and red wine. Hysterical, confined gonging. Smoked chili peppers. Garlic-and-peptic gall. The melancholy wail of a gypsy violinist playing hot jazz on a tuba. The sights and sounds and tastes and smells and feels that were the sensory images of the residents of Golden Groves interpenetrated the images of the inanimate world, blending and melding with them, until people and things became indistinguishable aspects of the chaotic whole.

Marvin's mind, except in isolated moments, consisted entirely of the combination of sensory impulses getting through to his brain at any given time. He existed as the confluence of these sensory images; in a sense, he *became* his sensory experience, no longer time-bound to memory and expectation, no longer a detached point of view sardonically bouncing around inside his own skull. Only in isolated stretches when his synesthetic flashes were at momentary ebbs did he step outside his own immediate experience, wonder at the strangeness in his own mind, watch himself moving through the trees and cabins and people of Golden Groves like some kind of automaton. At these times, he felt a certain vague sense of loss. He could not tell whether it was sadness at his temporary fall from a more sublime mental state, or whether his ordinary everyday consciousness was mourning its own demise.

One morning, when the granola in his mouth had scattered jeweled images of sparkling beads as he crunched it against a coffee backdrop of brown velvet, Harry Krell held him back as he started to walk out onto the porch for his morning booster session.

"This is day thirty for you, Marvin," Krell said.

Marvin stared back at him dumbly, hearing a hollow, brassy wail, seeing a rectangle of bright orange outlined against deep blue.

"I said this is the last day you've paid for. Either pony up another five hundred dollars, or send for someone to take you back to L.A. You won't be in any shape to drive for about a week."

Marvin's sensorium had changed again. He was standing in the cool living room near the open glass doors, through which sunlight seemed to extend in a solid chunk. "Thirty days?" he said dazedly. "Has it been *thirty days*? I've lost count." Lord, he thought, I was only supposed to be here a week or two! I haven't done any work in a month! I must be nearly broke, and the alimony payment is past due. My God, thirty days, and I can hardly remember them at all!

"Well I've kept good count," said Krell. "You've used up your five hundred dollars, and this is no charity operation. . . ."

Marvin found his mind racing madly like some runaway machine trying futilely to catch up with a world that had passed it by, desperately trying to sync itself back in gear with the real world of bank statements, alimony courts, four-day shooting schedules, rubber checks, vice-squad hassles, recalcitrant actresses, greasy backers. If I can cast something in three or four days, maybe I can use the same cast to shoot three quickies back-to-back, but I'll have to scout three different locations or it won't work. That should give me enough money to cover the monthly nut and keep Karen's lawyers off my back if I get all the money up front, pay them first and kite checks until—

"Well, Marvin, you want to write out another five hundred dollar check or—"

"What?" Marvin grunted. "Another five hundred dollars? No, no, hell, I'm broke, I've already been here too . . . I mean, I've got to get back to L.A. immediately."

"Well, maybe I'll see you around again sometime," said Harry Krell. He walked into the brilliant mass of sunlight, leaving Marvin standing alone in the shadowed living room, and, as he did, Marvin saw a brilliant pulse of sunshine yellow, heard an enormous chime, felt a terrible pang of paradise lost.

But there was no time to sort his head out. He had to call Earl Day, his regular cameraman, and get him to come out and drive him back to Los

Angeles in the Targa. They could put together three concepts on the way in, start casting tomorrow, and have some money in four or five days. Gotta make up for lost time fast, fast, fast!

For the barest moment, Bill Marvin was enveloped in rainbow fire which sputtered and crackled like color-TV snow, and he heard the zipping, syncopated whooshing of metal birds soaring past his ears, igniting phantom traces of memories almost forgotten after the frantic madness of grinding out three pornies in less than a month, slowing his racing metabolism, catching for a fleeting instant his psychic breath.

Then he was back stiff-spined in the driver's seat of his Porshe, his hands gripping the wheel like spastic claws, the engine growling at his back, barreling down the left lane of the Ventura Freeway at seventy-five miles per hour in moderate traffic. The flash had come and gone so quickly that he hadn't even had time to feel any sense of danger, unlike the first time he had tried to drive, only five days out of Golden Groves, when he nearly creamed out as the road became a sharp melody through rumbling drums up in the twisty Hollywood Hills. Now the synesthetic flashes were few—one or two a day—and so transient that they weren't much more dangerous behind the wheel than a strong sneeze. Each one slipped through his mind like a ghost, leaving only a peculiar echo of vague sadness.

The first couple of weeks of production on the other hand, had been a real nightmare. Up until maybe ten days ago, he had been flashing every half hour or so, and strongly enough so that he hadn't been able to do his own driving, so that takes had been ruined when he tripped out in the middle of them, so that the actors and crew sometimes thought he was stoned or flipping out and tried to take advantage of it. Fortunately, he had made so many pornies by now that he could just about do it in his sleep. The worst of it had been that making the films was so boring that he found himself actually waiting for the synesthetic flashes, concentrating on them when they came, even trying to anticipate them, and experiencing the actual world as something unreal, as marking time. He was never much interested in sex when he was shooting porn—after treating female bodies like meat all day it was pretty hard to get turned on by them at night—and the only time he had really felt alive was when he was flashing or involved in one of the hundreds of horrible hassles.

He made an abrupt three-lane jump and pulled off the freeway at Laurel Canyon Boulevard, drove across the ticky-tacky of the San Fernando Valley, began climbing up into the Hollywood Hills. The Valley side of the Hills was just more flatland style suburban plastic, but once across Mulholland Drive, which ran along the major ridge line, Laurel Canyon Boulevard curved and wound down toward the Sunset Strip, following an old dry stream bed through a deep gorge that cut through overgrown and twisted hills festooned with weird and half-hidden houses, a scene from some Disney Black Forest elf cartoon.

Usually, Marvin got a big lift out of leaving the dead plastic landscape of lowland Los Angeles for the shadowy, urbanized-yet-countrified world of the Canyon. Usually, he got a tremendous emotional surge out of having finished one film—let alone three—driving away from it all on the last day of cutting, with any one of a dozen readily available girls already waiting at the house for him to start a week-long lost weekend, his reward for a job well done.

But this time, the drive home did nothing for him, the end of the final cutting only left him empty and stale, and he hadn't even bothered to have a girl waiting for him at the house. He felt tapped out, bugged, emotionally flat, and the worst of it was that he didn't know why.

He pulled into his carport and walked around the side of his house into the seclusion of the unkempt, overgrown garden. Even the wild, lush vegetation of his private hillside seemed washed out, pallid, and somehow unreal. The bird sounds in the trees and underbrush seemed like so much Muzak.

He kicked irritably at a rock, then heard the phone ringing in the house. He went inside, plopped down in the black leather director's chair by the phone stand, picked up the living room extension, and grunted, "Yeah?"

It was Wally Bruner.

"What's going on, Bill? I haven't heard from you in nearly two months, ever since you started in on that matter we discussed. I heard you'd started shooting three weeks ago, so I knew you weren't dead, but why haven't you gotten in touch with me? Did you get what you went there for?"

Marvin stared out of the picture window into the garden, where the late afternoon sunlight cast shadows across scraggly patches of lawn under two big eucalyptus trees. Two dun-colored morning doves had ventured out of their wooded seclusion to nibble at seeds in the grass and gobble moodily to themselves like dowager aunts.

"What are you talking about, Wally?" Marvin said vacantly.

"Damn it, you know! Golden Groves. Harry Krell. Are we ready to proceed?"

Suddenly glowing bubbles of pastel shimmer were drifting languidly up through a viscous wine-colored liquid, and Marvin smelled the sweet aroma of perfect sunset; just for the tantalizing fraction of a moment, and then it was gone.

Marvin sighed, blinked, smiled.

"Forget it, Wally," he said. "I'm dropping the whole thing."

"What? Why on earth—"

"Let's just say that I went up on a mountain, came down, and want to make sure it's still there."

"What the hell are you talking about, Bill?"

"What the vintners buy," said Marvin.

"Bill, you sound like you've flipped."

"I'm okay," Marvin said. "Let's just say I don't give a damn what Karen spends her alimony on as long as I have to pay it, and leave it at that. Okay?"

"Okay, Bill. That's the advice I gave you in the first place."

After he hung up on Bruner, Marvin sat there looking out into his garden where ordinary dun-colored birds were pecking at a scruffy lawn, and the subtle gray tinge of smog was barely apparent in the waning light.

He sighed once, shuddered, shrugged, sighed again. Then he picked up the phone and dialed the number of Golden Groves.

Introduction to The Perils of Pauline

Living back in the Big Apple for the first time in years. East-West culture schlock. Heavy sexual and karmic currents. Nevertheless objects of caricature jump out of the landscape. Sidewalks of New York, yellow brick road of the mind.

Sanity seemed to call for a Busby Berkeley version. . . .

The Perils of Pauline

CHAPTER ONE: NEVER TRUST A GYPSY CABBIE

The telephone woke Pauline from tantalizing dreams of golden light pouring down over azure hills like hot butterscotch sauce over blueberry ice cream. Her head felt like a parade ground for the Wehrmacht and her mouth tasted like an old catcher's mitt—someone had slipped ipecac into her coke—but the phone bell drew her to it like a Tibetan gong summoning monks to prayer. She staggered across the painter's loft in cruel early morning light and found the instrument under a pile of evil-smelling paint rags. The fumes gave her a thirty second scopolomine flashback as she fished out the receiver.

Her sixth (seventh? It was hard to keep count) sense had not betrayed her. It was Caspar Johns summoning her to a yoga lesson. She hastily abluted herself with a lukewarm shower and a bottle of sesame oil she found in the roach-infested kitchen, threw her mink (a gift from the Quicksilver Kid, her djin godfather) around her naked body, and staggered down four flights of ominous stairs into the gray streets of lower New York, empty at this obscene hour save for an occasional bum blissfully asleep in his doorway. Extending her aura into a golden beam, she caused a cab to materialize from Canal Street. A gypsy cab, of course. Driven, of course, by a gypsy: Marlene Dietrich out of *Golden Earrings*.

"I see a tall lean man in your future," the cabbie said as they tore up Sixth Avenue, "driving a Stalin tank."

Caspar? Pauline wondered. It hardly seemed his style. Must be the Quicksilver Kid. The Kid never appeared on the same charger twice, whereas Caspar, for all his worldly success, drove a Volkswagen camper equipped with a glycerine-filled waterbed and embellished by Hari Krishna freaks with shaky designs out of the Bhagavad Gita.

Pauline forced her psychic attention away from the unattainable Quicksilver, and onto Caspar, whom she had met through the gift membership in the Guru of the Month Club given her last Christmas by her father, the Toilet Paper King of Sheboygan Wisconsin. December, January, February, March, and April had all been duds, but Caspar had proven to be worth the subscription. Author of *How To Mold a Prehensile Penis* ("Taught Nixon all he knew, child"), Caspar Johns had a softly muscular body and a thousand tasty little tricks. Satori seemed just as far away as ever, but Pauline could at least count on a blissful fifty minutes. (Caspar worked a fifty minute hour, like her shrink, Dr. Blackwish.)

At Caspar's West Village apartment house, she tossed Marlene a 50 zloty note and a Frank Perdue chicken, bustled past Billy Budd the beach boy doorman, and hurried up to Caspar's apartment, where she got her card in the timeclock just on the stroke of ten.

CHAPTER TWO: LIGHT ON THE MUSTARD

Caspar's living room was tastefully done up in framed Peter Max posters, Early Jack Kerouac antiques, and uptown garbage collages. The Great Man himself awaited her, his godlike body shrouded from neck to toes in a long black cloak. She had never before noticed how much his isolated head resembled that of William F. Buckley, Jr. "Welcome child," Caspar said. "Let us hasten to the meditative chamber. I've an appointment with Jacqueline Kennedy Onassis at eleven." Leapin' Lizards! Pauline thought as Caspar ushered her into the bedroom. He *sounds* like Buckley too!

The bedroom was all business: Madras tapestries from Azuma, a waterbed, a single glowing candle, an icon of Albert Ellis. But as she drew off her mink, Pauline could not escape the dread feeling that Gore Vidal was looking on from somewhere.

She positioned herself on the waterbed in the lotus position, but as Caspar disrobed, she saw that something was horridly amiss. His Apollolike member was all green and warty; it looked just like a cucumber!

Seeing her distress, Caspar flicked his tongue around a serpentine smile, and lifted the tip of the thing with thumb and forefinger, like one handling a very dead fish. Beneath the green cylinder was the genuine article, and Pauline thereby realized that it *was* in fact a cucumber, strapped around his shapely waist and buttocks dildo-fashion.

"We have progressed to the stage of the vegetative yab-yum ceremony, child," Caspar said, folding himself into lotus position before her. "Trust me. I shall prepare your yoni for the lingam." So saying, he arched gracefully toward her, and with a few chameleonlike darts of his subtle tongue, annointed her with a secretion strangely not unlike Prof. Himmelfarb's Wonderous Snake-Oil.

"We begin," he said, inserting the capacious cucumber into her yoni with the aid of an obsidian shoehorn. "You ain't gonna believe this, kid, but if you are truely worthy, the walls of thy yoni and the pureness of thy heart will in the passage of (he checked his Rolex) forty-eight minutes transform this humblest of vegetables into that paragon of transcendant lingamhood, a kosher pickle. Thus will you achieve satori."

Caspar wiggled his buttocks once, then assumed the Buddhalike stillness of true yab-yum and stared at her with his beagle-lizard eyes. "Meditate," he ordered. "Concentrate on the godhead. Fill your being with the essential sourness of Vishnu's Shiva aspect. Think of Katz' Delicatessen. Open yourself to true communion with my own ineffable being, let me be the Gulden's mustard on your pastrami sandwich."

Earnest as always, Pauline did as she was bade. Or tried to. But insidious thoughts kept disturbing her meditations. Lines from Bob Dylan songs. Gypsy prophecies. Daddy's latest creation, Duck Down Delight. Smokey Stover cartoons. Myra Breckenridge. God help her, Lobster Newburg on white toast points. How Protestant can you *get?* she thought mournfully. Will I never achieve satori. Will I never attain the pure golden light? Am I doomed to wander the Earth eternally like Little Orphan Annie, without even a Sandy's arf to recenter my being? Oh Lord Jesus, where is thy Punjab, oh Daddy, where is the Asp?

Time, as its habit, passed. Caspar's gaze remained inscrutable; was he meditating upon Jacqueline Kennedy Onassis, the bitch, or was he, unlike her, actually succeeding in filling his being with the essence of Katz' Delicatessen? Occasionally, Pauline felt a twinge within her, as of cucumber transforming itself into the holy substance, but her attention wandered, her faith failed.

Finally, the alarm on Caspar's watch sounded, and, with a sound like a beer-bung, he withdrew the lingam from her yoni. Unstrapping it from his body, he nibbled thoughtfully at its tip. Purple rage contorted his aristocratic features. He gobbled angrily at the green cylindroid with teeth that Pauline suddenly noticed had become razor-sharp and pointed.

Spitting fragments of pickle, he screamed: "A sweet gherkin! After all we've meant to each other, you insult me with a sweet gherkin! You have failed! I thrust you into the outer darkness, Whore of Sheboygan!" The room filled with a Jovian thunderhead. Lightnings crackled. Horns sprouted on Caspar's brow.

"But first, I must take holy vengeance," he hissed, snapping at her treasonous snatch.

"Get away from me, you creep!" Pauline shouted, vaulting off the bed, grabbing up the candle, and battering at Casper as the holy man, slavering, chased her around the meditative chamber, running now on all fours.

From somewhere, came the clattering roar of helicopter vanes, and a moment later, the Quicksilver Kid, ice-blue eyes, hair in the usual chrome-colored afro, burst through the fifth story window, wearing the natty scarlet and brown uniform of the Northwest Mounted Police and brandishing an antique Sten-gun. "I'm Captain Jenks of the Horse Marines . . ." he sang, firing a burst of automatic weapons fire into the waterbed, which began to bleed a clear viscous goo.

Caspar squealed, gibbered, and avaunted into a clothes-closet, locking the door behind him.

"Where the hell *were* you?" Pauline demanded.

"My Stalin tank threw a tread on Houston Street," the Quicksilver Kid said. "When are they going to fix those potholes?"

"Never trust a gypsy cabbie," Pauline sighed.

The doorbell rang. Pauline answered it, and a bull dyke in a Western Union uniform handed her a telegram and tweaked her nipple. It was from Houlihan O'Rourke, the Poet Laureate of Canarsie:

"I need my muse
And don't forget the booze."

"He needs me!" Pauline cried delightedly. "Give me a lift to the East Village, Quicksilver."

The Kid held his finely-chiseled nose. His blue eyes twinkled. His silver curls twanged like a thousand miniature sprung sofa-springs; his disdain was all too apparent. "For you, oh Princess of Sheboygan," he said, "even that." He threw her mink around her, grabbed her up by the waist, and leapt out the shattered bedroom window, catching the last rung of the helicopter ladder with a negligent hand. "Up, up and away!" he shouted at the pilot.

"When do I get to ball you?" Pauline asked for the thousandth time.

"When the swallows come back to Hoboken," the Kid answered as they ascended skywards. At least he never gave the same answer twice.

CHAPTER THREE: A GUINNESS GOODNIGHT IN LONDONDERRY TOWN

Pauline arrived at O'Rourke's lair lugging two fifths of Old Bushmill's. O'Rourke lay on his sprung sofa in an Oscar Wilde pose swilling Romilar from the bottle and coughing consumptively. A notepad and a Bic Banana with a goosefeather taped to it accented the crotch of his threadbare dressing gown.

"My daemon has deserted me," he moaned as Pauline kicked her way towards him through the debris of the living room. "I'm out of booze. I've been smoking kitty litter." As she knelt reverentially beside him, Pauline noted that the breath of the Poet Laureate of Canarsie did in fact smell like a catbox.

How the poor creature did suffer for his art, how she envied the knife-sharp goad of Olympus that drove his consciousness through the nether pits, the better to hone what was left of his purified mind for the holy task of carving truth out of gladly suffered pain! Would that it had been given to *her* to wallow heroically through the quagmire of maya towards that bright and distant shore! As it was, what was she but heiress to a Toilet Paper empire, fairy godchild to the Quicksilver Kid, seeker after sweet nirvana that seemed forever beyond her Midwestern grasp, enemy to those who make her an enemy, friend to those who have no friend.

Feebly, O'Rourke stroked her coal-black hair. "Ah, my flower of delight, you have come to succor me in my hour of darkest despair," he sighed. "Oh tempura, oh mores!" He snatched a whiskey bottle out of her hand. "Gimme!" he grunted, ripping out the stopper with his powerful teeth, and gargling down a third of the contents.

As the poet drew sustanence into his ravaged being, Pauline glanced at the lines of verse scribbled on his notepad. The deathless words had all been written atop each other, layer after layer on the same line. Pauline sighed. She had done the same thing, taking a sociology final on mescalin during her junior year at Vassar. It drew her soul towards him with dim maternal longings.

"Let me give what it is in me to give," she said, removing pad and pen, parting his dressing gown, and shooing a cockroach gently out of his navel. "Let me suckle in some small way the splendors of your creation."

"Sure kid," the poet said, still chugalugging the bottle of Old Bushmill's. "I can always use a good suckling. If the flesh is willing, as it were," he added uncertainly.

Pauline set to her noble if under the circumstances formidable task with holy dedication. She drew on her full resources, cycling her prana energy up from all chakras into the halolike interface between her lips and the quill of the Poet Laureate of Canarsie. She called upon the powers of the universe to fill her with their transcendant strength, to come to her aid in this moment of need. From somewhere, the pure golden light began to fill her, and she felt a tremulous communion with that which she had lifelong sought, the tentative tendrils of the Cosmic Connection.

Never before had she felt this close to total union with the unattainable. "Oh children," the voice of Mick Jagger sang in her head, "it's just a shot away. . . ." And while O'Rourke's limp flesh showed no signs of joining her in that land over the rainbow, the poet did give an ecstatic moan, and take up pad and Bic Banana. "Oh yeah, I feel it!" he cried. "The muse returneth." And he began to recite in barroom stentor:

"Twas a Guinness goodnight in Londonderry town
The world was opening up as the bars were shutting down. . . ."

All at once, the crystalline light was shattered by a commotion bursting through the door. "O'Rourke! At last I've found you!"

"Daddy!" Pauline groaned, as she looked up to see her gray-haired father, clad in a black pinstripe suit, making his way towards the couch.

"I'm the President of Feather-Bright Bathroom Tissue of Sheboygan Wisconsin," Daddy declaimed, "and I've got a commission for you. We're starting a new line called Epic Bathroom Parchment, a thousand wipes to a roll, and a heroic quatrain on each and every one of them! I'll pay you three dollars a panel."

O'Rourke beamed at him. "Enlightenment for the masses as they wipe their asses," he exclaimed, handing Daddy the severely-depleted bottle. "I'll be the Baudelaire of the Bathroom!"

Daddy poured himself a shot into a Dixie cup that he produced from a jacket pocket, downed it, and noticed Pauling kneeling at the foot of the erstwhile Baudelaire of the Bathroom.

"You've done it again, Daddy," Pauline sighed.

"Oh hullo Pauline," Daddy said mildly. "I've got a present for you in the car. A nice friendly doggie. His name is—"

"Don't tell me—Sandy."

"My little girl is psychic," Daddy said paternally, tilting his head proudly at O'Rourke.

CHAPTER FOUR: TAKE TWO AND HIT TO RIGHT

Out on the street again, trailed by a threadbare orange mutt with undotted eyeballs, Pauline accepted the homage of a green pill proffered by an aging hippie, tore up a few random parking tickets, read her fortune in a puddle of spilt beer, wandering south across Houston onto pushcart-choked Orchard Street, still searching for the ineffable. Which Daddy had once more snatched from her butterfingered grasp. "Arf," the dog commiserated, but she found that his word of wisdom moved her not a silly millimeter closer to true centeredness. One more legend down the willy-hole!

A bearded old man in a beaver hat and black frock coat accosted her confidentially from between a fruit cart and a stand purveying slightly defective rubber underwear. "Secrets of the Torah, kiddo, and for you, dirt cheap!"

She followed his crooked finger into a convenient alleyway. He unbuttoned his coat and flashed her a scroll sewn into the lining. "It's all here," he said. "Wisdom of the ages. Stock market tips. Dynamite recipe for gefilte fish. You name it, I got it, straight from heavies like Solomon and Moses, direct to you for a pittance."

"What do you have on nirvana?"

"What do *I* have for *you* on *nirvana*?" crowed the old sage. "Listen, in here is stuff on nirvana that Gautama Whatshisface got straight from my great-great-great-great-great granduncle Schmuel, his name be blessed. Only fifty kopecks."

Forlornly, Pauline searched her coat pockets. "No tengo," she shrugged.

"Well then, how about a little sweet potato pie for a hungry old man?"

Resignedly, Pauline opened her coat, leaned up against a brick wall, arched her pelvis towards him.

"*That's* not a sweet potato pie," the bearded sage said. "You got maybe a charlotte russe?"

Seeing her distress, the sage relented. "Okay, for you kiddo, a little spare change, as it were, not that you should think I'm usually a sucker for schnorrers." He bent close to her ear.

"Take two and hit to right, you can't go wrong," he whispered, and disappeared up the alley as the illusive meaning of his words reverberated just beyond her grasp.

CHAPTER FIVE: THE QUAINTEST LITTLE TEA-ROOM

"Quack," Pauline found herself abruptly observing. The green pill was starting to hit. A creature in a pantsless blue sailor suit scuttled across the alley. *Merde!* She had been fed Duck Tranquilizer again. Back on Orchard Street, everyone had sprouted bills and walked with a waddle.

"Help!" she telepathically wailed. Soundwise, it was just another "Quack."

Nevertheless, a moment later, the Quicksilver Kid appeared, this time in a flash of ectoplasm and dressed as Uncle Scrooge.

"Daisy, Daisy, give me your answer do . . ." he sang in a computer voice as he proffered a handful of dry corn, which Pauline gobbled up with her long yellow lips. She quacked one more time, and then Duckville faded into the morning mist like Brigadoon.

"When do I—"

"When shrimps learn to whistle," the Kid said, and vanished.

"Arf!" observed Sandy.

Turning, Pauline bumped behinds with a fat lady in a leopard skin coat who was scrutinizing a box of used rupture-easers through a whale-bone pince-nez.

"Mother!"

"Pauline, my only!" Mother exclaimed. "Still wearing that tacky old mink."

Actually, Pauline wasn't her only, but her brother Ogden had been disowned when, after eschewing the family product for thirty days in order to cop out of his induction physical, he had found that he *liked* what he called "The Rousseauian innocence of me unwiped arse." Poor Ogden had been banished to the nether reaches of Harvard Law School.

"We must have lunch together my precious," Mother declared. "I've discovered this quaintest little tea-room in Chinatown." So saying, Mother summoned her peach-colored Rolls, chauffeured by a bearded Cuban in matching livery, and whisked Pauline downtown to an alleyway off a hidden muse off an unknown sidestreet in the labyrinth of mysterious Chinatown, where she rapped three times with the ivory head of her umbrella on a graffitied green door.

A leering Chinese in a blue Mao suit admitted them to a large low-ceilinged room smogged with opium smoke. Racks of straw pallets climbed the walls, each supporting a comatose lotus-eater. A Nubian giant with a panga strapped to his waist passed the pipe around. A cockfight was being held in the far corner, and close by their table, Peter Lorre dropped a cageful of hamsters one by one into a tank of piranhas, giggling delicately. Arabs shot themselves up with syringes of black petroleum. A spirited auction of machineguns was taking place. Tarantulas scuttled across the floor, gingerly avoiding islands of broken glass. A befezzed Turk expired loudly with a scimitar in his back as they sat down.

"Isn't it *darling*?" Mother said as an Albanian dwarf brought evil-smelling cups of thick green tea. Mother sighed. "It's only a matter of time before *Cue Magazine* discovers the place and utterly *ruins* it."

Pauline took a gulp of tea and retched. Peyote. "The usual," Mother told the waiter. She slugged down half her cup of peyote tea. A peglegged pirate with a green vulture perched on his shoulder sat down at the next table, ordered grog, leered at them with his one bloodshot eye, and motioned a quartet of Arabs to him with his rusty hook.

A dead bat fell from the ceiling onto their table; Mother daintily picked it up with her chopsticks and dropped it onto the floor. "You really *must* let me choose a new wardrobe for you at Lord and Taylor's," she said. "You'll never make a decent match looking like *that.* And Antonio absolutely *must* redo your hair!"

The Albanian waiter angrily slammed a huge steaming platter of gray rice and stewed fish-heads down on the table. "Death to the revisionist lap-dogs of the Wall Street blood-suckers," he observed. "Henry Kissinger eats the hairy canary."

"You may go now," Mother told him, noblesse obligewise. She popped a smiling carp-head into her mouth and swallowed it with crunches and gurgles. "Absolutely authentic," she said, spitting a single fish-eye onto the plate. "I *must* get the recipe before we leave, do remind me, my precious."

Pauline poked nervously at her food with a single chopstick. Something about the place disquieted her—it was all so . . . so *pseudo.*

"You're not eating, child," Mother said. "You must eat your food." She picked up a fish-head with her chopsticks and shoved it in Pauline's face. "Eat it!" she commanded, blushing scarlet.

A vein pulsed purplely in her temple. "EAT IT!" she roared. "EAT IT, OR I'LL CRAM IT DOWN YOUR THROAT!"

"May we join you, ladies?" the one-eyed pirate asked, catching mother under the throat with his hook. An Arab conked her over the head with a baseball bat and stuffed her into a gunny sack. "The Sultan will pay well for this one, Black Pete," he promised. "Pieces of eight! Pieces of eight!" shrieked the vulture.

"Arr, what about the little girly?" Black Pete slavered, cuffing the bird with his meat hand.

"I'll take her on consignment," the Arab said, and Pauline found herself held aloft by the feet and dropped into a burlap darkness smelling of moldy potatoes.

CHAPTER SIX: MAMELUKE OF EXXON

"Well, it's not the Plaza, but it does have a certain raw charm," Mother said, leaning back against a mountain of plush velvet cushions and sipping grapejuice from a silver chalice. The huge tent was hung with Persian tapestries; a whole camel was being turned on a spit; gold trays of sweetmeats were everywhere; forty-seven beautiful women in harem costumes lounged about on pillows, plucking their eyebrows, teasing their hair, popping chewing gum and reading *Silver Screen*. A eunuch in red-and-green pantaloons dropped myrrh and frankincense on a charcoal brazier; another stood at the tentflap stroking a Thompson submachinegun.

"Daddy will be livid," Mother said. "I was supposed to meet him at the Forum at six. He'll probably get *drunk* and be picked up by some *hooker*. Just wait till I get him home, the beast!"

Mother fingered her mauve harem flimsies distastefully. "*As for this,*" she said, "they must've picked it up at *Klein's.* And it absolutely *clashes* with my eyeshadow!"

There was a flourish of off-key trumpets beyond the tentflap, a roll of tin drums, and then a reedy muzzein's voice proclaimed: "His Sultanic Majesty, Al-Arad-Al-Bul-Abdul-Ben-Dar-Kamir, Lion of the East, Sheik of the Burning Sands, Mameluke of Exxon, the Last of the Red Hot Lovers!"

Pauline looked up expectantly as the harem pressed their collective forehead to the Bigelow on the floor, and Mother raised her pince-nez, the better to regard the countenance of the fabulous sheik. "I'll bet he looks just like Rudolf Valendino, my precious," she cooed.

Through the tentflap came a stooped, emaciated little figure wearing tan Bermuda shorts and an Aloha shirt. His gray hair was greased into a pompadour-and-DA with a pound and a half of Vaseline. His pop-eyes, set a quarter of an inch apart, rolled in their sockets like spastic ball-bearings. Green drool spewed from his toothless mouth with which he furiously gummed a soggy green cigar.

"Pussy," slavered the Sultan. "Pussypus*sypussy*! Me want me *pussy*!"

His eyes chanced to fall on Pauline, and with a magnificent effort managed to stay there, staring at her like a frog's. He gummed his cigar to bits, spat out the fragments, and with a long warty tongue, licked at the pimple on the tip of his nose. "Pussy!" he howled, and scuttled across the tent towards her.

"QUICKSILVER!" Pauline screamed on all psychic wavelengths. "MAYDAY! MAYDAY! MAYDAY!"

From somewhere came the dopplering hoot of an approaching train whistle. A moment later, an eight-wheeled black iron locomotive burst through the fabric of the tent, bellowing steam, throwing red-hot cinders, and tossing Al-Arad-Al-Bul-Abdul-Ben-Dar-Kamir into a brass spittoon with its cowcatcher.

In the driver's cab was the Quicksilver Kid, wearing an Israeli general's fatigues, and a black patch over one eye. As the locomotive roared through the tent, he leaned down, snatched up Pauline, and bore her off into the trackless sun-seared wastes of the Arabian desert, singing "The Wabash Cannonball."

"When do I get to ball you, oh Djin of the Desert?" Pauline asked, as the Kid held her against the outside of the locomotive cab, steering nimbly with one hand. The encampment of the Sultan disappeared behind a horizon of endless dun sand dunes as the locomotive chugged merrily on into the horse latitudes of the desert sea.

"Inside the gates of Eden," the Kid said, depositing her on a sandy wavecrest. "Listen to the rumble, the lightning and the roar . . ." he sang in a hillbilly voice as the locomotive turned and disappeared into a convenient mirage.

CHAPTER SEVEN: THE SEVEN PILLARS OF WISDOM

For what seemed like the proverbial forty days and forty nights (forty years? She was not really up on Occidental religions), Pauline wandered in the desert under a klieg-light sun that never seemed to set, sustaining herself on random patches of psychedelic manna and the warm bottles of Coke littering the pristine desert sands. Long gone was her mink, her civilized persona, and about fifteen pounds of shapely flesh.

But as the desert sun tanned her skin, bleached her hair to starlet blond, wrung her dry like a Turkish towel, etched all surplus meat from her bones, and leeched her consciousness of all save the sparkly sand, golden sun, and baby blue sky, her spirit, her prana-energy, the essence of her Paulineishness, began to soar. Heat waves enveloped her in a perpetual silver aura. Her head seemed large enough to at last contain the cosmos. A clean sweat annointed her body with holy oil. The world was filled with light.

Satori flirted at her fingertips. Raga-rock rang in her ears. She felt herself closer than ever before to the ineffable oneness of it all, tiny lightning flashes of energy arcing between the Universal Mind and the points of her nipples, the golden tips of each strand of hair. Sipping warm Coke and striding like a goddess from dune to dune, she felt it was only a matter of time before the Connection was finally made.

Visitations appeared from out of the endless mirror mirage of the desert, travelled silently with her apace, then faded back into the shimmering void. An Englishman in a burnoose riding a camel. Country Joe and the Fish. The Maharishi. Mr. Natural. George Harrison. Mandrake the Magician. Yogi Berra. Winnie the Pooh.

Finally, with the inevitability of a Henny Youngman punchline, the Garden hove into sight, floating beyond the next ridge of sand dunes.

CHAPTER EIGHT: INSIDE THE GATES OF EDEN

Palm trees and junipers. Christmas trees dripping with sugar-plums and frosted with cocaine snow. Rivers of lemonade and pools of Gallo Hearty Burgundy. Soft green grass and Beatles Muzak. Hillocks of Baskin-Robbins Jamoca Almond Fudge ice cream. And under the mother-of-pearl gateway, an honest-to-Judy-Garland yellow brick road leading into the interior.

As Pauline followed the yellow brick road, munchkins giggled from behind banks of rosebushes, pink and white bunny rabbits gamboled beside her, patchouli incense wafted from giant lavender orchids, Bambi darted across her path, lions played jacks with lambs.

In the center of the Garden was an azure lake. In the center of the lake was a small island, lawned like an English park. In the center of the island grew a tall tree, heavy with bright red apples and festooned with No Trespassing signs. Under the tree grew a giant mushroom embellished with bright psychedelic scrimshaw like a Fillmore poster. Atop the mushroom sat the Quicksilver Kid, naked except for a golden loincloth.

CHAPTER NINE: WHEN THE SWALLOWS COME BACK TO HOBOKEN

As Pauline swam through the warm water, shrimp in its limpid depths began to whistle "Bolero". And she knew at last the swallows were returning to far-off Hoboken.

Glistening, Pauline emerged from the lake and walked across the lawn to the kid's mushroom. Sinuously, he debarked from it and stood before her.

His hair was a Buddha's silver mandala. His ice blue eyes were lidded with wisdom. His ears had grown to the Bodhisattva-like magnificence of a Lyndon Johnson's. The transcendental hush was broken only by the OM-like chant of bright neon hummingbirds.

"At last," Pauline said. "At last my search is over." For the moment of Enlightenment was surely at hand. Golden light was the world.

"The time to hesitate is through," the Kid sang. "Got no time to wallow in the mire. . . ."

With a tremulous hand, Pauline drew aside his golden loincloth, the last veil of maya, and beheld—

A pelvis as smooth and featureless as a Barbie Doll's.

"You can't always get what you want," sang the Quicksilver Kid, ascending skywards on a royal blue cloud.

"Arf!" said the faithful Sandy, who had appeared at her side. *Poit!* Satori! It was time to return to Hoboken.

Introduction to The Last Hurrah of the Golden Horde

This story was first conceived as a fantasy movie extravaganza with a cast of thousands and a budget the size of the national debt. "The Last Hurrah of the Golden Horde" remained an unmakeable movie and an unwriteable story until I met Jerry Cornelius or Michael Moorcock or whoever.

As a film spectacular, it would be a studio-breaker, and as a story it had no central character, since lack of a centrality was part of the point.

When I arrived in London, however, I found that a literary experiment was going on aimed at playing with this very notion of lack of centrality, among other things. Michael Moorcock had written a novel called The Final Program*, the first part of a tetralogy, in which he created the character of Jerry Cornelius and "stated the themes" of a kind of four part novelistic symphony. In the three succeeding novels, he would use all this material as unstated mythic substructure so that* subsequent "Jerry Cornelius stories" would be structured by allusion to an "artificial myth" that was not necessarily in the readers' repertoires. At the center might be void.

Mike not only wrote the four novels, not only wrote many Jerry Cornelius stories in addition to the books, not only called into being a Jerry Cornelius movie and a Jerry Cornelius comic strip, but encouraged over half a dozen other writers to write "their Jerry Cornelius story."

How did he do this? It's very hard to explain. Each of us had our own different reasons for participating in Mike's weird experiment. In my case, Jerry Cornelius gave me a bankable dark star and turned "The Last Hurrah of the Golden Horde" into a shootable story.

Or would you rather buy a duck?

The Last Hurrah of the Golden Horde

Eastward across the Gobi, three hundred old men ride upon three hundred shaggy, wizened Mongolian ponies. The ponies, like their riders, are the tag-end of a dying breed. The men are dressed in filthy, cracked, badly-tanned leathers. Across their backs are strapped short Mongolian bows; swords dangle from their waists and they carry lances in their horny hands as they ride toward the sunrise.

In the dingy storefront on Sullivan Street identified as the D'Mato Social Club by the peeling green letters on the fly-specked translucent area above the black-painted area of the plate glass window that hid the cave-like interior from the view of casual assassins in the street, Jerry Cornelius, a not-so-casual (or in his own way a *more* casual) assassin, sat on a gray-enameled metal folding chair facing a gnarled old man with a Jimmy Durante nose across the cracked surface of a rickety card-table. Jerry wore a carefully-dated black suit, a black silk shirt, a white tie, and white boots. His black vinyl raincoat was draped across a counter which paralleled one wall of the room and which held a display of candy bars and a cardboard showcase of De Nobili cigars. Behind the counter hung a faded photograph of Franklin D. Roosevelt framed in black. The man with the Jimmy Durante nose was smoking a De Nobili and the semipoisonous smoke that he blew across the table was clearly designed to blow Jerry's cool. Jerry, however, had expected this, and as a counter-measure kept his violin case close at hand. It seemed a draw.

"This is a big one, Cornelius," the old man said.

"Flesh is flesh, Mr. Siciliano," Jerry replied. "Metal is metal."

"Have you ever hit a Cabinet-level official before?"

Jerry pondered. "It's open to doubt," he finally admitted. "I got a head of state once, but it was a benevolent despotism."

The old man chewed his cigar, much to Jerry's disgust. "It'll have to do," he said. "You've got the contract. How soon can you be in Sinkiang?"

"Three days. I'll have to change passports again."

"Make it two."

"I'd have to pull strings. It'll cost you."

The old man shrugged. "Do it," he said.

Jerry grinned. "My motto, Mr. Siciliano. Who's the contract on?"

"Mao Tze Tung's heir-apparent."

"Who's that these days?" Jerry asked. The situation in China had gotten somewhat muddled.

"That's your problem," Durante-nose said.

Jerry shrugged. "And my cover?"

"Arrange it yourself."

Jerry got up clutching his violin case, ran his hand through his great bush of blonde natural, retrieved his raincoat, took a De Nobili from the counter, and said with an evil smirk: "Don't say I didn't warn you."

The railroad train consisted of a locomotive, a sealed boxcar, three flatcars and a caboose. The boxcar contained one ton of (uncut?) heroin. The open flatcars held three hundred members of the People's Army of China armed with machine-guns, protected from the elements by the thought of Chairman Mao. The caboose held the negotiating team. The locomotive was a diesel job.

"You'll be working with the Russians on this, Inspector Cornelius," Q said. "Our interests happen to coincide."

Jerry frowned. The last time he had worked with a Russian, he had contracted the clap. "I don't trust those buggers," he told Q.

"Neither do we," Q said crisply, "but it's the only way we can get you into Sinkiang. You leave for Moscow on Aeroflot in the morning."

"*Aeroflot?*" whined Jerry. Christ, those Russian stewardesses! he thought. "I get airsick on Aeroflot," he complained.

Q glared at Jerry firmly. "We're getting the family plan discount," he explained.

"But I'm flying alone. . . ."

"Precisely."

"Dramamine?"

"If you insist," Q said primly. "But the Bureau frowns on foreign substances."

"My mission?" Jerry asked.

"Catch the Chinks and the Maf in the act. Bust them."

"But we have no jurisdiction."

"Hence the Russians," said Q. "Use your head."

"They have no jurisdiction either."

"You're not that naive, Cornelius."

"I suppose not," Jerry said wistfully.

According to the thought of Chairman Mao, the village was an anachronism: one hundred and fifty-three flea-bitten nomads, along with their animals (mostly diseased horses and threadbare yaks) encamped in a cluster of leather yurts on the margin of the Gobi. From the correct point of view, the village might be said not to exist.

From this same point of view (as well as from several others) the three hundred old men who galloped in from the wastes of the Gobi might also be said to be nonexistent. Nevertheless, the nomad encampment had a certain reality for the old warriors; in fact an archetypal reality stretching back in a line of unbroken tradition from the days of the Great Khan and his Golden Horde still burning clearly in their ancestral memory to the misty and arthritic present.

Village. Burn. Pillage. Rape. Kill.

Outside the umbrella of the thoughts of Chairman Mao, the old barbarians existed in a happier reality of simple, straightforward traditional imperatives.

Therefore, unmindful of the fact that the village was an anachronism, the old warriors, in the time-honored tradition of the Golden Horde, rode into the encampment, slew the men and children, made a pass at raping the women to death, slaughtered the animals, burned the yurts, and continued to ride eastward, secure in the knowledge that they had fulfilled another quantrum of their timeless destiny.

A long concrete runway broke the monotony of the Sinkiang wastelands with the more absolute monotony of its geometric perfection. At right angles to the runway, a railroad spur wandered off toward the horizon. From the viewpoint of the pilot of the C-5A approaching this three-dimensional nexus, the runway and the railroad spur formed a T with a finite bar and an infinite upright. If anything, the pilot thought this sloppy. It is likely that he did not fully comprehend the thought of Chairman Mao; a more erudite man might have appreciated the symbolism.

"It is a clear demonstration of the cynical perfidy of the Chinese gangster element enshrined behind the facade of the Maoist clique, Comrade Cornelius," Commissar Krapotkin observed genially, drawing a glass of tea from the silver samovar and handing it across the table to Jerry. Krapotkin was a short barrel of a man who wore his double-breasted Mod suit like a uniform. Perhaps it is a uniform, Jerry thought, as he took a spiked sugar-cube out of his mother-of-pearl pillbox and inserted it between his teeth. The Russians were doing their best to be hip these days and it was hard to keep up.

As Jerry sipped tea through the sugar-cube between his teeth, Krapotkin lit up an Acapulco Gold and continued to make small-talk: "While they gibber and squeak their anti-Soviet obscenities in Peking, they deal with the worst gangster element of the decadent capitalist society by their back door in Sinkiang, which, by the way, is of course rightfully Soviet territory."

"I wouldn't call the Maf the *worst* gangster element of decadent capitalist society," Jerry observed mildly.

Krapotkin produced a metallic sound which Jerry tentatively identified as a laugh. "Ah, very good, Comrade Cornelius. Indeed, one might argue that the distribution of heroin, contributing as it does to the further corruption of the already decadent West, is an act which contributes to the long range progress of the working-class."

"But providing the reactionary adventurist regime in Peking with hard American currency does not," Jerry rejoined.

"Exactly, Comrade! Which is why my government has decided to cooperate with the American narcs. Once the Maoist clique has been exposed in the act of selling heroin to the Maf, we should have no trouble totally discrediting them with progressive elements throughout the world."

"And of course the Mafia will be discredited as well."

"?"

"The Maf is essentially a patriotic organization like the K.K.K. or the Loyal Order of Moose."

Krapotkin roached his joint. "Enough of the pleasantries, Comrade," he said. "Are you prepared for the drop?"

Jerry fingered his violin case. "My cover?" he inquired.

"You will be a Mafia hit man assigned a contract on the heir-apparent to Mao Tze Tung," Krapotkin said. "Our agents in Palermo have uncovered just such a plot."

"The real hit man?"

Krapotkin smiled. "He has been disposed of, I assure you."

From a certain viewpoint, Jerry reflected, Krapotkin was right.

Not 90 seconds after the C-5A had taxied to a halt with its tail facing the juncture of the rail-spur-runway T as if preparing to fart along the track, the great doors in the nose opened like the petals of an aluminium flower, a ramp was lowered, and a black Cadillac disgorged, pulling a house trailer of grandiose proportions and Miami-Beach-Gothic design. The C-5A continued to disgorge Cadillacs like a pregnant guppy, each one pulling a trailer larger and more rococo than the last.

Something less than three hundred old men galloped haltingly across the wastes of Sinkiang on faltering ponies. A dozen or more of the Mongol warriors had burst blood vessels in their tired old brains from the excitement of the last massacre. The blood was running thin. Where once the steppes had echoes to the pounding hooves of the Golden Horde as the whole world trembled before a tide of barbarians that filled the field of vision from horizon to horizon, now there was naught but an expiring handful of decrepit savages. *Sic transit gloria mundi.* The spirit was willing, but the flesh was practically moribund. The survivors envied those few of their comrades lucky enough to have died a warrior's death sacking the last village in an endless chain reaching back to the glory days when the villages had names like Peking and Samarkand and Damascus.

But something—call it pride or manly virtue—kept the pitiful remnant of the Horde going, riding ever eastward into the sunrise. Perhaps it was the hope that somewhere on the endless steppe there still remained a village large enough (but not *too* large) to bring them all the glory of death in one last gory, triumphant, final massacre. Flailing like tattered battle flags in their befuddled old brains the simple imperatives which shaped their lives and hopes and destinies: Village. Burn. Pillage. Rape. Kill.

Jerry Cornelius, still clutching the violin case, stood alone in the gray wasteland, and watched the Russian helicopter disappear into the slate-colored sky with a certain sense of foreboding. You just can't trust those Russians, he thought. Now where was the car?

To the east was a large boulder. Behind it, and not without a certain sense of relief, Jerry found a late model black Cadillac sedan, well-waxed and shiny. So far, so good.

Inside the car, Jerry found his new persona. Doffing his clothes, he assumed the persona: a black pin-striped suit with pegged pants and thin lapels, a white button-down shirt, a white tie, a diamond stickpin, pointed black Italian loafers, argyl socks, a box of De Nobilis, and jars of black shoe polish and vaseline, with which he gave himself a Rudolph Valentino job, atop which he affixed a green porkpie hat with a leopard skin band. Thus accoutered, and with a round toothpick in his mouth at a jaunty angle, he sealed the car, turned on the air-conditioning, and set out across the wasteland.

Only when he discovered that the radio would bring in nothing but Radio Moscow and that the tape library contained naught but Tschaikowsky did the full extent of Krapotkin's treachery become apparent.

As the train hove into sight of the rail-spur-runway junction, the soldiers of the People's Army were able to contain cries of awe, amazement and dismay only by diligent application of the thought of Chairman Mao.

For there in the depths of Sinkiang was, considering the circumstances, quite a decent facsimile of Las Vegas. A semicircle of trailers rimmed a large kidney-shaped swimming pool. Done up in pastels, sporting picture windows, and sprouting numerous extensions, wings, and breezeways, the trailers resembled the lower or casino floors of Las Vegas hotels. Complex mazes of cabanas, beach chairs, bocci courts, pavillions, greenhouses, handball courts and pidgeon coups which filled the interstices between the trailers completed the illusion. Behind the semicircular Las Vegas facade towered the tail of the C-5A, reminiscent, somehow, of Howard Hughes and all that his shadowy persona implied. Parked among the spectral casino hotels were an indeterminate number of black Cadillacs.

Around the pool, waiters in red tuxedoes served tepid Collinses to fat men in sunglasses stretched out in beach chairs, warming themselves with complex arrays of sunlamps. Starlets in bikinis paraded their pinchable asses by the poolside.

The officials in the caboose immediately called for the reserve train which had been parked fifty miles down the track in anticipation of such a necessity.

Approaching his destination from the south, Jerry Cornelius spotted a cluster of pagodas, huts and barracks, among which huge billboards had been erected bearing immense portraits of Mao, Lenin, Stalin, Enver Hoxha, and other popular personalities of the People's Republic of China. Everything was festooned with calligraphy like a wedding cake. Intermittent strings of firecrackers exploded. Hatchet men chased each other through the winding streets. Soldiers of the People's Army performed the calisthenics. The sharp syllables of Chinese dialects filled the air like razorblades. Gongs sounded. Paper dragons danced in the streets. Perpetual twilight hovered over the scene, which, upon closer inspection, proved to be constructed of balsa wood, rice paper and papier-mâché.

Warily, Jerry swung the Cadillac wide of this Chinese version of Disneyland and circled toward the tail of a C-5A which dominated the landscape. Soon reality (such as it was) changed and he found himself on the outskirts of what appeared to be a suburb of Las Vegas: the lower stories of casino hotels mounted on wheels and parked in a semicircle around a huge kidney-shaped pool, facing the Chinese apparition across the chlorinated waters.

Having spied a heavily-guarded boxcar behind

the facade of the Chinese reality, Jerry was not surprised to see a dozen thugs with machineguns guarding the C-5A. The $50,000,000 must be on the plane.

For a moment, Jerry parked the Cad along the Orient-Vegas interface, playing at pondering his next move.

Shortly, he drove on into the Mafia camp, parked the Cadillac next to a fire hydrant outside a barbershop, and melted into the scene with barely a ripple. Yes indeed, this was his kind of town!

Eastward across the wastelands, here and there a rider dead on his horse, a scungy pony faltering under its rider, the spirit burning brighter as the blood thinned as if their ancient flesh were ecto-plasmating into naught but the weathered parchment-dry quintessence of tradition-cum-desire, the desperate determination not to die a peasant's death, the image of the Final Massacre burning its forlorn hope into the backs of what was left of their arteriosclerotic brains, the husks of the Golden Horde doddered onward, ever on-ward.

"Ya get da Big Picture, Cornelius?" The Rock said, sipping at his Collins as he and Jerry lay side by side in beach chairs, sunning themselves at poolside. Jerry, dressed in neon-blue bathing suit, contrasting yellow terrycloth robe, Japanese rub-ber sandals and silvered Air Force shades, had resisted the dangerous urge to order Pernod, and as a consequence was nursing a foul rum concoc-tion. Only the presence of his violin case close at hand soothed his jangled nerves. And the sunlamps threatened to melt the shoe-polish in his hair.

"I'm not paid to get the Big Picture, Rock," Jerry said, keeping in character, though from a certain viewpoint what he was saying was true.

The Rock scratched his hairy paunch with one hand and with the other, clawlike, pinched the ass of a passing starlet, who giggled appropriately.

"I like yer style, kid," The Rock said. "But doncha have any curiosity?"

"Curiosity killed a cat."

"I'm a dog man myself, Cornelius, so who gives a shit? What I say is dese Chinks have been asking for it. Just because da punks got a few H-bombs and ICBMs is no reason for them to get the idea they can burn the Maf and live ta talk about it. Yeah, after ya hit their number two *padron*, that smart-ass punk in Peking will have ta look over his shoulder a few times before he tries putting milk-sugar in our heroin again."

"Just who is their number two?"

Rock pointed his De Nobili at the empty raft anchored out in the center of the kidney-shaped pool. "Da Big Boy will make this year's deal out on da raft—neutral turf. Whatever Chink is out there with him—zap!"

"Won't the Reds . . .?" Jerry inquired.

"Da Cads are full of heavies with choppers," The Rock grinned. "When you hit da number two, dey hit da People's Army." The Rock chucked himself under the chin with his right forefinger as if flicking a bead of sweat at the giant posters of Mao, Stalin, Hoxha and Lenin glowering like spectral Internal Revenue agents across the moat-waters of the pool.

Jerry decided to develop a sudden hankering for Egg Foo Yung.

Major Sung passed the opium pipe across the black-lacquered table to Jerry, who inhaled the sweet smoke and fingered his violin case voluptuously as Major Sung caressed his copy of the Little Red Book obscenely and said: "Of course I am familiar with your work in England, Colonel Kor Ne Loos."

"Your English is excellent, Major," Jerry lied. "Harvard?"

"Berlitz."

"I should be reporting to the honorable Heir-Apparent to godlike Mao," Jerry chided.

Major Sung frowned and kicked the brass gong which sat upon the table. Kung-fu, Jerry noted warily. He revised his estimate of Major Sung laterally. "As you of course know," Sung said with an oriental leer, "the peacock often hides his egg behind an embroidered fan."

Jerry started—he certainly hadn't expected anything like this! "The dragon has been known to preen his scales before he pounces," he rejoined.

Outside the pagoda, a chorus of two hundred kindergarten students were chanting the latest Number One on the Chinese Top 40, "Death To The Violators Of The Spirit Of Mao's Urine." Jerry tapped his fingers on the table in time to the catchy rhythm, which he recognized as a variation on "Rock Around The Clock."

"May I take that to imply that the pasta contains an asp?" Major Sung said. It was clearly not a question.

Jerry smiled. "As Confucius says, a fox with a dagger may behead a drunken lion."

Major Sung laughed. "As Chairman Mao has observed, the enemies of the Revolution will devour their own entrails if they can make a fast buck in the process."

Bowing and scraping, a Sergeant in a kimono entered the chamber with tea and fortune cookies.

Major Sung cracked open his pastry and read aloud: "Death to the revisionist running dogs of the Wall Street imperialists and their would-be lackies in Prague."

Jerry's fortune cookie said: "Tension, apprehension and dissension have begun."

As Jerry, in his pin-stripe suit, porkpie hat, and Italian loafers, lounged against the right front fender of the Cadillac, which he had parked inconspicuously at poolside, a fat man in a flowered Hawaiian shirt and black Bermuda shorts boarded a speedboat at the Vegas end of the pool. Stuffed between his thick lips was an El Ropo Supremo Perfecto Grande. Set jauntily on his bald head was a red sailor cap on the brim of which "The Big Boy" had been embroidered in Atlantic City in bold blue thread.

As a Meyer Davis orchestra in one of the poolside cabanas struck up "Amore" and a stripper began to peel on the diving board, the white speedboat set out across the pool toward the raft.

Meanwhile across the pool, fifty soldiers of the

People's Army marched back and forth bearing placards serializing the menu of Hong Fat's restaurant in severe calligraphy and psychedelic posters of Mao, Stalin, Lenin and Jim Morrison while the People's Army Brass Band played "Chinatown, My Chinatown" to which a chorus of Red Guards waving the Little Red Book sung the "Internationale" in Sinosized Albanian. To this heady send-off, an old bearded Chinese in a military tunic (with a curious if superficial resemblance to Ho Chi Minh) rowed a punt toward the raft in neutral waters.

At poolside, Jerry's trained eye picked out heavies in blue serge suits moving unobtrusively toward their Cadillacs. They all carried violin cases. Jerry placed a bet with a convenient bookie that the cases did not contain violins. The best he could get was the wrong end of 9-4 odds.

Alone on the raft at last, The Big Boy and the Heir-Apparent swapped bon mots as the strains of "High Hopes" mingled with the thin voices of schoolchildren chanting "My Mao Can Lick Your Mao" in a corrupt Canton dialect.

"Ya dirty mother, last year's dope was cut with milk-sugar."

"As Chairman Mao has observed, when dealing with corrupt mercenaries of the exploitative class, the doctrine of 'no tickee, no washee' is fully justified."

"Remember what happened to Bugsy Siegal!"

"Confucius once said that a toothless dragon does not fear the orthodontist."

Behind the Chinese Disneyland, the People's

Army had placed six machinegun nests in a circle around the boxcar of heroin.

Twenty heavies with choppers ringed the C-5A. Inside, five more heavies guarded $50,000,000 in unmarked small bills.

"Fifty million! That's robbery. You Chinks are crooks."

The Meyer Davis orchestra played "It Takes Two To Tango." The People's Army Brass Band countered with a Chinese version of "Die Fahne Hoch."

"As Chairman Mao has said," the Heir-Apparent threatened, "I may not be the best man in town, but I'll be the best till the best comes round."

Hidden behind a facade of placards, posters, pagodas, dancing paper dragons, hatchet men, schoolchildren performing calisthenics, rioting Red Guards, captured American airmen in chains, opium dens and filthy peasant huts, three hundred soldiers of the People's Army of the People's Republic of China girded themselves for a human wave attack.

"We only deal with you Commie pinko Chink bastards because you're the only mass suppliers of heroin aside from the Federal narcs that we can find."

"As Chairman Mao has said, tough, shit."

Ominously, the Meyer Davis orchestra began playing "Hawaiian War Chant."

Jerry Cornelius stubbed out his roach and

reached for his violin case. "The time has come, the Walrus said, to speak of many things," he observed as, out on the raft, The Big Boy gave the finger to the Heir-Apparent.

"Fifty million for the boxcar, take it or leave it," the Heir-Apparent said.

The People's Army Brass Band broke into "Light My Fire" as seven hundred Red Guards doused themselves with gasoline and immolated themselves while singing "Chairman Mao ist unser Fuehrer" contrapuntally, but since they were all off-key, the ploy was a failure.

"As Al Capone once observed, play ball, or we lean on you."

Jerry Cornelius opened his violin case and withdrew a violin. To the untrained observer, it appeared to be merely an ordinary electric violin with self-contained power supply, built-in amp and speaker rated at 100 watts. However, an Underground electronics expert on 150 mg of methedrene had made a significant modification: the high notes registered well into the ultrasonic and the lows were deep down in the subsonic, while all audible frequencies were eliminated.

When Jerry tucked the violin under his chin and began to play "Wipeout," the brains of everyone within a five mile radius began to vibrate to the beat of a drummer who was ultra-and-supersonic as well as different and nonexistent. To the naked human ear, Jerry appeared to be playing "The Sounds of Silence."

Out on the raft, The Big Boy was growing quite

cross as the subliminal strains of "Wipeout" inflamed cells deep within his paretic brain. "Mao Tze Tung eats shit!" he informed the Heir-Apparent.

"Al Capone was a faggot, according to the infallible thought of Mao Tze Tung!"

The Meyer Davis orchestra began to play "The Battle Hymn of the Republic."

The People's Army Brass Band immolated their tuba-player.

As Jerry segued into a subliminal rendition of "Heartbreak Hotel," fifty slot machines produced spontaneous jackpots. Cadillacs gunned their engines, whores' poodles howled, thirteen plate glass windows shattered, and every starlet at poolside achieved climax. (Some of them had not come since their first screentests.)

Hatchet men began chopping at papier-mâché pagodas. A paper dragon set itself on fire. Three hundred soldiers preparing themselves for a human wave attack began to drool and got erections. Seven hundred chanting kindergarten children achieved satori and began to devour an American flag drenched with soy sauce. A giant poster of Stalin broke into a grin and thumbed its nose at a poster of Mao.

"Mao Tze Tung eats the hairy canary!"
"The Maf sucks!"
"Faggot!"
"Creep!"
"Chink!"
"Wop!"

"ARGH!"

Salivating, The Big Boy leapt at the Heir-Apparent, chomping his El Ropo Supremo Perfecto Grande to bits, and buried teeth and cigar in the old Chinaman's beard, setting it aflame. The two men wrestled on the raft, biting, spitting and cursing for a few moments, then toppled each other into the pool, which proved to be filled with crocodiles.

Pleased with his work, Jerry Cornelius began to play "Fire."

A phalanx of Cadillacs screamed around the pool and barreled into the People's Army Brass Band spewing machinegun bullets which ripped into a poster of Mao Tze Tung, enraging a rioting mob of Red Guards who set themselves on fire and threw themselves under the wheels of the cars, causing them to skid into a balsa wood pagoda which toppled into the pool in splinters which were devoured by the blood-crazed crocodiles who expired in agony from the splinters in their stomachs some time later.

Three hundred soldiers of the People's Army launched a human wave attack, firing their machineguns at random.

Jerry continued to play "Fire," seeing no particular reason to change the tune.

Major Sung shrieked: "Capitalistic running dogs of the demographic People's revisionist lackies of Elvis Presley have over-run the ideological manifestations of decadent elements within the amplifier of the pagoda!" and committed harakiri.

The Rock began smashing slot machines with a baseball bat.

Starlets tore off their bikinis and chased terrified hatchet men around the poolside.

The human wave reached the pool, dove in, and proceeded to beat moribund crocodiles to death with their gunbutts.

A suicide squad hurled itself through the plate glass window of a trailer and devoured the rug.

Cadillacs circled the boxcar of heroin like hostile Indians, filling the air with hot lead.

The sopping remnants of the human wave reached the trailer camp and began beating thugs to death with dead crocodiles.

Red Guards showered the C-5A with ink bottles.

Tongues of flame were everywhere.

Explosions, contusions, fire, gore, curses, looting, rape.

Jerry Cornelius began playing "All You Need Is Love," knowing that no one was listening.

Riding eastward across the wastelands on their

diseased ponies, something under two hundred decrepit remnants of what once had been the glorious Golden Horde, most of them incoherent with exhaustion, spied a great conflagration on the horizon.

Flaccid adrenals urged near-moribund hearts to beat faster. They flayed their ponies with the shafts of their spears. Drool flecked the lips of doddards and ponies alike. Their backbrains smelled blood and fire in the air.

The smells of gunpowder, gasoline, burning balsa wood and papier mâché, sizzling flesh, gave Jerry Cornelius a slight buzz as he began to play "Deck the Halls With Boughs of Holly." The swimming pool was colored a bright carnelian, which did little to mask the chlorine odor. Bits of anodized aluminum struggled to keep afloat amid scraps of charred balsa wood and shards of placards.

A dented Cadillac careened through a barricade of beach chairs and into a squad of Chinese soldiers beating a starlet to death with copies of the Little Red Book before sliding over the rim of the pool to sink bubbling into the churning depths.

The pillar of fire consuming the Chinese Disneyland reminded Jerry of the Dresden firestorm. Sentimentally, he began to play "Bongo, Bongo, Bongo, I Don't Want To Leave The Congo."

In a strange display of gallantry, Red Guards, hit men, capa mafiosas and Chinese soldiers joined hands in a ring around the ruined trailer camp, screaming "*Burn*, baby, burn!" in English, Mandarin, Cantonese, Italian, Pidgin, and Yiddish. At each "*burn*" a canister of napalm dropped from somewhere onto the conflagration.

Reduced to sentimentality despite himself, Jerry played "God Save The Queen."

Two hundred or so pairs of rheumy eyes lit up with feral joy at the sight of a great city (by current Horde standards anyway) going up in flames, at the sight of smashed cars, broken bodies, naked starlets shrieking, and a great pool of what appeared to be blood.

Weeping great nostalgic tears, the last generation of the Golden Horde shouldered their spears, whipped their ponies into a stumbling gallop and charged in a body into the fray, the image of the Final Massacre burning like a city in the fevered brains of the aged savages:

Village! Burn! Pillage! Rape! Kill!

Mongolian ponies wheezing and gasping under them, the crazed doddards reached the conflagration and found to their chagrin that there was precious little unburnt, unpillaged, unraped, unkilled.

They found a boxcar guarded by machinegunners and charged it en masse, sacrificing half their number to impale the befuddled Chinese troops on their spears and set the boxcar aflame. As a strangely-intoxicating aromatic smoke billowed from the burning boxcar, the remnant of the remnant scattered, looking for more things or people to burn, rape, and kill.

A dozen of the doddards expired attempting to rape an aged whore to death, and another dozen were compelled to shamefacedly trample her to death under the hooves of their ponies, eight of which expired from the effort.

Fifteen of the Horde had heart attacks trying to beat Cadillacs to death.

A half-dozen doddards died of broken hearts when the slot machines they were torturing failed to cry out in pain.

Several of the Horde fell to devouring the corpses of crocodiles and choked to death on the splinters.

As the last Khan of the Golden Horde watched in senile befuddlement, the great silver bird issued a terribly battlecry and began to move. The doddard's bleary eyes bugged as the C-5A picked up speed, shot by him, and actually left the ground!

A feeble nervous impulse traveled spastically from his optic nerve into his brain, and thence to his arm and throat.

"Kill!" he wheezed asthmatically, and hurled his spear at the unnatural thing.

The spear was sucked into the intake of the left inboard jet engine, lodged in the turbine, and shattered it. The jet engine exploded, shearing off the wing. The C-5A nearly completed a loop before it crashed upside-down to the runway and exploded into flames.

From an aerial viewpoint, the runway and the railroad spur formed a T with a finite bar and an infinite upright, but the only living being in the area did not notice the symbolism. Riding into the sunset on his pony, his back to what in the distance seemed naught but a smoldering refuse-heap, the last Khan of the Golden Horde, sole survivor of the Final Massacre, filled his dying brain with one thought, like a dwindling chord: fulfillment; Golden Horde died in glory; village; burned; pillaged; raped; killed; ancestors proud.

This thought flared brightly in his brain like a dying ember and then he went to that Great Carnage Heap in the Sky. The wheezing pony tripped over a rock, dislodging the body, which fell to the ground in a twisted heap. A vulture descended, pecked at the body, sniffed, and departed.

The pony staggered on for a few steps, then halted, its dim brain perhaps mesmerized by the glare of the setting sun.

The Mongolian pony was still standing there an hour later when Jerry Cornelius, in his pin-stripe suit, porkpie hat, and Italian loafers, wandered dazedly up to it out of the wasteland.

"Here's a bit of luck," Jerry muttered, perking up a bit. (The short-circuiting of his electric violin had seriously vexed him.)

Jerry mounted the pony, kneed its flanks and shouted: "Git 'em up, Scout!"

The pony waddled forward a few steps, puked, and died.

Jerry extricated himself from the corpse, brushed himself off, and consulted a fortune cookie he had secreted in a pocket.

"It's a long way to Tipperary," the fortune cookie informed him.

Munching the soggy rice pastry, Jerry trudged off into the setting sun whistling "Dem bones, dem bones, dem dry bones, now hear de word of de Lord. . . ."

Introduction to Holy War on 34th Street

If there is a courtyard of Mammon in New York City, it is Herald Square, a stonehenge circle of giant department stores. A few years ago, proselytizers for any number of paths to enlightenment took to working the hordes of shoppers who poured across the intersection of Broadway and 34th Street. Moonies, and Hare Krishnas, and Scientologists, and Jews for Jesus, and the Lubevitch Society, and a whole gang of others vied in their fervor to preach The Word according to whoever. On a hot summer's day it came to resemble some Ganges flea market of gurus and movements.

This, understand, on one of the most screwed-up intersections in Manhattan's snarling traffic. This story could have erupted at any moment. . . .

Holy War on 34th Street

There oughta be a law, or if there ain't a law, then there oughta be a place where all the loonies can do their thing without driving a poor cop nuts. Like they have in London, where I took the wife and kids on my last vacation—Hyde Park, where all the religious kooks can stand up on their soap-boxes and yell at each other without screwing up traffic. We got enough trouble on the streets of New York with stoned out hippies thinking they're on LA freeways, buses hogging three lanes, crazy cabbies think they own the streets, winos gorking out in the middle of intersections, and trucks parking anywhere they damn please and to tell with all the citizens leaning on their horns behind them. What we sure enough don't need is thirty-one different flavors of religious fruitcakes crapping up traffic too, let me tell you, Charlie.

Especially not at 34th Street and Herald Square, which is a traffic cop's nightmare to begin with. You got Sixth Avenue and Broadway criss-crossing and 34th punching right across both of them, all three being major arteries, islands, and three-way traffic lights and a pattern so confusing that some out-of-town yuk is always panicking and creating a balls-up. It ain't bad enough, you got Macy's and Gimbel's and Korvette's and a major subway station pumping mobs of pedestrians into the intersection, just to keep things interesting.

Down on 33rd Street is the McAlpin Hotel, where the Scientology nuts have got a whole floor. A weird-looking crew—got eyes that seem too close together, if you know what I mean, and they like to *stare* at you with them. There are always a few of them hanging around on the corners trying to rope in the marks with some kind of free aptitude test or something, but that's for the bunco squad to worry about, they never gave traffic any trouble. Not until, that is . . .

No, I think the whole mess really started when the Hare Krishnas staked out the northeast corner of 34th and Broadway. Now even in New York, which is a twenty-four-hour freak-show, the Hare Krishnas are major league weirdos for my money. Barbled-looking kids in orange robes, the guys with their heads shaved, some kind of white gook on their noses sometimes, playing drums and bells and cymbals and dancing up and down and chanting "Hare Krishna, Hare Krishna Krishna Krishna, Hare Hare . . . ." Over and over again till you know the words by heart, whatever they mean. They peddle incense and magazines too, but what the heck, there didn't seem to be any percentage in trying to move kooks like that along as long as they didn't do it in front of Macy's and really screw the sidewalks up. Live and let live, right? *Wrong*, Charlie, as I was to find out the hard way.

Because eventually the Scientologists got to notice the crowds they were drawing. There would be maybe a dozen or so of these bozos in orange robes chanting, jumping up and down, and staring into space; naturally, they would draw a crowd of shoppers from Macy's, tourists from Keokuk, hippies from the East Village, and grease from the Bronx and Brooklyn. "Street Theater," what they call it, and so much of it goes on in New York that we don't try to bust it up unless it really impedes traffic or starts turning ugly, I mean who wants to turn a little free-lance craziness into something for the riot squad.

But the Scientologists, working the sidewalks like Orchard Street pullers, started homing in on these crowds of stationary people—easier to run their spiel on marks just standing there than trying to catch them on the fly.

Trouble was that the Hare Krishnas had their *own* goods to peddle—magazines and incense and religion—and they were into hard-sell techniques too. While most of them were drawing the crowds with their dingo act, two or three of the least spaced-out types would be pushing incense and magazines and catching citizens in raps.

Some poor schmuck from out of town comes walking down the street with the little lady, staring up at the Empire State Building or gawking at the free freak-show, and all of a sudden he's staring into a pair of spaced-out eyes attached to a weirdo in an orange robe saying loudly: "Have you heard about our Lord Hare Krishna?"

"Uh. . . ."

"Are you a religious man?"

"Ah. . . ."

"Well then wouldn't you like to know more about our beautiful Lord?"

"Uk . . ."

"This magazine will tell you, go on, take it, it's yours!"

And he hands the mark the magazine, and the guy, who by now wants nothing more than to get the hell away from this nut, nods thank you, and starts to escape.

At which point he finds the Hare Krishna freak standing in front of his face with his palm out: "That'll be a dollar." Maybe six times out of ten, the yuk will give him the buck just to get free.

Well when the Scientologists started working the same crowd, the scene began to change. They started competing. The same poor schmuck wanders down the street, stops to look, and all of a sudden he is accosted by *two* loonies.

"Have you heard about our Lord, Hare Krishna—"

"Pardon me sir, I'm a student and my school is offering these free personality profile tests to—"

"—beautiful Lord—"

"—right around the corner at the Church of Scientology—"

Both of them trying to stare him down with the same kind of crazy eyes, you know, too close together and too close to his face. "Huh? What? Jeez, Maude—" He starts to freak.

"Here, take this magazine—"

"If you'll just come this way, sir—"

They start shoving magazines and personality profiles in his puss and grabbing him by the sleeve. "What the—? Buncha crazy people here, come on Iris, let's go to the top of the Empire State Building or somewheres . . . ." And he brushes the weirdos away and pulls the old lady double-time down the street like a kid's balloon.

In the beginning, this was about all that happened, but once it began happening often enough, the Hare Krishnas and the Scientologists started *noticing* each other. You might think that this was stating the obvious, but Charlie, these were people who had trouble noticing *anything* outside their own brands of craziness, let alone each other. It must have taken them at least a week or two to finally realize that the *other* loonies were costing them customers. And from there to realizing that there *was* another flavor of nut out there. In that order.

At which point, they started taking *each other* for marks. Why not? To the Scientologists, the Hare Krishnas were just more crazy citizens in need of what they call it, "processing," and to the Hare Krishnas, the Scientologists were just more unenlightened citizens who by rights oughta be wearing orange robes, shaving their heads, chanting, and jumping up and down like jungle bunnies. I think the main reason they started really glomming onto each other, though, was that both brands of loonie were heavy into *staring*.

You must've been in staring contests when you were a kid, you know, first kid to blink or laugh or say something is the loser. Silent staring contests, we used to call 'em. Well, the Scientologists and the Hare Krishnas got themselves into jabbering staring contests, nothing silent about 'em, let me tell you, Charlie.

The rube drags his wife up the street away from them, and they're left alone giving the heavy staring act to each other, close enough to smell pastrami on each other's breath.

"Come on, chant with us and experience the pure joy of—"

"—seem to be fixated at a very low energy level, but the Church of Scientology—"

"—Hare Krishna, Hare Krishna—"

"—possible to reach a high pre-clear level in only eight weeks of—"

"—Krishna Krishna, Hare Hare—"

"—come on, stop this suppressive behavior and—"

"—Hare Rama, Rama Rama, Rama Rama, Hare Hare—"

"—you're really in desperate need of the help only Scientology—"

"HARE KRISHNA, HARE KRISHNA—"

"—reach beyond your natal engrams to—"

"KRISHNA KRISHNA, HARE HARE—"

All the while staring at each other, and the Krishna freak jumping up and down finally, and clapping his hands in time with his goombahs.

At this point it was that the northeast corner of Broadway and 34th Street became something of a hassle for the traffic detail. Because sometimes these contests would really go on and get heavy. The Hare Krishnas would come in behind their boy like sidemen, and the whole bunch of them would practically surround the poor Scientologist, bouncing up and down, playing their drums and bells, chanting, and giving him the collective goggle-eye. Now if it was you or me in there, Charlie, we would instantly remove ourselves from such a hard-sell television commercial, right, I mean it's like having an armpit shoved in your face. Not your Scientologist. To him, it's a challenge or something. He stands there staring right back, clutching his clipboard of personality tests and playing to the crowd.

Because by now there *is* a real crowd, and they are all watching the contest to see who flinches. I mean, after all, here you have a dozen crazies dancing up and down, playing their instruments, and chanting at the top of their lungs, giving their all to put this one guy on their trip, and him a beady-eyed character who's giving them the Big Stare right back. Even for New York, this is pretty good Street Theater stuff, right, so the crowd grows and grows and pretty soon it's slopping over into the gutter of 34th Street and they're not paying attention to the traffic lights any more and traffic trying to turn right onto 34th gets blocked and ties up Broadway and cabbies start leaning on their horns and pick-pockets start working the crowd and truck drivers are turning the air brown with their mouths and a poor son of a bitch traffic cop has to run over and break it up before some old fart in an Oldsmobile has a heart attack and *really* screws traffic up.

Who knew who would win? Every time it really got going, we had to step in and break it up. And it was always a somewhat surly crowd to move along, because they wanted to see how the show would end. Hard to blame them. After busting up these weirdo contests two or three times a day for half a week, I got to wondering how it would come out too. Sergeant Kelly, in his gentle way, told me later that this was my downfall, my ticket to my present beat up here in Fort Apache in the wilds of the East Bronx, where *patrol cars* have to travel in pairs. Like what they say about curiosity and the cat . . . .

Not that I was crazy enough to do anything more than think about it. I don't care what Kelly says, I didn't purposely create the "Holy War on 34th Street," as the *Daily News* called it. You think I *wanted* a thing like that to happen on my beat? You think I wanted to be up here in yehupetz dodging bricks and rousting savage junkies? Sure, I admit I had this fantasy about letting the Heavyweight Staring Championship of the World go on till a KO, but I had no intention of letting it actually happen, no matter what Kelly says. All that happened was that this curiosity *slowed me down* a little, that much I will admit.

But even that would've been okay if the damn Mitzvah Mobile hadn't been the first vehicle to get caught trying to make a right turn from Broadway onto 34th. Picture this crummy old rented truck, a covered delivery type, the back of which is filled with these characters in black hats and long black coats. I mean coats made out of horseblanket material—in June, with the thermometer hitting 85! And they've all got scroungy beards and long scruffy sideburns—Hassidim, Jewish hippie holy rollers from Williamsburg, something called the "Lubevitch Society," which I know on account of this is written on the side of what is also labeled the "Mitzvah Mobile," along with a lot of Hebrew graffiti and a picture of a mezzuzah which is also some kind of ICBM.

There I am, standing on the Herald Square island halfway across the intersection, pausing for just a minute, honest Charlie, to watch the show before I break it up. The whole width of 34th Street is blocked with people and the crowd is starting to spill into Broadway. I can see the shaved heads of at least a dozen Hare Krishnas bouncing together above the crowd, and the chanting is shriller and louder than I've ever heard it before, even over the sounds of horns and the screams of cabbies. There's a little gang of street hoods in the crowd and they're starting to cheer and yell, they seem a little loaded. Hippies are clapping their hands in time to the chanting. Even some ordinary citizen types are cheering and applauding.

I cross over to the edge of the crowd, but instead of waving my nightstick, blowing my whistle, and telling them to get their stupid asses moving, I elbow my way quietly through them. All right, all right, I admit it, I wanted to see what all the excitement was about before I broke it up this time.

In the middle of the crowd, a dozen Hare Krishnas were dancing and chanting at the top of their lungs, as expected, but what wasn't expected, Charlie, was that there were *six* Scientology nuts standing there with their arms folded and staring at them. And I mean, those boys were staring! Shoulder to shoulder like statues of the Rockettes, making like Bela Lugosi on methadone, you could hang your clothes out to dry on the lines between the Krishna freaks and their spaced-out eyeballs. Let me tell you, like the hippies say, the vibes there were really strange. The Scientologists just stood like fireplugs and stared, and that just made the Hare Krishnas jump up and down faster and faster and chant louder and louder.

"HARE KRISHNA, HARE KRISHNA, KRISHNA KRISHNA, HARE HARE . . . ."

And the crazier the Hare Krishna freaks went at it, the harder and colder the Scientologists stared. It got so heavy that the crowd was lining up between the silent starers and the jumping jacks, and something was going to give pretty soon.

At this point, let me tell you, I unfroze fast, and started to move in, but, damn it, I was about a second too late. All of a sudden comes this incredibly loud blast of incredibly tinny hora music to the tune of which a chorus line of weirdos in beaver hats and long black coats dances in between the Hare Krishnas and the Scientologists.

"What's this goyisha mishegas?" says a Hassid who looks like a fullback for Yeshiva University.

Another of the beards accosts a thin pimply Scientologist. "Are you Jewish?" he demands.

"All right, move it along!" I shout, waving my billie and stepping right into the fruitsalad. But it's too late, the loonie bin has hit the fan.

Everyone is shoving their literature in everyone else's faces. Half of the Hare Krishnas are jumping up and down and chanting half-heartedly while the others are trying to brush away Hassids who are trying to reach down the front of their robes to see if they're wearing mezzuzahs. The Scientologists have seized the main chance and are pushing their free personality tests on the crowd that has now moved right into the middle of everything.

"—Krishna Krishna, Rama Rama—"

"—Tsalis and Tvillen are the strategic deterrant of the Jewish people—"

"—it'll only take an hour of your time, and it could change your whole life—"

"—Hare Krishna, Hare Krishna—"

"—Bal Shem Tov—"

"—L. Ron Hubbard—"

I try my best to break it up, but I ask you Charlie,

what could I do? It's wall to wall people now, and everybody is screaming at the top of his lungs, and the horns from the clogged traffic on Broadway sound like a dinosaur convention, and Scientologists keep pushing their clipboards under my nose, and the Yeshiva University fullback even has the nerve to frisk *me* for a mezzuzah. Who can hear me blowing my whistle like an idiot? Who can tell a goose-along from my billie from somebody's elbow in his back? What was I supposed to do, start hitting people over the head and firing my pistol into the air? How was I to know that the Mitzvah Mobile had a bullhorn?

All of a sudden over the squawking hora music comes this wheezy old voice in a thick Jewish accent, only loud enough to rattle your fillings: "Without study of the Torah, in the streets comes chaos!"

And this old bird in a beaver hat and black coat gives me a knee in the butt as he pushes past me jabbering into his portable bullhorn. "A Mitzvah a day keeps der Teufel away!" He looks like Moses as played by Sam Jaffe, if you know what I mean, Charlie, and he makes straight for the line of chanting Krishna freaks, drowning them all out with his amplified grandpa voice. "—stop dancing around like a Minsky's chorus line and dance for joy in the name of the Lord—"

At which point, all the Hassids grab people at random—Hare Krishnas, Scientologists, hippies, street hoods, yuks from Keokuk—and start whirling them around in a hora. Whirl, whirl, whirl, then change partners like a square dance. One of them even grabs me, and I find myself spinning around like a yo-yo. Everyone is whirling around, then staggering into each other like drunks, then whirling again, orange robes, black coats, satin jackets, shirtsleeves and skirts.

And then comes the moment when I know for sure that I have had it, when I can feel the pavements of Fort Apache slamming my size nines. Hoo-boy! Here comes the Jews for Jesus!

These characters everybody knows about because they've stuck up their "Jews for Jesus" posters all over the city, and what flavor *they* are is self-evident. What is also self-evident, unfortunately, is that somewhere in Fun City is another crowd that doesn't like their trip, because the city is also plastered with posters that read "Not Wanted: Jews for Jesus." Lately, the phantom opposition has taken to spraypainting out Jews for Jesus posters, and the Jews for Jesus have taken to painting out the "Not Wanted" on enemy posters, cleverly converting them to more of their own.

And here come a dozen Boy Scouts with five o'clock shadows in Jew for Jesus T-shirts chain-ganging through the fruitsalad hora like that Carrie Nation and her bad-ass biddies busting up a saloon. Can you imagine if it's the *Lubevitch Society* that's been fighting the poster war with them?

"Accept the Lord Jesus Christ King of the Jews!" they scream, actually loud enough to make themselves heard, they must be in practice.

"*Bite* your *tongue*, you should say such a thing!" Sam-Jaffe-in-the-black-coat lectures back through his bullhorn.

"GOYIM!" shout the Hassids.

I try to step in between the front lines, but there aren't any front lines anymore, the Jews for Jesus and the Hassids are suddenly all over the place going at each other in groups of two or three.

"—as Jewish as you are, bubelah, and don't you forget it—"

"—look at *this* mishegas and tell me the Messiah's already come—"

The Lubevitchers are trying to check the Jews for Jesus for mezzuzahs, who are trying to push them away, and the Krishna freaks have gotten their act back together again and are jumping up and down, and dozens of weirdos in the crowd are still horaing on their own. The Scientologists have gone whacko or something; they're handing out free personality profile tests to everyone within reach and trying to get them to fill them out right on the spot. A Salvation Army lady in her blue uniform appears playing a tambourine. Two black guys in white robes selling newspapers. Indians in turbans with signs in Hindu lettering. Hassids are whirling unwilling Jews for Jesus around by the wrists. Somehow I find myself dancing with a Hare Krishna. Somehow I find myself putting a quarter in a collection can shoved in my face. Somehow I find myself filling out a free personality profile test.

Then I hear sirens—the riot squad to the rescue!

But what pushes aside the mob like bowling pins and comes to a panic stop in front of me is not the riot bus but Sergeant Kelly's squad car.

And what comes howling up out of it is Sergeant Kelly, his face so red it's purple, his eyes rolling like Groucho Marx', veins standing out like cables on his forehead—believe me, Charlie, a sight that would make Godzilla crap in his pants.

"WHATDAHELLISDISGETYERASSESOUTA HERE!" Sergeant Kelly suggested to the crowd like King Kong on bennies. A division of Marines would've backed off from Kelly in this state, and instantly the war was over and the parties concerned were streaming away from Kelly's squad car in every direction while Kelly continued to bellow like a bull moose in heat to encourage their cooperation.

He was still in top form when he turned his attention to me. Me, standing there holding a half-completed free personality profile test.

Fade out Broadway, fade in Fort Apache.

But you know, Charlie, I got to admit it, I still kind of wonder how it all would have come out.

Introduction to Blackout

When the lights went out for days during New York City's last fun-filled blackout, TV newspapers went too. The papers couldn't print, and nobody could receive television transmissions. But some radio stations stayed on the air, and lots of people had battery radios.

Even that much media-deprivation makes the modern mind a wee bit paranoid; we're too used to knowing what's happening out there, and we start to wondering what might be going on in all those suddenly dark corners. But if there were simply no news, none at all . . .

Blackout

In Orange County California, Freddie Dystrum took an afterdinner Coors into the living room and sat down in his favorite chair as his wife Mildred turned on the ABC nightly network news. While he preferred the authoritative dignity of Walter Cronkite, Mildred was addicted to the sophisticated folksiness of Harry Reasoner, and, in return for drawing a bye on the battleax bellowings of *Maude*, Reasoner it was. By such negotiated settlements was domestic tranquility maintained.

After the station break, Reasoner's calm smiling face came onto the screen and began talking about the latest governmental crisis in Spain or Nigeria or someplace like that—with his belly stuffed with Colonel Sanders' finest, Freddie was drifting off into his customary python-like post-prandial stupor and one unstable foreign government seemed much like any other.

Then it happened, jolting him wide awake.

A hand suddenly appeared on camera from the left, shoving a piece of paper in Reasoner's face. It seemed to have some kind of military cuff on its sleeve, and when the indignant Reasoner turned to glare at the off-camera personage, his face went pale, and for the first time in Freddie's memory this man, who had reeled off every sort of world disaster for decades with professional calm and aplomb, seemed visibly shaken. The military hand silently shook the paper in front of Harry Reasoner's face, and the newscaster finally took it in a quavering hand and read it aloud.

"All television and radio newscasts and newspaper publication have been indefinitely suspended by government order until . . . until. . . ." Reasoner's eyes bugged as if he couldn't believe what he was reading. He looked off-camera quizzically, swallowed hard, then continued. "Until the Department of Defense has gotten to the bottom of the flying saucer phenomenon. . . ."

The screen abruptly became a hissing field of multicolored static. Then an announcer's voice said: "In place of our regularly scheduled newscast, we bring you *Antelopes of the West*, already in progress." And a scared-looking faun was bounding across the prairie.

On 88th Street in Manhattan, New York, Archie and Bill sat on the edge of their bed pulling on their clothes, quite ready to believe that they were going to find Martians parading down Broadway in armored personnel carriers. Wasn't that the way superior invading forces always made their appearance on the 7:00 news?

"Can you believe this is happening?" Archie chortled. "Can you see the look on the President's face?"

"Lead me to your taker?"

"My god, do you really think there are tentacled monstrosities out there tearing the brass brassieres off Earthwomen?"

"You're assuming that they're straight?"

Out on Broadway, people were milling about, not so much in a panic as in a state of bleary stupefaction, rubbing the glaze out of their eyes and staring at the transformation of the sky from sunset violet to fathomless black.

"It must be some kind of television stunt like that Orson Welles thing on radio," a tweedy man was saying to his wife.

"On all channels, Maxwell?"

Archie walked up to a cop leaning up against his squad car and staring at the sky. "Have any flying saucers landed in New York yet?" he asked the rough-looking cop. Ten minutes ago, he would have gotten a snarl and a scowl or something worse, but now the cop simply said "Search me," and studied the now-dark sky with undisguised dread.

Then something bright flashed across the southern horizon from west to east, like a slow-motion shooting star or a speeded-up satellite. The crowd oohed and then sent up an unsettling subterranean growl of fear.

Bill looked around nervously. "If we're going to be invaded, perhaps it would be wise to take to the hills," he said. "Far from our fellow man and juicy targets."

"Jesus, Bill, do you really think this is *real*?"

Something flared brightly, north above Harlem.

As soon as the alarm woke him up, Freddie Dystrum crawled out of bed, staggered into the kitchen, and tried to find some news on the radio. There was nothing but music on all the AM and FM stations, punctuated by the usual commercials and introductions, but not a word of anything else. There were no news shows, no talk shows, and all the all-news stations were off the air.

Mildred was already in the kitchen making breakfast as if it were just another Tuesday. "What are you doing? What's happening?" Freddie rumbled as he gave up on the radio.

"Your breakfast is just about ready, Timmy is in the bathroom, and Kim is finally getting out of bed," Mildred said, turning over a pancake.

"Jeez, Mildred, what about last night? What about the radio?"

"What's wrong with the radio?" Mildred asked mildly.

"There's no news on it. All the news stations are off the air."

"You mean that flying saucer thing on Harry Reasoner last night?" Mildred said, finally looking up at him. "It wasn't a joke?"

"It doesn't seem to be," Freddie said. "There's no news on the radio, just like Harry Reasoner said."

Mildred now began to look worried. "Maybe you should call Charlie, doesn't he get the *Times* in the morning?"

"Yeah, he does," Freddie said, and he went into the den to call Charlie. Charlie hadn't gotten his morning paper. Charlie hadn't gotten to sleep till after 2:00 after hearing the announcement about flying saucers on Walter Cronkite, and about 1:30, he had seen repeated bright flashes of light zip across the horizon far away to the north. Charlie was scared.

Freddie told him it could have been missiles

from Vandenburg, but he had to admit that that might not exactly be a soothing explanation.

Back in the kitchen, Timmy and Kim had heard about the blackout via the mysterious ectoplasmic kiddie grapevine, and had decided it was a good excuse not to go to school.

"You're not going to send us out there with flying saucers landing and Martian monsters running around, are you Dad?" Timmy said slyly. "With tentacles and big teeth and ray guns?"

Freddie wasn't having any of *that*. "Nobody said anything about Martians landing in flying saucers, Timmy," he said. "They said no news until they get to the bottom of the flying saucer thing, not that we were being invaded."

"Why would they do that if nothing's happening, Daddy?" Kim asked.

"I don't know," Freddie snapped. He eyed the kids significantly. "Maybe your double-dome *teachers* will have it figured out when you get to school, and then you can tell me. That's what we pay our property tax for."

That ended that, and Freddie dropped the kids off at school on his way to the plant as usual. But after he dropped them off and drove back down the Santa Ana Freeway, he had second thoughts as he watched a long convoy of army vehicles monopolizing the high-speed northbound lane, grim, brown, and sinister-looking as they highballed towards Los Angeles.

"I tell you I don't like it, I don't like it at all," Karl Bendtsen said, staring glumly across his southern cornfield at the heavy midmorning traffic on the Interstate. "All those cars coming out of

Omaha. Damn fools are likely to panic and swarm all over everything like locusts. Wish I had put barbed wire on the fences."

"Lot of good that'd do if we're being invaded by space people," Ben the foreman said, spitting a stream of tobacco juice in the general direction of Washington.

Karl snorted. "They got you believing that nonsense too?" he said. "*Flying saucers*! It'll turn out to be just the eastern press liberals trying to stir up some trouble. I read only last week in *TV Guide* that they're out to embarrass the government and they don't much care how."

"Was the government that made the announcement, Mr. Bendtsen."

"Arrr!" Karl threw up his hands. "Maybe they had some crazy flying saucer scare they were going to broadcast and for once someone in Washington had sense enough to shut them up before they stirred up a hornets' nest."

Ben nodded towards the highway. "Don't seem to have worked too well, do it?" he said.

A loud sustained roar caused both men to whirl and look to the west. A squadron of B-52s, maybe a dozen of the things, was lumbering ominously high across the sky like vultures, headed north towards the Arctic Circle.

"Maybe it's the Russians," Karl decided. "For sure, they're up to no good."

Willis Cohen's big editorial lunch with Harrison Gaur had turned into a disaster. Why did his big chance to pitch some article ideas to the editor of the best-paying magazine in New York have to coincide with . . . with whatever this damned thing was? Gaur could think of nothing else, and people kept coming up to their table to swap paranoias.

"It *can't* be anything as simple as an invasion from outer space," Gaur was assuring a tweedy longhair. "It smacks of the CIA. It's got to be a cover for something."

"Must be heavy, if *this* is the cover-up, man!"

"Maybe it's a coup," Cohen said, trying for the tenth time to reassert his presence. This time, he finally succeeded.

"*A coup?*" Gaur said, fixing his full attention on Cohen. "You think there's a coup going on *right now*?"

I've got his attention, Cohen thought, grasping for conspiracy theories. If I lay it on thick, maybe he'll buy an article on it. "What if there really are spaceships visiting Earth and the government knows about it?" he said off the top of his head. "What if there are rival factions within the Administration? The hawks want to keep the whole thing secret until they can develop a weapon to knock down the saucers and then use it to drive a big increase in the Pentagon budget through Congress. The moderates want to inform the world and try to negotiate with the saucer people and thus strengthen detente. One side started to make its move and the other side is moving against them."

"The CIA versus the State Department—"

"Maybe the CIA versus the White House, even—"

"With the Army using the power struggle as an excuse to seize control—

"Not necessarily—"

Suddenly there was a loud surge of voices at the bar around a man who had just sat down.

"—passing under the Verrazano Bridge—"

"—my wife called me at the office—"

Gaur turned and shouted at a silver-bearded man at the bar. "Ken? What's going on?"

"There's an aircraft carrier moving up the Hudson River!" the bearded man shouted, creating instant bedlam in the restaurant. Everyone was talking loudly at once and a dozen people abruptly got up to leave.

Including Harrison Gaur. "That does it!" he said, pushing his chair away from the table. "Sorry about this, Will, but I've got to get going."

"Get going *where?*" Cohen said despairingly.

Gaur paused, looked at him, started to sit down again. "I don't really know where," he said in surprise. Then he was off again. "But I can't just sit here," he said. And Cohen, left out in the cold again, began to wonder if the whole thing weren't a plot against *him*. Peculiar that it all should have been timed to his meeting with Harrison Gaur.

Bill had insisted that they put as much distance as possible between themselves and nightfall in New York, so he and Archie drove northwest all day through lush upstate farmland and rolling wooded hills in the general direction of Montreal, staying off the main roads, which Archie figured would be jammed and dangerous if getting the jump on a general exodus turned out to have been a good idea.

As 6:30 approached 7:00, however, it seemed necessary to get a motel fast, so as to be in front of a television set when the network news did or didn't come on. They stopped at a cluster of wooden cabins in the ass-end of nowhere, where the owner charged them $35 for a grim cubicle with a black and white set, take it or leave it, the next motel is twenty miles away, and I reckon I'm going to have all the business I can handle later on tonight.

They got the set on just at the station break, and they sat on the edge of the bed while commercials for dog food, deodorant, and huggable toilet paper reeled on in insane normalcy. "I'll bet we drove all the way up here and spent $35 for nothing," Archie said. "Now good old Walter Cronkite will come on and tell us it's all some outre joke."

But good old Walter did not come on at all. Instead, there was an idiotic old pilot for a show that had never gotten on the air, about a loveable family of misunderstood Transylvanian peasants living in John Wayne's Texas.

"At least they could have run an old *Twilight Zone*," Bill said wanly.

"Or Gore Vidal getting it on with William Buckley," Archie said, turning off the tube. They sat there for a few minutes silently trying to absorb the reality of what was going on and failing to connect. Then, without saying anything to each other, they went outside into the empty parking lot.

Night had come on, and here in the country, the sky was an immensity of stars glowing over the black outlines of the hills. Occasionally, a lone car moved down the road, ghostly bright and loud in the dark silence.

There was traffic up there among the stars. They could see it. A blinking red light moving across the western horizon. A star that moved in a deliberate parabolic curve across the top of the heavens. Things flying in formation far to the east.

"You know Archie, out here you can believe it," Bill said. "You can just about believe it."

"But what would they want with us? Our cities are fetid sties, millions of us are starving, we're ungrateful, vicious creatures, and welfare is bankrupting us. Wouldn't any self-respecting space monster look for a tonier neighborhood to move into?"

"Maybe we're a rare French delicacy to them," Bill suggested. "Like a good moldy Roquefort. Haven't you ever been cruised by a fart-sniffer?"

Archie giggled nervously, but his flesh crawled.

Something loud was moving across the sky unseen, far away. Dogs began to howl. A helicopter buzzed across the sky, lit by its own strobe. Uneasiness seemed to creep across the heavens like roaches in a dark apartment.

Bill shuddered and nodded suggestively towards their cabin. "Maybe there's a Bette Davis movie on inside?" he suggested.

Freddie Dystrum awoke to glare and blare and a steeringwheel rim in the gut. A bunch of people had gotten together at Frank's house after a second evening without the news, and when everyone said they were going to keep their kids out of school and go to the mountains or Big Sur or Mexico if it wasn't over by morning, Freddie figured he'd be smart and beat the morning crush. All night they had driven northeast towards the Sierras in thick moving traffic, not because they wanted to, but because it was already impossible to find an empty motel room. When they finally gave up about 1:00 AM and tried to sleep four in the car, with the kids giggling over endless Martian jokes and Mildred jumping at every strange noise, Freddie decided he hadn't been so smart after all.

But now, waking up in the middle of a Hollywood Freeway traffic jam way up here in the wilderness, Freddie felt smart again.

For as far as the eye could see—and in this long straight valley that was saying something—the northbound lanes of the highway were crammed with barely moving cars. Horns shouted, radiators steamed, engines snarled and coughed and died, and a long plume of smog hung over the highway, baking in the heat. The shoulders of the road were full of parked cars—overheated, flat-tired, or full of people sleeping by the road like his own family. Helicopters buzzed around the mess like flies over horseshit. It looked as if it went all the way south to Los Angeles and all the way north to Nome.

"Good Lord," Mildred grunted, sliding up the back of the seat beside him. "It's like the Fourth of July at Disneyland!"

"Can we get breakfast now, Daddy?" Kim piped up from the back seat. "I'm hungry."

"I gotta go to the bathroom," Timmy whined. *"Real bad."*

Freddie looked north up the road. He needed a john too. Not a motel, gas station, or Pancake House in sight, and it could take all day to go twenty miles in that screaming, coughing, crawling jungle of chrome, gas, and rubber. Looking south, he saw nothing either, but the southbound lanes were clear and empty and would probably be that way all the way back to Torrence.

"ARROARR!!" Freddie jumped out of his seat as a squadron of Phantom jets swooped low over the highway and roared northeast at treetop level.

"That does it!" Freddie snapped. "If it's the end of the world, it's the end of the world, and at least we can spend it near a toilet. We're going home."

"But Daddy—"

"No buts!" Freddie snarled, starting the engine. He made a ninety degree turn, stuck the front of the car into the first available hole in the crawling traffic, wedged his way past shaking fists across the northbound lanes, made a U onto the sweet clear southbound highway, and floored it.

Highballing south along the empty roadway, Freddie shouted at the idiots in the northbound traffic jam. "Lemmings, is what you are! Buncha goddamn lemmings!"

"What's a lemming, Daddy?"

It was a clear day in San Francisco, and from Coit Tower, Ted and Veronica could see the packed traffic on the Golden Gate, loops of empty freeway snaking along the hills and valleys of San Francisco, the deserted Bay Bridge, and the ominous concentration of warships at the Oakland Navy Yard.

Ted had wanted to hitchhike up the coast towards redwood country until the coup was over, and then either go home to Berkeley or head for the Canadian border, depending on the gravity of what came down. But Veronica had pointed out that hitchhiking on the road would be the worst place to be when the long night of repression began. Hitchhikers would be the first people they'd scoop up into concentration camps. So they decided they might as well await the inevitable hidden in the belly of the beast. They were on too many Berkeley pig lists not to feel totally paranoid there.

"In a way, maybe this is a positive thing," Veronica said. "The beast finally shows its true colors. Maybe people will wake up when they see tanks in the street."

Ted grunted dubiously. He hadn't seen any tanks—though there seemed to be a lot of helicopter activity and comings and goings at the Navy Yard—and the People had either taken to the hills running from Martians or stood around sullenly in confused, isolated little groups. The city had a dazed and empty look, as if an enormity had already occurred.

"You know," he said, "I think whoever planned it this way was a genius. The cities are emptied out, troops can maneuver at will and secure all the strong points, and when people finally drag themselves home, sweaty and beat, it's already all over and there's no energy to resist."

"Unless . . . unless . . ." Veronica looked north across the Bay where something strange shimmered like a mirage, bright and formless. "Unless it's for real."

Archie and Bill took a long walk in the woods in the morning after a slow breakfast, had greasy hamburgers for lunch, watched "Godzilla" on TV, looked at the jam of cars on the road, then had an early supper, killing agonizingly slow time waiting for the hour of the seven o'clock news.

Stupifying bucolic boredom had made them decide that they would head home unless . . . unless there was an announcement that the Army really *was* battling invaders from outer space in the streets of New York. The coitus interruptus was just too enervating.

At 6:50, they went inside and turned on the tube, watched the last ten minutes of a *Star Trek*, in which Captain Kirk had been forced to change bodies with a woman, then turned to Channel 4, hoping for the soothing moderation of positive old John Chancellor.

Commercials for beer, pantyhose, vaginal spray, and chicken chow mein, and then the NBC logo, and the familiar announcer's voice: "The NBC Nightly News, with John Chancellor"!

And there was John Chancellor, crisp, unruffled, and utterly normal, going into his rundown of the major news stories. An imminent coup was feared in Lebanon. The cost of living was up half a percent. A jet had crashed en route from New York to Shannon. The Secretary of State was flying to Rio. The Israelis had killed three Palestinian terrorists.

On and on and on. Someone had hit five home runs in a doubleheader. Drought threatened the midwestern corn crop. NASA had launched a weather satellite. Workers were striking in Cleveland.

Bill and Archie watched the nightly pablum unreel in numb amazement, speaking only during the commercials, their nerves rubbed raw by the screaming ordinariness.

"What's happening? What's happening?"

"Looks like nothing's happening. Looks like the last two days didn't happen after all."

The last commercial ended, and John Chancellor looked earnestly and forthrightly straight at them, as was his wrap-up habit.

"Finally tonight," he said breezily, "the Defense Department's thorough investigation of the flying saucer phenomenon. After thorough satellite reconnaissance, a complete review of all available evidence, and exhaustive analysis, the Pentagon has announced that there are no such things as flying saucers. Absolutely and definitively. Good night for NBC News."

Freddie Dystrum sat woodenly in front of his television set, feeling the cool wetness of the beer can in his hand, picturing the people dragging their silly asses back to the city, and wondering what the boys would have to say to each other at work tomorrow.

Beside him, Mildred sat shaking her head as she munched on a cold chicken leg. "What happened to the Martians?" Kim piped up.

"There weren't any Martians, stupid," Timmy told her. "It was just a dumb joke."

"A dumb joke all right," Freddie muttered, imagining the dull morning-after throb at work tomorrow. Yet he wondered as he sat there watching the "Hollywood Squares" why he had this dread feeling in his gut that everything had changed, and not at all for the better.

PHASE TWO

New Worlds Coming

Introduction

The only thing we can be sure of is that the future will not be like the present, as American realities continue to mutate along an exponential vector. Indeed, changes seem to be coming so fast that in a way the *present* isn't even much like what most people are comfortable with in real-time. This is why "Future Shock" is a common popular cliche.

Of course the future shock of the masses is the sense of wonder of the sf-reading elite. The sense of disorientation in the face of ongoing mutational change that bothers poor Joe Prole becomes a kind of high for the futures-oriented mutant. Indeed, that is the very nature of his mutational consciousness. This positive attitude towards the future is definitely a survival factor, but it frequently tends to go a little too far.

Too often the future worlds of science fiction draw their chrome-plated optimism from disassociation with the full range of textures of the science fiction reality of America unfolding all around them. We'd all love to live in nice clean zero-g suburban orbital utopias without ghettos or human shitheadedness or dogshit on the street. In such a sterling stellar empire, all our wars will be righteous and involve no atrocities, at least not on camera. And we all know that we good guys can handle Darth Vader in the crunch because the Force is on our side.

Not that such optimism isn't a valuable counter to the downbeat rhythm of bummer times. Nor can it be said that science fiction has been remiss in its creation of monumental disasters, 1984s, and post-catastrophe blues.

But what's missing in most of them is a sense of connection to continuity with the moral and psychic reality of the realtime reader. Lester del Rey once attempted to define "science fiction" in such a way that my novel *Bug Jack Barron* was excluded. What he came up with was the notion that *Bug Jack Barron* wasn't science fiction because it was too obviously and smoothly an evolutionary outgrowth of the times in which it was written.

As a formal definition of what science fiction *should* be, this is for the birds as far as I'm concerned, but as a descriptive definition of much of what has been written it is all too accurate. The worlds of science fiction all too seldom can be comprehended as projections of vectors we're traveling in our own times. They all take place on the other side of some Great Discontinuity, be it a million years of time, or parsecs of space, or the great atomic war, or a Velikovsky two-cushion shot. Here the agonies and problems of our own times have been erased and cartoon heroes play out television scenarios. Distopian warnings or logical positivist space opera, neither of them connects up to history.

Which is why both the cry-sayers of doom and the space-age optimists miss the point. Which is that the future, alas, *is* going to be just more history.

True, we stand a significant chance of blowing ourselves to bits and/or poisoning our planet through our historical tradition of assholery. But unless we do succeed in totally exterminating ourselves—always a possibility now that we're playing with atoms—the chances are overwhelming that there will be no Great Discontinuity, no merciful annihilation of history.

After all, any catastrophe that still left significant numbers of humans alive would also leave zillions of tons of books, magazines, videotapes, films, computer memories, home movies, comic books, records, and advertising copy for them to brood over. Even our remote descendants are likely to know exactly who they are and how they got there.

Furthermore, the march of science is not likely to erase our time-honored species traditions of violence, oppression, psychosis, revolution, honor, justice, humor, love, fear and hate.

Try as we will to evade the truth, the future arises out of what goes on in the present. Destiny arises out of karma, and the future we get will be the future we make.

Realistically, we can expect to do this in our usual fashion—in the name of commerce and art and political rights and tribal hatreds, moved by love and fear and murky cravings, in a world too complex for even the best of us to fully comprehend, and in one way or another quite often in a bent state of mind.

Introduction to The National Pastime

As I write this, the Yankees have just beaten the Dodgers in the 1978 World Series after being 14 games out in July and down 2 games to Los Angeles. New York has retrieved some of its tarnished pride by destroying the Big Red Cheeses from Boston in their own lair and then humiliating first the mid-Americans from Kansas City and then the show-biz team from Los Angeles.

You think people don't take this seriously? The Dodgers invoked the astral ministrations of their late coach Jim Gilliam, who died just before the Series, before every game, and solemnly dedicated the proceedings to his shade. Reggie Jackson owned that God might be a Yankee fan this year because a victory for the team would be a victory for the downtrodden populace of New York. Same downtrodden populace, aka the "animals" in the stands at Yankee Stadium, were the Dodgers' alibi for booting so many plays. The ferocity of the fans admittedly daunted them.

If this seems ominously nuts, remember that for

*a certain stretch–curiously enough during the Viet Nam War—*football *had replaced baseball as the National Pastime. It may be a measure of our relatively greater current sanity that baseball has made such a comeback. Let us hope football will not soon once more replace it as our number one tribal sports drama.*

Because when you act out the national passion-play on the football *field. . . .*

The National Pastime

The Founding Father

I know you've got to start at the bottom in the television business, but producing sports shows is my idea of cruel and unusual punishment. Sometime in the dim past, I had the idea that I wanted to make films, and the way to get to make films seemed to be to run up enough producing and directing credits on television, and the way to do *that* was to take whatever came along, and what came along was an offer to do a series of sports specials on things like kendo, sumo wrestling, jousting, Thai boxing, in short, ritual violence. This was at the height (or the depth) of the anti-violence hysteria, when you couldn't so much as show the bad guy getting an on-camera rap in the mouth from the good guy on a moronic Western. The only way you could give the folks what they really wanted was in the All-American wholesome package of a sporting event. Knowing this up front—unlike the jerks who warm chairs as network executives—I had no trouble producing the kind of sports specials the network executives knew people wanted to see without quite knowing why, and, thus, I achieved the status of boy genius. Which, alas, ended up in my being offered a long-term contract as a producer in the sports department that was simply too rich for me to pass up. I mean, I make no bones about being a crass materialist.

So try to imagine my feelings when Herb Dieter, the network sports programming director, calls me in to his inner sanctum and gives me The Word. "Ed," he tells me, "as you know, there's now only one major football league, and the opposition has us frozen out of the picture with long-term contracts with the NFL. As you also know, the major-league football games are clobbering us in the Sunday afternoon ratings, which is prime time as far as sports programming is concerned. And as you know, a sports programming director who can't hold a decent piece of the Sunday afternoon audience is not long for this fancy office. And as you know, there is no sport on God's green earth that can compete with major-league football. Therefore, it would appear that I have been presented with an insoluble problem.

"Therefore, since you are the official boy genius of the sports department, Ed, I've decided that you must be the solution to my problem. If I don't come up with something that will hold its own against pro football by the beginning of next season, my head will roll. Therefore, I've decided to give you the ball and let you run with it. Within ninety days, you will have come up with a solution, or the fine-print boys will be instructed to find a way for me to break your contract."

I found it very hard to care one way or the other. On the one hand, I liked the bread I was knocking down, but on the other, the job was a real drag and it would probably do me good to get my ass fired. Of course, the whole thing was unfair from my point of view, but who could fault Dieter's logic; he personally had nothing to lose by ordering his best creative talent to produce a miracle or be fired. Unless I came through, he would be fired, and then what would he care about gutting the sports department? It wouldn't be his baby anymore. It wasn't very nice, but it was the name of the game we were playing.

"You mean all I'm supposed to do is invent a better sport than football in ninety days, Herb, or do you mean something more impossible?" I couldn't decide whether I was trying to be funny or not.

But Dieter suddenly had a twenty-watt bulb come on behind his eyes (about as bright as he could get). "I do believe you've hit on it already, Ed," he said. "We can't get any pro football, and there's no existing sport that can draw like football, so you're right, you've got to *invent* a sport that will outdraw pro football. Ninety days, Ed. And don't take it too hard; if you bomb out, we'll see each other at the unemployment office."

So there I was, wherever *that* was. I could easily get Dieter to do for me what I didn't have the willpower to do for myself and get me out of the stinking sports department—all I had to do was *not* invent a game that would outdraw pro football. On the other hand, I liked living the way I did, and I didn't like the idea of losing *anything* because of failure.

So the next Sunday afternoon, I eased out the night before's chick, turned on the football game, smoked two joints of Acapulco Gold, and consulted my muse. It was the ideal set of conditions for a creative mood: I was being challenged, but if

I failed, I gained, too, so I had no inhibitions on my creativity. I was stoned to the point where the whole situation was a game without serious consequences; I was hanging loose.

Watching two football teams pushing each other back and forth across my color television screen, it once again occurred to me how much football was a ritual sublimation of war. This seemed perfectly healthy. Lots of cultures are addicted to sports that are sublimations of the natural human urge to clobber people. Better the sublimation than the clobbering. People dig violence, whether anyone likes the truth or not, so it's a public service to keep it on the level of a spectator sport.

Hmmm . . . that was probably why pro football had replaced baseball as the National Pastime in a time when people, having had their noses well-rubbed in the stupidity of war, needed a war-substitute. How could you beat something that got the American armpit as close to the gut as that?

And then from the blue-grass mountaintops of Mexico, the flash hit me: the only way to beat football was at its own game! Start with football itself, and convert it into something that was an even *closer* metaphor for war, something that could be called—

!!COMBAT FOOTBALL!!

Yeah, yeah, Combat Football, or better, *Combat* Football. Two standard football teams, standard football field, standard football rules, except:

Take off all their pads and helmets and jerseys and make it a warm-weather game that they play in shorts and sneakers, like boxing. More meaningful, more intimate violence. Violence is what sells football, so give 'em a bit more violence than football, and you'll draw a bit more than football. The more violent you can make it and get away with it, the better you'll draw.

Yeah . . . and you could get away with punching; after all, boxers belt each other around and they still allow boxing on television; sports have too much All-American Clean for the antiviolence freaks to attack; in fact, where their heads are at, they'd *dig* Combat Football. Okay. So in ordinary football, the defensive team tackles the ball-carrier to bring him to his knees and stop the play. So in Combat, the defenders can slug the ball-carrier, kick him, tackle him, why not, anything to bring him to his knees and stop the play. And to make things fair, the ball-carrier can slug the defenders to get them out of his way. If the defense slugs an offensive player who doesn't have possession, it's ten yards and an automatic first down. If anyone but the ball-carrier slugs a defender, it's ten yards and a loss of down.

Presto: Combat Football!

And the final touch was that it was a game that any beer-sodden moron who watched football could learn to understand in sixty seconds, and any lout who dug football would have to like Combat better.

The boy genius had done it again! It even made sense after I came down.

Farewell to the Giants

Jeez, I saw a thing on television last Sunday you wouldn't believe. You really oughta watch it next week; I don't care who the Jets or the Giants are playing. I turned on the TV to watch the Giants game and went to get a beer, and when I came back from the kitchen I had on some guy yelling something about today's professional combat football game, and it's not the NFL announcer, and it's a team called the New York Sharks playing a team called the Chicago Thunderbolts, and they're playing in L.A. or Miami, I didn't catch which, but someplace with palm trees anyway, and all the players are bare-ass! Well, not really bare-ass, but all they've got on is sneakers and boxing shorts with numbers across the behind—blue for New York, green for Chicago. No helmets, no pads, no protectors, no jerseys, no nothing!

I check the set and, sure enough, I've got the wrong channel. But I figured, I could turn on the Giants game anytime. What the hell, you can see the Giants all the time, but what in hell is *this*?

New York kicks off to Chicago. The Chicago kick-returner gets the ball on about the ten—bad kick—and starts upfield. The first New York tackler reaches him and goes for him and the Chicago player just belts him in the mouth and runs by him! I mean, with the ref standing there watching it, and no flag thrown! Two more tacklers come at him on the twenty. One dives at his leg, the other socks him in the gut. He trips and staggers out of the tackle, shoves another tackler away with a punch in the chest, but he's slowed up enough so that three or four New York players get to him at once. A couple of them grab his legs to stop his motion, and the others knock him down at about the twenty-five. Man, what's going on here?

I check my watch. By this time the Giants game

has probably started, but New York and Chicago are lined up for the snap on the twenty-five, so I figure what the hell, I gotta see some more of this thing, so at least I'll watch one series of downs.

On first down, the Chicago quarterback drops back and throws a long one way downfield to his flanker on maybe the New York forty-five. It looks good, there's only one player on the Chicago flanker; he beats this one man and catches it, and it's a touchdown, and the pass looks right on the button. Up goes the Chicago flanker, the ball touches his hands—and pow, right in the kisser! The New York defender belts him in the mouth and he drops the pass. Jeez, what a game!

Second and ten. The Chicago quarterback fades back, but it's a fake; he hands off to his fullback, a gorilla who looks like he weighs about two-fifty, and the Chicago line opens up a little hole at left tackle and the fullback hits it holding the ball with one hand and punching with the other. He belts out a tackler, takes a couple of shots in the gut, slugs a second tackler, and then someone has him around the ankles; he drags himself forward another half yard or so, and then he runs into a good solid punch and he's down on the twenty-eight for a three-yard gain.

Man, I mean *action!* What a game! Makes the NFL football look like something for faggots! Third and seven, you gotta figure Chicago for the pass, right? Well, on the snap, the Chicago quarterback just backs up a few steps and pitches a short one to his flanker at about the line of scrimmage. The blitz is on and everyone comes rushing in on the quarterback and, before New York knows what's happening, the Chicago flanker is five yards downfield along the left sideline and picking up speed. Two New York tacklers angle out to stop him at maybe the Chicago forty, but he's got up momentum and one of the New York defenders runs right into his fist—I could hear the thud even on television—and falls back right into the other New York player, and the Chicago flanker is by them, the forty, the forty-five; he angles back toward the center of the field at midfield, dancing away from one more tackle, then on maybe the New York forty-five a real fast New York defensive back catches up to him from behind, tackles him waist-high, and the Chicago flanker's motion is stopped as two more tacklers come at him. But he squirms around inside the tackle and belts the tackler in the mouth with his free hand, knocks the New York back silly, breaks the tackle, and he's off again downfield with two guys chasing him. Forty, thirty-five, thirty, twenty-five, he's running away from them. Then from way over the right side of the field, I see the New York safety man running flat out across the field at the ball-carrier, angling toward him so it looks like they'll crash like a couple of locomotives on about the fifteen, because the Chicago runner just doesn't see this guy. Ka-boom! The ball-carrier running flat-out runs right into the fist of the flat-out safety at the fifteen and he's knocked about ten feet one way and the football flies ten feet the other way, and the New York safety scoops it up on the thirteen and starts upfield, twenty, twenty-five, thirty, thirty-five, and then, slam, bang, whang, half the Chicago team is all over him, a couple of tackles, a few in the gut, a shot in the head, and he's down. First and ten for

New York on their own thirty-seven. And that's just the first series of downs!

Well, let me tell you, after that, you know where they can stick the Giants game, right? This Combat Football, that's the real way to play the game; I mean, it's football and boxing all together, with a little wrestling thrown in—it's a game with *balls.* I mean, the *whole game* was like that first series. You oughta take a look at it next week. Damn, if they played the thing in New York, we could even go out to the game together. I'd sure be willing to spend a couple of bucks to see something like that.

Commissioner Gene Kuhn Addresses the First Annual Owners' Meeting of the National Combat Football League

Gentlemen, I've been thinking about the future of our great sport. We're facing a double challenge to the future of Combat Football, boys. First of all, the NFL is going over to Combat rules next season, and since you can't copyright a sport (and if you could, the NFL would have us by the short hairs anyway) there's not a legal thing we can do about it. The only edge we'll have left is that they'll have to at least wear heavy uniforms because they play in regular cities up north. But they'll have the stars, and the stadiums, and the regular hometown fans and fatter television deals.

Which brings me to our second problem, gentlemen, namely, that the television network which created our great game is getting to be a pain in our sport's neck, meaning that they're shafting us in the crummy percentage of the television revenue they see fit to grant us.

So the great task facing our great National Pastime, boys, is to ace out the network by putting ourselves in a better bargaining position on the television rights while saving our million-dollar asses from the NFL competition, which we just cannot afford.

Fortunately, it just so happens that your commissioner has been on the ball, and I've come up with a couple of new gimmicks that I am confident will insure the posterity and financial success of our great game while stiff-arming the NFL and the TV network nicely in the process.

Number one, we've got to improve our standing as a live spectator sport. We've got to start drawing big crowds on our own if we want some clout in negotiating with the network. Number two, we've got to give the customers something the NFL can't just copy from us next year and clobber us with.

There's no point in changing the rules again because the NFL can always keep up with us there. But one thing the NFL is locked into for keeps is the whole concept of having teams represent cities; they're committed to that for the next twenty years. We've only been in business for a year and our teams never play in the damned cities they're named after because it's too cold to play bare-ass Combat in those cities during the football season, so it doesn't have to mean anything to us.

So we make two big moves. First, we change our season to spring and summer so we can play up north where the money is. Second, we throw out the whole dumb idea of teams representing cities; that's old-fashioned stuff. That's crap for the coyotes. Why not six teams with *national* followings? Imagine the clout that'll give us when we renegotiate the TV contract. We can have a flexible schedule so that we can put any game we want into any city in the country any time we think that city's hot and draw a capacity crowd in the biggest stadium in town.

How are we gonna do all this? Well, look boys, we've got a six-team league, so, instead of six cities, why not match up our teams with six national groups?

I've taken the time to draw up a hypothetical league lineup just to give you an example of the kind of thing I mean. Six teams: the Black Panthers, the Golden Supermen, the Psychedelic Stompers, the Caballeros, the Gay Bladers, and the Hog Choppers. We do it all up the way they used to do with wrestling; you know, the Black Panthers are all spades with naturals, the Golden Supermen are blond astronaut types in red-white-and-blue bunting, the Psychedelic Stompers have long hair and groupies in miniskirts up to their navels and take rock bands to their games, the Caballeros dress like gauchos or something, whatever makes Latin types feel feisty, the Gay Bladers and Hog Choppers are mostly all-purpose villains—the Bladers are black-leather-and-chain-mail faggots, and the Hog Choppers we recruit from outlaw motorcycle gangs.

Now is that a *league*, gentlemen? Identification is the thing, boys. You gotta identify your teams with a large enough group of people to draw crowds, but why tie yourself to something local like a city? This way, we got a team for the spades, a team for the frustrated Middle Americans, a team for the hippies and kids, a team for the spics, a team for the faggots, and a team for the motorcycle nuts and violence freaks. And any American who can't identify with any of those teams is an odds-on bet to hate one or more of them enough to come out to the game to see them stomped. I mean, who wouldn't want to see the Hog Choppers and the Panthers go at each other under Combat rules?

Gentlemen, I tell you, it's creative thinking like this that made our country great, and it's creative thinking like this that will make Combat Football the greatest gold mine in professional sports.

Stay Tuned, Sports Fans. . . .

Good afternoon, Combat fans, and welcome to today's major-league Combat Football game between the Caballeros and the Psychedelic Stompers, brought to you by the World Safety Razor Blade Company, with the sharpest, strongest blade for your razor in the world.

It's ninety-five degrees on this clear New York day in July, and a beautiful day for a Combat Football game, and the game here today promises to be a real smasher, as the Caballeros, only a game behind the league-leading Black Panthers, take on the fast-rising, hard-punching Psychedelic Stompers, and perhaps the best running back in the game today, Wolfman Ted. We've got a packed house here today, and the Stompers, who won the toss, are about to receive the kickoff from the Caballeros. . . .

And there it is, a low bullet into the end zone, taken there by Wolfman Ted. The Wolfman crosses the goal line, he's up to the five, the ten, the fourteen. He brings down Number 71, Pete Lopez, with a right to the windpipe, crosses the fifteen, takes a glancing blow to the head from Number 56, Diaz, is tackled on the eighteen by Porfirio Rubio, Number 94, knocks Rubio away with two quick rights to the head, crosses the twenty, and takes two rapid blows to the midsection in succession from Beltran and Number 30, Orduna, staggers, and is tackled low from behind by the quick-recovering Rubio, and slammed to the ground under a pile of Caballeros on the twenty-four.

First and ten for the Stompers on their own twenty-four. Stompers quarterback Ronny Seede brings his team to the line of scrimmage in a double flanker formation with Wolfman Ted wide to the right. A long count—

The snap, Seede fades back to—

A quick handoff to the Wolfman charging diagonally across the action toward left tackle, and the Wolfman hits the line on a dead run, windmilling his right fist, belting his way through one, two, three Caballeros, getting two, three yards, then taking three quick ones to the rib cage from Rubio, and staggering right into Number 41, Manuel Cardozo, who brings him down on about the twenty-seven with a hard right cross.

Hold it! A flag on the play! Orduna, Number 30, of the Caballeros, and Dickson, Number 83, of the Stompers, are smashing away at each other on the twenty-six! Dickson takes two hard ones and goes down, but as Orduna kicks him in the ribs,

Number 72, Merling, of the Stompers, grabs him from behind, and now there are six or seven assistant referees breaking it up. . . .

Something going on in the stands at about the fifty, too—a section of Stompers' rooters mixing it up with the Caballero fans—

But now they've got things sorted out on the field, and it's ten yards against the Caballeros for striking an ineligible player, nullified by a ten-yarder against the Stompers for illegal offensive striking. So now it's second and seven for the Stompers on their own twenty-seven—

It's quieted down a bit there above the fifty-yard line, but there's another little fracas going in the far end zone and a few groups of people milling around in the aisles of the upper grandstand—

There's the snap, and Seede fades back quietly, dances around, looks downfield, and throws one intended for Number 54, Al Viper, the left end, at about the forty. Viper goes up for it, he's got it—

And takes a tremendous shot along the base of his neck from Number 94, Porfirio Rubio! The ball is jarred loose. Rubio dives for it, he's got it, but he takes a hard right in the head from Viper, then a left. Porfirio drops the ball and goes at Viper with both fists! Viper knocks him sprawling and dives on top of the ball, burying it and bringing a whistle from the head referee as Rubio rains blows on his prone body. And here come the assistant referees to pull Porfirio off as half the Stompers come charging downfield toward the action—

They're at it again near the fifty-yard line! About forty rows of fans going at each other. There goes a smoke bomb!

They've got Rubio away from Viper now, but

three or four Stompers are trying to hold Wolfman Ted back, and Ted has blood in his eye as he yells at Number 41, Cardozo. Two burly assistant referees are holding Cardozo back. . . .

There go about a hundred and fifty special police up into the midfield stands. They've got their Mace and prods out. . . .

The head referee is calling an official's time out to get things organized, and we'll be back to live National Combat Football League action after this message. . . .

The Circus Is in Town

"We've got a serious police problem with Combat football," Commissioner Minelli told me after the game between the Golden Supermen and the Psychedelic Stompers last Sunday, in which the Supermen slaughtered the Stompers, 42-14, and during which there were ten fatalities and one hundred eighty-nine hospitalizations among the rabble in the stands.

"Every time there's a game, we have a riot, your honor," Minelli (who had risen through the ranks) said earnestly. "I recommend that you should think seriously about banning Combat Football. I really think you should."

This city is hard enough to run without free advice from politically ambitious cops. "Minelli," I told him, "you are dead wrong on both counts. First of all, not only has there *never* been a riot in New York during a Combat Football game, but the best studies show that the incidences of violent crimes and social violence diminishes from a period of three days before a Combat game clear through to a period five days afterward, not only here, but in every major city in which a game is played."

"But only this Sunday ten people were killed and nearly two hundred injured, including a dozen of my cops—"

"In the *stands*, you nitwit, not in the streets!" Really, the man was too much!

"I don't see the difference—"

"Ye gods, Minelli, can't you see that Combat Football keeps a hell of a lot of violence off the streets? It keeps it in the stadium, where it belongs. The Romans understood that two thousand years ago! We can hardly stage gladiator sports in this day and age, so we have to settle for a civilized substitute."

"But what goes on in there is murder. My cops are taking a beating. And we've got to assign two thousand cops to every game. It's costing the taxpayers a fortune, and you can bet . . . *someone* will be making an issue of it in the next election."

I do believe that the lout was actually trying to pressure me. Still, in his oafish way, he had put his finger on the one political disadvantage of Combat Football: the cost of policing the games and keeping the fan clubs in the stands from tearing each other to pieces.

And then I had one of those little moments of blind inspiration when the pieces of a problem simply fall into shape as an obvious pattern of solution.

Why bother keeping them from tearing each other to pieces?

"I think I have the solution, Minelli," I said.

"Would it satisfy your sudden sense of fiscal responsibility if you could take all but a couple dozen cops off the Combat Football games?"

Minelli looked at me blankly. "Anything less than two thousand cops in there would be mincemeat by halftime," he said.

"So why send them in there?"

"Huh?"

"All we really need is enough cops to guard the gates, frisk the fans for weapons, seal up the stadium with the help of riot-doors, and make sure no one gets out till things have simmered down inside."

"But they'd tear each other to ribbons in there with no cops!"

"So let them. I intend to modify the conditions under which the city licenses Combat Football so that anyone who buys a ticket legally waives his right to police protection. Let them fight all they want. Let them really work out their hatreds on each other until they're good and exhausted. Human beings have an incurable urge to commit violence on each other. We try to sublimate that urge out of existence, and we end up with irrational violence on the streets. The Romans had a better idea—give the rabble a socially harmless outlet for violence. We spend billions on welfare to keep things pacified with bread, and where has it gotten us? Isn't it about time we tried circuses?"

As American as Apple Pie

Let me tell it to you brother, we've sure been waiting for the Golden Supermen to play the

Panthers in *this* town again, after the way those blond mothers cheated us, 17-10, the last time and wasted three hundred of the brothers! Yeah, man, they had those stands packed with honkies trucked in from as far away as Buffalo—we just weren't ready is why we took the loss.

But this time we planned ahead and got ourselves up for the game even before it was announced. Yeah, instead of waiting for them to announce the date of the next Panther-Supermen game in Chicago and then scrambling with the honkies for tickets, the Panther Fan Club made under-the-table deals with ticket brokers for blocks of tickets for whenever the next game would be, so that by the time today's game was announced, we controlled two-thirds of the seats in Daley Stadium and the honkies had to scrape and scrounge for what was left.

Yeah, man, today we pay them back for that last game! We got two-thirds of the seats in the stadium and Eli Wood is back in action and we gonna just go out and *stomp* those mothers today!

Really, I'm personally quite cynical about Combat; most of us who go out to the Gay Bladers games are. After all, if you look at it straight on, Combat Football is rather a grotty business. I mean, look at the sort of people who turn out at Supermen or Panthers or, for God's sake, *Caballero* games: the worst sort of proletarian apes. Aside from us, only the Hogs have any semblance of class, and the Hogs have beauty only because they're so incredibly up-front gross; I mean, all that shiny metal and black leather!

And, of course, that's the only real reason to go to the Blader games: for the spectacle. To see it and to be part of it! To see seminaked groups of men engaging in violence and to be violent yourself—and especially with those black-leather-and-chain-mail Hog Lovers!

Of course, I'm aware of the cynical use the loathsome government makes of Combat. If there's nastiness between the blacks and PR's in New York, they have the league schedule a Panther-Caballero game and let them get it out on each other safely in the stadium. If there's college campus trouble in the Bay area, it's a Stompers-Supermen game in Oakland. And us and the Hogs when just *anyone* anywhere needs to release general hostility. I'm not stupid; I know that Combat football is a tool of the Establishment. . . .

But, Lord, it's just so much bloody *fun!*

We gonna have some fun today! The Hogs is playing the Stompers and that's the wildest kind of Combat game there is! Those crazy freaks come to the game stoned out of their minds, and you know that at least Wolfman Ted is playing on something stronger than pot. There are twice as many chicks at Stompers games than with any other team the Hogs play because the Stompers chicks are the only chicks besides ours who aren't scared out of their boxes at the thought of being locked up in a stadium with twenty thousand hot-shot Hogger rape artists like us!

Yeah, we get good and stoned, and the Stomper fans get good and stoned, and the Hogs get stoned, and the Stompers get stoned, and then we all groove on beating the piss out of each other, *whoo-whee!* And when we win in the stands, we drag off the pussy and gang-bang it.

Oh, yeah, Combat is just good clean dirty fun!

It makes you feel good to go out to a Superman game, makes you feel like a real American is supposed to, like a *man*. All week you've got to take crap from the niggers and the spics and your goddamned crazy doped-up kids and hoods and bums and faggots in the streets, and you're not even supposed to think of them as niggers and spics and crazy doped-up kids and bums and hoods and faggots. But Sunday you can go out to the stadium and watch the Supermen give it to the Panthers, the Caballeros, the Stompers, the Hogs, or the Bladers and maybe kick the crap out of a few people whose faces you yourself don't like.

It's a good healthy way to spend a Sundy afternoon, out in the open air at a good game when the Supermen are hot and we've got the opposition in the stands outnumbered. Combat's a great thing to take your kid to, too!

I don't know, all my friends go to the Caballero games. We go together and take a couple of sixpacks of beer apiece, and get *muy boracho,* and just have some crazy fun, you know? Sometimes I come home a little cut up and my wife is all upset and tries to get me to promise not to go to the Combat games anymore. Sometimes I promise, just to keep her quiet—she can get on my nerves—but I never really mean it.

Hombre, you know how it is; women don't understand these things like men do. A man has got to go out with his friends and feel like a man sometimes. It's not too easy to find ways to feel *muy macho* in this country, *amigo*. The way it is for us here, you know. It's not as if we're hurting anyone we shouldn't hurt. Who goes out to the Caballero games but a lot of dirty *gringos* who want to pick on us? So it's a question of honor, in a way, for us to get as many *amigos* as we can out to the Caballero games and show those *cabrones* that we can beat them anytime, no matter how drunk we are. In fact, the drunker we are, the better it is, *tu sabes*?

Baby, I don't know what it is, maybe it's just a chance to get it all out. It's a unique trip, that's all. There's no other way to get that particular high, that's why I go to Stompers games. Man, the games don't mean anything to me as games; games are like *games*, dig. But the whole Combat scene is its own reality.

You take some stuff—acid is a groovy high, but you're liable to get wasted; lots of speed and some grass or hash is more recommended—when you go in, so that by the time the game starts you're really loaded. And then, man, you just groove behind the violence. There aren't any cops to bring you down. What chicks are there are there because they dig it. The people you're enjoying beating up on are getting the same kicks beating up on you, so there's no guilt hang-up to get between you and the total experience of violence.

Like I say, it's a unique trip. A pure violence high without any hang-ups. It makes me feel good and purged and kind of together just to walk out of that stadium after a Combat Football trip and know I survived; the danger is groovy, too. Baby, if you can dig it, Combat can be a genuine mystical experience.

Hogs Win It All, 21-17, 1578(23)—989(14)!

Anaheim, October 8. It was a slam-bang finish to the National Combat Football League Pennant Race, the kind of game Combat fans dream about. The Golden Supermen and the Hog Choppers in a dead-even tie for first place playing each other in the last game of the season, winner take all, before nearly sixty thousand fans. It was a beautiful, sunny ninety degree Southern California day as the Hogs kicked off to the Supermen before a crowd that seemed evenly divided between Hog lovers, who had motorcycled in all week from all over California, and Supermen fans, whose biggest bastion is here in Orange County.

The Supermen scored first blood midway through the first period when quarterback Bill Johnson tossed a little screen pass to his right end, Seth West, on the Hog twenty-three, and West slugged his way through five Hog tacklers, one of whom sustained a mild concussion, to go in for the touchdown. Rudolf's conversion made it 7-0, and the Supermen fans in the stands responded to the action on the field by making a major sortie into the Hog lover section at midfield, taking out about twenty Hog lovers, including a fatality.

The Hog fans responded almost immediately by launching an offensive of their own in the bleacher seats, but didn't do much better than hold their own. The Hogs and the Supermen pushed each other up and down the field for the rest of the period without a score, while the Supermen fans seemed to be getting the better of the Hog lovers, especially in the midfield sections of the grandstand, where at least one hundred and twenty Hog lovers were put out of action.

The Supermen scored a field goal early in the second period to make the score 10-0, but more significantly, the Hog lovers seemed to be dogging it, contenting themselves with driving back continual Supermen fan sorties, while launching almost no attacks of their own.

The Hogs finally pushed in over the goal line in the final minutes of the first half on a long pass from quarterback Spike Horrible to his flanker Greasy Ed Lee to make the score 10-7 as the half ended. But things were not nearly as close as the field score looked, as the Hog lovers in the stands were really taking their lumps from the Supermen fans who had bruised them to the extent of nearly five hundred takeouts including five fatalities, as against only about three hundred casualties and three fatalities chalked up by the Hog fans.

During the half-time intermission, the Hog lovers could be seen marshaling themselves nervously, passing around beer, pot, and pills, while the Supermen fans confidently passed the time entertaining themselves with patriotic songs.

The Supermen scored again halfway through the third period, on a handoff from Johnson to his big fullback Tex McGhee on the Hog forty-one. McGhee slugged his way through the left side of the line with his patented windmill attack, and burst out into the Hog secondary swinging and kicking. There was no stopping the Texas Tornado, though half the Hog defense tried, and McGhee went forty-one yards for the touchdown, leaving three Hogs unconscious and three more with minor injuries in his wake. The kick was good, and the Supermen seemed on the way to walking away with the championship, with the score 17-7, and the momentum, in the stands and on the field, going all their way.

But in the closing moments of the third period, Johnson threw a long one downfield intended for his left end, Dick Whitfield. Whitfield got his fingers on the football at the Hog thirty, but Hardly Davidson, the Hog cornerback, was right on him, belted him in the head from behind as he touched the ball, and then managed to catch the football himself before either it or Whitfield had hit the ground. Davidson got back to midfield before three Supermen tacklers took him out of the rest of the game with a closed eye and a concussion.

All at once, as time ran out in the third period, the ten-point Supermen lead didn't seem so big at all as the Hogs advanced to a first down on the Supermen thirty-five and the Hog lovers in the stands beat back Supermen fan attacks on several fronts, inflicting very heavy losses.

Spike Horrible threw a five-yarder to Greasy Ed Lee on the first play of the final period, then a long one into the end zone intended for his left end, Kid Filth, which the Kid dropped as Gordon Jones and John Lawrence slugged him from both sides as soon as he became fair game.

It looked like a sure pass play on third and five, but Horrible surprised everyone by fading back into a draw and handing the ball off to Loser

Ludowicki, his fullback, who plowed around right end like a heavy tank, simply crushing and smashing through tacklers with his body and fists, picked up two key blocks on the twenty and seventeen, knocked Don Barnfield onto the casualty list with a tremendous haymaker on the seven, and went in for the score.

The Hog lovers in the stands went Hog-wild. Even before the successful conversion by Knuckleface Bonner made it 17-14, they began blitzing the Supermen fans on all fronts, letting out everything they had seemed to be holding back during the first three quarters. At least one hundred Supermen fans were taken out in the next three minutes, including two quick fatalities, while the Hog lovers lost no more than a score of their number.

As the Hog lovers continued to punish the Supermen fans, the Hogs kicked off to the Supermen, and stopped them after two first downs, getting the ball back on their own twenty-four. After marching to the Supermen thirty-one on a sustained and bloody ground drive, the Hogs lost the ball again when Greasy Ed Lee was rabbit-punched into a fumble.

But the Hog lovers still sensed the inevitable and pressed their attack during the next two Supermen series of downs, and began to push the Supermen fans toward the bottom of the grandstand.

Buoyed by the success of their fans, the Hogs on the field recovered the ball on their own twenty-nine with less than two minutes to play when Chain-Mail Dixon belted Tex McGhee into a fumble and out of the game.

The Hogs crunched their way upfield yard by yard, punch by punch, against a suddenly shaky Supermen opposition, and, all at once, the whole season came down to one play: with the score 17-14 and twenty seconds left on the clock, time enough for one or possibly two more plays, the Hogs had the ball third and four on the eighteen-yard line of the Golden Supermen.

Spike Horrible took the snap as the Hog lovers in the stands launched a final all-out offensive against the Supermen fans, who by now had been pushed to a last stand against the grandstand railings at fieldside. Horrible took about ten quick steps back as if to pass, and then suddenly ran head down, fist flailing, at the center of the Supermen line with the football tucked under his arm.

Suddenly Greasy Ed Lee and Loser Ludowicki raced ahead of their quarterback, hitting the line and staggering the tacklers a split-second before Horrible arrived, throwing them just off-balance enough for Horrible to punch his way through with three quick rights, two of them k.o. punches. Virtually the entire Hog team roared through the hole after him, body-blocking, elbowing, and crushing tacklers to the ground. Horrible punched out three more tacklers as the Hog lovers pushed the first contingent of fleeing Supermen fans out onto the field, and went in for the game and championship-winning touchdown with two seconds left on the clock.

When the dust had cleared, not only had the Hog Choppers beaten the Golden Supermen 21-17, but the Hog lovers had driven the Golden Supermen fans from their favorite stadium, and had racked up a commanding advantage in the casualty statistics, 1578 casualties and 23 fatalities inflicted, as against only 989 and 14.

It was a great day for the Hog lovers and a great day in the history of our National Pastime.

The Voice of Sweet Reason

Go to a Combat Football game? Really, do you think I want to risk being injured or possibly killed? Of course, I realize that Combat is a practical social mechanism for preserving law and order, and, to be frank, I find the spectacle rather stimulating. I watch Combat often, almost every Sunday.

On television, of course. After all, everyone who is anyone in this country knows very well that there are basically two kinds of people in the United States: people who go out to Combat games, and people for whom Combat is strictly a television spectator sport.

Introduction to It's A Bird! It's A Plane!

Honest, I swear I wrote this story years before anyone even thought of doing a big Superman movie, and if you don't believe me just check the copyright page of this book. I predict nothing. The movie hasn't even come out as I write this. I am responsible for nothing. I didn't do it, honest I didn't!

Honest, really, please believe me for your own good. Superman does not exist. He's only a character in a comic book and a movie and merchandising campaigns and dirty jokes. He's entirely a figment of poor nebbishy Clark Kent's imagination. You do believe that, don't you. . . ?

It's a Bird! It's a Plane!

Dr. Felix Funck fumblingly fitted yet another spool onto the tape recorder hidden in the middle drawer of his desk as the luscious Miss Jones ushered in yet another one. Dr. Funck stared wistfully for a long moment at Miss Jones, whose white nurse's smock advertised the contents most effectively without revealing any of the more intimate and interesting details. If only x-ray vision were really possible and not part of the infernal Syndrome. . . .

Get a hold of yourself, Funck, get a hold of yourself! Felix Funck told himself for the seventeenth time that day.

He sighed, resigned himself, and said to the earnest-looking young man whom Miss Jones had brought to his office, "Please sit down, Mr. . . .?"

"Kent, Doctor," said the young man, seating himself primly on the edge of the overstuffed chair in front of Funck's desk. "Clark Kent!"

Dr. Funck grimaced, then smiled wanly. "Why not?" he said, studying the young man's appearance. The young man wore an archaic blue double-breasted suit and steel-rimmed glasses. His hair was steel-blue.

"Tell me . . . Mr. Kent," he said, "do you by some chance know where you are?"

"Certainly, Doctor," replied Clark Kent crisply. "I'm in a large public mental hospital in New York City!"

"Very good, Mr. Kent. And do you know why you're here?"

"I think so, Dr. Funck!" said Clark Kent. "I'm suffering from partial amnesia! I don't remember how or when I came to New York!"

"You mean you don't remember your past life?" asked Dr. Felix Funck.

"Not at all, Doctor!" said Clark Kent. "I remember everything up till three days ago when I found myself suddenly in New York! And I remember the last three days here! But I don't remember how I got here!"

"Well, then, where did you live before you found yourself in New York, Mr. Kent?"

"Metropolis!" said Clark Kent. "I remember that very well! I'm a reporter for the Metropolis *Daily Planet!* That is, I am if Mr. White hasn't fired me for not showing up for three days! You must help me, Dr. Funck! I must return to Metropolis immediately!"

"Well, then you should just hop the next plane for home," suggested Dr. Funck.

"There don't seem to be any flights from New York to Metropolis!" exclaimed Clark Kent. "No buses or trains either! I couldn't even find a copy of the *Daily Planet* at the Times Square newsstand! I can't even remember where Metropolis is! It's as if some evil force has removed all traces of Metropolis from the face of the Earth! That's my problem, Dr. Funck! I've got to get back to Metropolis, but I don't know how!"

"Tell me, Mr. Kent," said Funck slowly, "just

why is it so imperative that you return to Metropolis immediately?"

"Well . . . uh . . . there's my job!" Clark Kent said uneasily. "Perry White must be furious by now! And there's my girl, Lois Lane! Well, maybe she's not my girl yet, but I'm hoping!"

Dr. Felix Funck grinned conspiratorially. "Isn't there some more pressing reason, Mr. Kent?" he said. "Something perhaps having to do with your Secret Identity?"

"S-secret Identity?" stammered Clark Kent. "I don't know what you're talking about, Dr. Funck!"

"Aw come on, Clark!" Felix Funck said. "Lots of people have Secret Identities. I've got one myself. Tell me yours, and I'll tell you mine. You can trust me, Clark. Hippocratic Oath, and like that. Your secret is safe with me."

"*Secret*? What secret are you talking about?"

"Come, come, Mr. Kent!" Funck snapped. "If you want help, you'll have to come clean with me. Don't give me any of that meek, mild-mannered reporter jazz. I know who you really are, Mr. Kent."

"I'm Clark Kent, meek, mild-mannered reporter for the Metropolis *Daily Planet!*" insisted Clark Kent.

Dr. Felix Funck reached into a desk drawer and produced a small chunk of rock coated with green paint. "Who is in reality, Superman," he exclaimed, "faster than a speeding bullet, more powerful than a locomotive, able to leap tall buildings at a single bound! Do you know what this is?" he shrieked, thrusting the green rock in the face of the hapless Clark Kent. "It's Kryptonite, that's what it is, genuine, government-inspected Kryptonite! How's *that* grab you, Superman?"

Clark Kent, who is in reality the Man of Steel, tried to say something, but before he could utter a sound, he lapsed into unconsciousness.

Dr. Felix Funck reached across his desk and unbuttoned Clark Kent's shirt. Sure enough, underneath his street clothing, Kent was wearing a pair of moth-eaten longjohns dyed blue, on the chest of which a rude cloth "S" had been crudely sewn.

"Classic case . . ." Dr. Funck muttered to himself. "Right out of a textbook. Even lost his imaginary powers when I showed him the phony Kryptonite. Another job for Supershrink!"

Get a hold of yourself, Funck, get a hold of yourself! Dr. Felix Funck told himself again.

Shaking his head, he rang for the orderlies.

After the orderlies had removed Clark Kent #758, Dr. Felix Funck pulled a stack of comic books out of a desk drawer, spread them out across the desktop, stared woodenly at them and moaned.

The Superman Syndrome was getting totally out of hand. In this one hospital alone, there are already 758 classified cases of Superman Syndrome, he thought forlornly, and lord knows how many Supernuts in the receiving ward awaiting classification.

"Why? Why? Why?" Funck muttered, tearing at his rapidly thinning hair.

The basic, fundamental, inescapable, incurable reason, he knew was, of course, that the world was full of Clark Kents. Meek, mild-mannered men. Born losers. None of them, of course, had self-images of themselves as nebbishes. Every mouse has to think of himself as a lion. Everyone has a Secret Identity, a dream image of himself, possessed of fantastic powers, able to cope with normally impossible situations. . . .

Even psychiatrists had Secret Identities, Funck thought abstractedly. After all, who but Supershrink himself could cope with a ward full of Supermen?

Supershrink! More powerful than a raving psychotic! Able to diagnose whole neuroses in a single session! Faster than Freud! Abler than Adler! Who, disguised as Dr. Felix Funck, balding, harried head of the Superman Syndrome ward of a great metropolitan booby-hatch, fights a never-ending war for Adjustment, Neo-Freudian Analysis, Fee-splitting, and the American Way!

Get a hold of yourself, Funck, get a hold of yourself!

There's a little Clark Kent in the best of us, Funck thought.

That's why Superman had long since passed into folklore. Superman and his alter ego Clark Kent were the perfect, bald statement of the human dilemma (Kent) and the corresponding wish-fulfillment (The Man of Steel). It was normal for kids to assimilate the synthetic myth into their grubby little ids. But it was also normal for them to outgrow it. A few childhood schizoid tendencies never hurt anyone. All kids are a little loco in the coco, Funck reasoned sagely.

If only someone had shot Andy Warhol before it was too late!

That's what opened the whole fetid can of worms, Funck thought—the Pop Art craze. Suddenly, comic books were no longer greasy kid stuff. Suddenly, comic books were Art with a big, fat capital "A." They were hip, they were in, so-called adults were no longer ashamed to snatch them away from the brats and read the things themselves.

All over America, meek, mild-mannered men went back and relived their youths through comic books. Thousands of meek, mild-mannered slobs were once more coming to identify with the meek, mild-mannered reporter of the Metropolis *Daily Planet*. It was like going home again. Superman was the perfect wish-fulfillment figure. No one doubted that he could pulverize 007, leap over a traffic jam on the Long Island Expressway in a single bound, see through women's clothing with his x-ray vision, and *voilá*, the Superman Syndrome!

Step one: the meek, mild-mannered victim identified with that prototype of all *schlemiels*, Clark Kent.

Step two: they began to see themselves more and more as Clark Kent; began to dream of themselves as Superman.

Step three: a moment of intense frustration, a rebuff from some Lois Lane figure, a dressing-down from some irate Perry White surrogate, and something snapped, and they were in the clutches of the Superman Syndrome.

Usually, it started covertly. The victim procured a pair of longjohns, dyed them blue, sewed an "S" on them, and took to wearing the costume under his street clothes occasionally, in times of stress.

But once the first fatal step was taken, the Superman Syndrome was irreversible. The victim took to wearing the costume all the time. Sooner or later, the stress and strain of reality became too much, and a fugue-state resulted. During the fugue, the victim dyed his hair Superman steel-blue, bought a blue double-breasted suit and steel-rimmed glasses, forgot who he was, and woke up one morning with a set of memories straight out of the comic book. He *was* Clark Kent, and he had to get back to Metropolis.

Bad enough for thousands of nuts to waltz around thinking they were Clark Kent. The horrible part was that Clark Kent was the Man of Steel. Which meant that thousands of grown men were jumping off buildings, trying to stop locomotives with their bare hands, tackling armed criminals in the streets and otherwise contriving to commit *hara-kiri*.

What was worse, there were so many Supernuts popping up all over the place that everyone in the country had seen Superman at least once by now, and enough of them had managed to pull off some feat of daring—saving a little old lady from a gang of muggers, foiling an inexpert bank robbery simply by getting underfoot—that it was fast becoming impossible to convince people that there *wasn't* a Superman.

And the more people became convinced that there was a Superman, the more people fell victim to the Syndrome, the more people became convinced. . . .

Funck groaned aloud. There was even a well-known television commentator who jokingly suggested that maybe Superman *was* real, and the nuts were the people who thought he wasn't.

Could it be? Funck wondered. If sanity was defined as the norm, the mental state of the majority of the population, and the majority of the population believed in Superman, then maybe anyone who *didn't* believe in Superman had a screw loose. . . .

If the nuts were sane, and the sane people were really nuts, and the nuts were the majority, then the truth would have to be. . . .

"Get a hold of yourself, Funck!" Dr. Felix Funck shouted aloud. "There is no Superman! There is no Superman!"

Funck scooped the comics back into the drawer and pressed a button on his intercom.

"You may send in the next Supertwitch, Miss Jones," he said.

Luscious Miss Jones seemed to be blushing as she ushered the next patient into Dr. Funck's office.

There was something unsettling about this one, Funck decided instantly. He had the usual glasses and the usual blue double-breasted suit, but on him they looked almost good. He was built like a brick outhouse, and the steel-blue dye job on his hair looked most professional. Funck smelled money. One of the powers of Supershrink, after all, was the uncanny ability to instantly calculate a potential patient's bank balance. Maybe there would be some way to grab this one for a private patient. . . ."

"Have a seat, Mr. Kent," Dr. Funck said. "You are Clark Kent, aren't you?"

Clark Kent sat down on the edge of his chair, his broad back ramrod-straight. "Why, yes, Doctor!" he said. "How did you know?"

"I've seen your stuff in the Metropolis *Daily Planet*, Mr. Kent," Funck said. Got to really humor this one, he thought. There's money here. That dye job's so good it must've set him back fifty bucks! *Indeed* a job for Supershrink! "Well just what seems to be the trouble, Mr. Kent?" he said.

"It's my memory, Doctor!" said Clark Kent. "I seem to be suffering from a strange form of amnesia!"

"So-o . . ." said Felix Funck soothingly. "Could it possibly be that . . . that you suddenly found yourself in New York without knowing how you got here, Mr. Kent?" he said.

"Why that's amazing!" exclaimed Clark Kent. "You're one hundred percent correct!"

"And could it also be," suggested Felix Funck, "that you feel you must return to Metropolis immediately? That, however, you can find no plane or train or bus that goes there? That you cannot find a copy of the *Daily Planet* at the out-of-town newsstands? That, in fact, you cannot even remember where Metropolis is?"

Clark Kent's eyes bugged. "Fantastic!" he exclaimed. "How could you know all that? Can it be that you are no ordinary psychiatrist, Dr. Funck? Can it be that Dr. Felix Funck, balding, harried head of a ward in a great metropolitan booby-hatch is in reality . . . *Supershrink?*"

"Ak!" said Dr. Felix Funck.

"Don't worry, Dr. Funck," Clark Kent said in a warm, comradely tone, "your secret is safe with me! We superheroes have got to stick together, right?"

"Guk!" said Dr. Felix Funck. How could he possibly know? he thought. Why, he'd have to be . . . *ulp!* That was ridiculous. Get a hold of yourself, Funck, get a hold of yourself! Who's the psychiatrist here, anyway?

"So you know that Felix Funck is Supershrink, eh?" he said shrewdly. "Then you must also know that you can conceal nothing from me. That I know your Secret Identity too."

"*Secret Identity?*" said Clark Kent piously. "Who me? Why everyone knows that I'm just a meek, mild-mannered reporter for a great metropolitan—"

With a savage whoop, Dr. Felix Funck suddenly leapt halfway across his desk and ripped open the shirt of the dumbfounded Clark Kent, revealing a skin-tight blue uniform with a red "S" insignia emblazoned on the chest. Top-notch job of tailoring too, Funck thought approvingly.

"Aha!" exclaimed Funck. "So Clark Kent, meek, mild-mannered reporter, is, in reality, *Superman!*"

"So my secret is out!" Clark Kent said stoically. "I sure hope you believe in Truth, Justice and the American way!"

"Don't worry, Clark old man. Your secret is safe with me. We superheroes have got to stick together, right?"

"Absolutely!" said Clark Kent. "Now about my problem, Doctor . . ."

"Problem?"

"How am I going to get back to Metropolis?" asked Clark Kent. "By now, the forces of evil must be having a field day!"

"Look," said Dr. Funck. "First of all, there is no Metropolis, no *Daily Planet,* no Lois Lane, no Perry White, and *no Superman.* It's all a comic book, friend."

Clark Kent stared at Dr. Funck worriedly. "Are you feeling all right, Doctor?" he asked solicitously. "Sure you haven't been working too hard? Everybody knows there's a Superman! Tell me, Dr. Funck, when did you first notice this strange malady? Could it be that some childhood trauma has caused you to deny my existence? Maybe your mother—"

"Leave my mother out of this!" shrieked Felix Funck. "Who's the psychiatrist here, anyway? I don't want to hear any dirty stories about my mother. There is no Superman, you're not him, and I can prove it!"

Clark Kent nodded his head benignly. "Sure you can, Dr. Funck!" he soothed.

"Look! Look! If you were Superman you wouldn't have any problem. You'd—" Funck glanced nervously about his office. It was on the tenth floor. It had one window. The window had steel bars an inch and a quarter thick. He can't hurt himself, Funck thought. Why not? Make him face reality, and break the delusion!

"You were saying, Doctor?" said Clark Kent.

"If you were Superman, you wouldn't have to worry about trains or planes or buses. You can fly, eh? You can bend steel in your bare hands? Well then why don't you just rip the bars off the window and fly back to Metropolis?"

"Why . . . why you're absolutely right!" exclaimed Clark Kent. "Of course!"

"Ah . . ." said Funck. "So you see you have been the victim of a delusion. Progress, progress. But don't think you've been completely cured yet. Even Supershrink isn't *that* good. This will require many hours of private consultation, at the modest hourly rate of a mere fifty dollars. We must uncover the basic psychosomatic causes for the—"

"What are you talking about?" exclaimed Clark Kent, leaping up from the chair and shucking his suit with blinding speed, revealing a full-scale Superman costume, replete with expensive-looking scarlet cape which Funck eyed greedily.

He bounded to the window. "Of course!" said Superman. "I can bend steel in my bare hands!" So saying, he bent the inch-and-a-quarter steel bars in his bare hands like so many lengths of licorice whip, ripped them aside and leapt to the windowsill.

"Thanks for everything, Dr. Funck!" he said. "Up! Up! And away!" He flung out his arms and leapt from the tenth-floor window.

Horrified, Funck bounded to the window and peered out, expecting to see an awful mess on the crowded sidewalk below. Instead:

A rapidly-dwindling caped figure soared out over the New York skyline. From the crowded street below, shrill cries drifted up to the ears of Dr. Felix Funck.

"Look! Up there in the sky!"

"It's a bird!"

"It's a plane!"

"It's SUPERMAN!!"

Dr. Felix Funck watched the Man of Steel execute a smart left bank and turn due west at the Empire State Building. For a short moment, Dr. Funck was stunned, nonplussed. Then he realized what had happened and what he had to do.

"He's nuts!" Felix Funck shouted. "The man is

crazy! He's got a screw loose! He thinks he's Superman, and he's so crazy that he *is* Superman! The man needs help! *This* is a job for SUPER-SHRINK!"

So saying, Dr. Felix Funck bounded to the windowsill, doffed his street clothes, revealing a gleaming skin-tight red suit with a large blue "S" emblazoned across it, and leapt out the window screaming "Wait for me, Superman, you pathetic neurotic, you, wait for me!"

Dr. Felix Funck, who is, after all, in reality Supershrink, turned due west and headed out across the Hudson for Metropolis, somewhere beyond Secaucus, New Jersey.

Introduction to The Entropic Gang Bang Caper

Written in England under the influence of the "condensed novels" of J. G. Ballard and the "programmed" humorous fiction of John T. Sladek and first published in New Worlds, *"The Entropic Gang Bang Caper" is probably the most thoroughly and forthrightly experimental and "New Wave" piece I've ever written. Funny how my whole image in certain quarters apparently seems based upon this obscure 1500 word story.*

Okay, all you Second Foundationeers, this is as hard-core a "New Wave" story as you're going to get to gnash your teeth over in this book. The real stuff, the kind pseudo-intellectuals like!

Near as I can make out, what the hard core English "New Wave" school was trying to do was replace the notion of linear plot entirely and create fiction which the reader experienced not as a "story" but as a succession of interpenetrating images. Think of it as fiction formally organized like film. Montage replaces plot as the organizing principle. Since what the reader is experiencing is montage and not story, you don't necessarily need continuing characters, or indeed characters at all. Meaning is conveyed by or arises from the juxtaposition of images, of slices of realities. The prose glides lightly and allusively over the phenomenological surface while what depth there is comes from the interaction of the readers' own various minds with the ambiguity of what's on paper.

Condense it as far as possible. Ballard's "condensed novels" really are *full formal novels in miniature when they work, multifaceted fictional realities.*

John Sladek was doing his separate weirdness. He was "writing" some amusing short stories by taking words and phrases and running them through a syntax program that organized them into sentences, paragraphs, and, by proper choice of input data, into "stories."

In "The Entropic Gang Bang Caper," I tried to combine both processes and carry them a bit further. I concocted a program for assembling story elements, an equation in which each term would be chosen from the appropriate class of "raw footage." But first I went out and "shot" the raw footage in the typewriter, keeping the assembly scenario in mind. In other words, I went out and shot sequential takes of the classes of prose elements I was going to use, and then edited them with a simple program.

But I took it even a little further than that. I programmed in a random factor. Every time the program called for a certain class of prose footage, I would choose which "take" went in that slot by coin flip. The result is a "condensed novel" written in collaboration with both a program and random chance.

Yes Virginia, there was a New Wave. . . .

The Entropic Gang Bang Caper

PBA THREATENS STRIKE OVER
DEMONSTRATION TACTICS

New York, N.Y. The President of the Patrolmen's Benevolent Association threatened to call a general police strike unless all riot police were immediately disarmed. "Armed police have a tough time getting laid at demonstrations," he explained. "It's bad for morale."

The Arsenal of Entropy

Some common human phobias include fear of close spaces, fear of heights, fear of spiders, fear of suffocation, fear of dogs, fear of injury to the eyes, fear of rats, fear of faeces, fear of insects, fear of slime, fear of injury to the genitals, fear of buggery, fear of impotence, fear of a public display of cowardice.

Scenario One:

War is any means of breaking the will of the enemy. Violence is a means of waging war. A violence-war breaks the will of the enemy through fear. In a violence-war, the enemy is defeated when his fear of further violence is greater than his fear of the consequences of defeat.

VIOLENCE IS THE LAST RESORT OF DESPERATE MEN ARE THE LAST RESORT OF VIOLENCE IS DESPERATE RESORT OF THE LAST MEN

The Arsenal of Entropy

DMSO is a chemical which when combined with a wide spectrum of liquids will cause the liquid with which it is mixed to be absorbed into the bloodstream, through skin-contact.

Spray-guns may be purchased on the open market.

LSD is a colorless, odorless, tasteless liquid which may be introduced into any fluid medium without fear of detection.

Scenario Two:

War is any means of breaking the will of the enemy. Revulsion is a means of waging war. A revulsion-war breaks the will of the enemy through disgust. In a revulsion-war, the enemy is defeated when his disgust for further conflict is greater than his fear of the consequences of defeat.

WAR NEGOTIATIONS SUSPENDED

Miami Beach, Fla. Negotiations were suspended until next Friday today between the Pentagon and the Military Association of Soldiers, Sailors and Airmen over the unresolved issue of combat coffee-breaks. Although MASSA has accepted the Pentagon proposal of a $2.25 an hour wage-increase for enlisted men, to be spread out over the duration of the next three-year contract, MASSA spokesmen indicated that the Pentagon refusal to grant combat coffee-breaks could lead to an indefinite prolongation of the current strike.

Regular coffee-breaks have been standard procedure in most other industries for years, MASSA negotiators pointed out, in refusing the Pentagon's counter-proposal of double-time for night patrols.

REVOLUTION IS THE OPIUM OF THE INTELLECTUAL CLASS IS THE OPIUM REVOLUTION IS INTELLECTUAL OPIUM IS THE CLASS REVOLUTION OF THE INTELLECTUAL CLASS OPIUM IS THE REVOLUTION.

Scenario Three:

War is any means of breaking the will of the enemy. Sour grapes is a means of waging war. A sour-grapes-war breaks the will of the enemy through envy. In a sour-grapes-war, the enemy is defeated when his envy of the pleasures enjoyed by the opponent is greater than his fear of the consequences of defeat.

The Arsenal of Entropy

Many men (including police, public officials and military personnel) strongly relish the prospect of sexual intercourse with young, nubile, willing, attractive women. They have been known to abandon more onerous tasks when confronted with the immediate prospect of a good lay. Other men (including police, public officials and military personnel) experience an equivalent reaction at the prospect of sexual congress with young, nubile, willing, attractive men. A small minority of men (including police, public officials, and military personnel) have similar lust for sexual objects such as dogs, goats, or dirty sweatsocks. Science has discovered few men in whom a sexual desire cannot be provoked.

YOU CAN NEVER FIND A COP WHEN YOU NEED ONE COP A NEED WHEN YOU FIND ONE COP NEVER NEED A COP CAN NEVER FIND YOU WHEN YOU NEED YOU CAN NEVER FIND A NEED WHEN YOU COP ONE

Scenario Four:

War is any means of breaking the will of the enemy. Lust is a means of waging war. A lust-war breaks the will of the enemy through tantalization. In a lust-war, the enemy is defeated when his sexual lust for the enemy is greater than his fear of the consequences of defeat.

SCOTUS RULES ON CONSTITUTIONAL ISSUE

Washington, D.C. The Supreme Court, in a unanimous decision today, declared the Constitution Unconstitutional. "There is no provision whatsoever in the Constitution for the Constitution," the Court decision pointed out.

The Arsenal of Entropy

Many human beings experience a violent disgust-reaction when showered with the entrails of freshly-killed animals.

A violently nauseous man is incapable of violence.

A variety of readily-obtainable substances provoke an irresistible biological urge to vomit.

Scenario Five:

War is any means of breaking the will of the enemy. Love is a means of waging war. A love-war breaks the will of the enemy through desire. In a love-war, the enemy is defeated when his desire to be loved by the enemy is greater than his fear of the consequences of defeat.

VD EPIDEMIC AMONG POLICE LAID TO HIPPY DEMONSTRATORS VD EPIDEMIC LAID TO POLICE LAID AMONG HIPPY DEMONSTRATORS VD EPIDEMIC AMONG POLICE LAID TO VD EPIDEMIC AMONG HIPPY DEMONSTRATORS LAID TO POLICE VD

LA COPS MOBBED BY GROUPIES

Los Angeles, Calif. Three hundred Los Angeles riot police were brutally sexually assaulted today by a screaming mob of several thousand naked fifteen-to-eighteen-year-old groupies. Five rock stars had to be summoned to restore order using charisma and amplified guitars. The management of the Shrine Auditorium threatened to revoke the LAPD's entertainment license if this outrage were to be repeated.

"Blue cloth and brass buttons turn me on," explained the seventeen-year-old President of the Cop-You-Laters, the new fan club which is causing serious concern in anti-government circles. "I just can't help it, the sight of a nightstick makes me throb inside."

"Shocking!" declared a rock star who preferred to remain anonymous. "These groupies should be setting an example for our impressionable police. Do they treat their fathers like that?"

Scenario Six:

War is any means of breaking the will of the enemy. Guilt is a means of waging war. A guilt-war breaks the will of the enemy through remorse. In a guilt-war, the enemy is defeated when his remorse for the actions he is committing is greater than his fear of the consequences of defeat.

The Arsenal of Entropy

Shit is a substance easily obtained by anyone. It is neither colorless, odorless, nor tasteless. Its odor, taste, appearance, and concept provoke severe disgust in many people, including police, public officials, and military personnel.

UNIVERSITY DEMANDS DEMONSTRATOR CONTROL OF POLICE

Berkeley, Calif. At a news conference called after the latest Berkeley riot, the Chancellor of the University of California demanded tighter demonstrator control of police. "The situation would never have gotten out of hand if the police had been forced to summon demonstrators earlier," he declared. "It's time the anarchists stopped coddling the police."

Scenario Seven:

War is any means of breaking the will of the enemy. Reality-alteration is a means of waging war. A reality-alteration-war breaks the will of the enemy through alienation. In a reality-alteration-war, the enemy is defeated when his fear of alienation from the current reality is greater than his fear of the consequences of defeat.

IF YOU CAN'T BEAT 'EM EAT 'EM IF YOU BEAT 'EM YOU CAN'T EAT 'EM IF YOU CAN'T BEAT 'EM YOU CAN'T EAT 'EM

MUGGER CLEARED OF POLICE BRUTALITY RAP

New York, N.Y. Superior Court Judge Arthur Cranz today dismissed charges of intent to commit police brutality against Herbert Smith, 29. Smith, a member of the International Brotherhood of Muggers, had been accused of police brutality against Patrolman David MacDougal of the New York City Vice Squad, when the latter's nightstick was buggered during a routine mugging in New York's Central Park. Judge Cranz ruled that since both men were under the influence of capitalist propaganda at the time, intent could not be proven. However, all three paternity suits arising out of the incident are still pending in civil court.

Scenario Eight:

War is any means of breaking the will of the enemy. Identity is a means of waging war. An identity-war breaks the will of the enemy through absorption. In an identity-war, the enemy is defeated when his degree of merger with the enemy is greater than his fear of the consequences of defeat.

SECRETARY OF TREASURY ABSCONDS

New York, N.Y. The Secretary of the Treasury today announced his formal abscondence with the National Debt at a press conference held in a Wall Street crash-pad. He told reporters that he planned to sell the Debt to the Mafia as a tax-loss, deposit the proceeds in municipal bonds, and accept a Presidential appointment to the Mothers of Invention.

Scenario Nine:

War is any means of breaking the will of the enemy. Chaos is a means of waging war. A chaos-war breaks the will of the enemy through entropy. In a chaos-war, the enemy is defeated when further action on his part becomes the consequences of defeat.

BECAUSE WE LOVE EACH OTHER,
THAT'S WHY!

Reno, Nevada. At a press conference in Reno today, the President and the Vice President announced that they had been married during the night in a private ceremony conducted by the Chief of Naval Operations.

"I just don't see what all the fuss is about," the Vice President said. "We're just two people in love, that's all."

"This time it's for keeps!" the President assured reporters as the newlyweds left for a two-week honeymoon in Niagara Falls.

Introduction to The Big Flash

This story came close to being suppressed for the sake of the body politic. Hot off the typewriter, I had sent it to Damon Knight, both as a submission to Orbit *and as a workshop story for the imminent Milford Science Fiction Writers Conference.*

When I got to Milford, Damon greeted me with an evil look in his eye, and ushered me into the kitchen, cackling maniacally. There on the countertop he had arranged a display for my amusement. He had gone into the woods and picked several radioactive-looking toadstools and lettered the words "Do It" on each mushroom cap.

He told me he loved the story, that he was going to buy it, and he thought his little fungus display was very funny. I thought it was funny too, uh, sort of, I was glad he liked the story, and happy that he was going to buy it. But somehow I was beginning to feel a little peculiar. . . .

When the story was workshopped, Damon joined in the general literary admiration, and said that he thought he was going to buy it, but. . . .

But he wasn't so sure the story ought to be published at all. After all, look what it had caused a relatively sane person such as himself to go out and do! Was this story constructed with such artful evil that publication of it might tend to make it a self-fulfilling prophecy?

Well, okay, maybe he did have a point, but was I going to let that stand in the way of a sale? Besides, it was pointed out by myself and others that a fictional catharsis might contrariwise defuse the awful reality.

So free press and commerce triumphed and Damon published the story in Orbit 5.

A few months later the Jefferson Airplane's new album appeared. There was a great big ecstatic atomic mushroom cloud on the cover. It was called "The Crown of Creation."

The Big Flash

T minus 200 days . . . and counting. . . .

They came on freaky for my taste—but that's the name of the game: freaky means a draw in the rock business. And if the Mandala was going to survive in L.A., competing with a network-owned joint like The American Dream, I'd just have to hold my nose and out-freak the opposition. So after I had dug the Four Horsemen for about an hour, I took them into my office to talk turkey.

I sat down behind my Salvation Army desk (the Mandala is the world's most expensive shoestring operation) and the Horsemen sat down on the bridge chairs sequentially, establishing the group's pecking order.

First the head honcho, lead guitar, and singer, Stony Clarke—blond shoulder-length hair, eyes like something in a morgue when he took off his steel-rimmed shades, a reputation as a heavy acid-head, and the look of a speed-freak behind it. Then Hair, the drummer, dressed like a Hell's Angel, swastikas and all, a junkie, with fanatic eyes that were a little too close together, making me wonder whether he wore swastikas because he grooved behind the Angel thing or made like an Angel because it let him groove behind the swastika in public. Number three was a cat who called himself Super Spade and wasn't kidding—he wore earrings, natural hair, a Stokeley Carmichael sweatshirt, and on a thong around his neck a shrunken head that had been whitened with liquid shoe polish. He was the utility infielder: sitar, base, organ, flute, whatever. Number four, who called himself Mr. Jones, was about the creepiest cat I had ever seen in a rock group, and that is saying something. He was their visuals, synthesizer, and electronics man. He was at least forty, wore early-hippie clothes that looked like they had been made by Sy Devore, and was rumored to be some kind of Rand Corporation dropout. There's no business like show business.

"Okay, boys," I said, "you're strange, but you're my kind of strange. Where you worked before?"

"We ain't baby," Clarke said. "We're the New Thing. I've been dealing crystal and acid in the Haight. Hair was drummer for some plastic group in New York. The Super Spade claims it's the reincarnation of Bird and it don't pay to argue. Mr. Jones, he don't talk too much. Maybe he's a Martian. We just started putting our thing together."

One thing about this business, the groups that don't have square managers, you can get cheap. They talk too much.

"Groovy," I said. "I'm happy to give you guys your start. Nobody knows you, but I think you got something going. So I'll take a chance and give you a week's booking. One A.M. to closing, which is two, Tuesday through Sunday, four hundred a week."

"Are you Jewish?" asked Hair.

"What?"

"Cool it," Clarke ordered. Hair cooled it. "What

it means," Clarke told me, "is that four hundred sounds like pretty light bread."

"We don't sign if there's an option clause," Mr. Jones said.

"The Jones-thing has a good point," Clarke said. "We do the first week for four hundred, but after that it's a whole new scene, dig?"

I didn't feature that. If they hit it big, I could end up not being able to afford them. But, on the other hand, four hundred dollars *was* light bread, and I needed a cheap closing act pretty bad.

"Okay," I said. "But a verbal agreement that I get first crack at you when you finish the gig."

"Word of honor," said Stony Clarke.

That's this business—the word of honor of an ex-dealer and speed-freak.

T minus 199 days . . . and counting. . . .

Being unconcerned with ends, the military mind can be easily manipulated, easily controlled, and easily confused. Ends are defined as those goals set by civilian authority. Ends are the conceded province of civilians; means are the province of the military, whose duty it is to achieve the ends set for it by the most advantageous application of the means at its command.

Thus the confusion over the war in Asia among my uniformed clients at the Pentagon. The end has been duly set: eradication of the guerrillas. But the civilians have overstepped their bounds and meddled in means. The generals regard this as unfair, a breach of contract, as it were. The generals (or the faction among them most inclined to paranoia) are beginning to see the conduct of the war, the political limitation on means, as a ploy of the civilians for performing a putsch against their time-honored prerogatives.

This aspect of the situation would bode ill for the country, were it not for the fact that the growing paranoia among the generals has enabled me to manipulate them into presenting both my scenarios to the President. The President has authorized implementation of the major scenario, provided that the minor scenario is successful in properly molding public opinion.

My major scenario is simple and direct. Knowing that the poor flying weather makes our conventional air power, with its dependency on relative accuracy, ineffectual, the enemy has fallen into the pattern of grouping his forces into larger units and launching punishing annual offensives during the monsoon season. However, these larger units are highly vulnerable to tactical nuclear weapons, which do not depend upon accuracy for effect. Secure in the knowledge that domestic political considerations preclude the use of nuclear weapons, the enemy will once again form into division-sized units or larger during the next monsoon season. A parsimonious use of tactical nuclear weapons, even as few as twenty one-hundred-kiloton bombs, employed simultaneously and in an advantageous pattern, will destroy a minimum of two hundred thousand enemy troops, or nearly two-thirds of his total force, in a twenty-four hour period. The blow will be crushing.

The minor scenario, upon whose success the implementation of the major scenario depends, is far more sophisticated, due to its subtler goal: public acceptance of, or, optimally, even public clamor for, the use of tactical nuclear weapons. The task is difficult, but my scenario is quite sound, if somewhat exotic, and with the full, if to some extent clandestine, support of the upper military hierarchy, certain civil government circles and the decision-makers in key aerospace corporations, the means now at my command would seem adequate. The risks, while statistically significant, do not exceed an acceptable level.

T minus 189 days . . . and counting. . . .

The way I see it, the network deserved the shafting I gave them. They shafted me, didn't they? Four successful series I produce for those bastards, and two bomb out after thirteen weeks and they send me to the salt mines! A discotheque, can you imagine they make me producer at a lousy discotheque! A remittance man they make me, those schlockmeisters. Oh, those schnorrers made the American Dream sound like a kosher deal—twenty percent of the net, they say. And you got access to all our sets and contract players; it'll make you a rich man, Herm. And like a yuk, I sign, being broke at the time, without reading the fine print. I should know they've set up the American Dream as a tax loss? I should know that I've *gotta* use their lousy sets and stiff contract players and have it written off against my gross? I should know their shtick is to run the American Dream at a loss and then do a network TV show out of the joint from which I don't see a penny? So I end up running the place for them at a paper loss, living on salary, while the network rakes it in off the TV show that I end up paying for out of my end.

Don't bums like that deserve to be shafted? It isn't enough they use me as a tax-loss patsy; they gotta tell me who to book! "Go sign the Four Horsemen, the group that's packing them in at the Mandala," they say. "We want them on 'A Night with the American Dream.' They're hot."

"Yeah, they're hot," I say, "which means they'll cost a mint. I can't afford it."

They show me more fine print—next time I read the contract with a microscope. I *gotta* book whoever they tell me to and I gotta absorb the cost on my books! It's enough to make a Litvak turn anti-semitic.

So I had to go to the Mandala to sign up these hippies. I made sure I didn't get there until twelve-thirty so I wouldn't have to stay in that nuthouse any longer than necessary. Such a dive! What Bernstein did was take a bankrupt Hollywood-Hollywood club on the Strip, knock down all the interior walls, and put up this monster tent inside the shell. Just thin white screening over two-by-fours. Real schlock. Outside the tent, he's got projectors, lights, speakers, all the electronic mumbo-jumbo, and inside is like being surrounded by movie screens. Just the tent and the bare floor, not even a real stage, just a platform on wheels they shlepp in and out of the tent when they change groups.

So you can imagine he doesn't draw exactly a class crowd. Not with the American Dream up the street being run as a network tax loss. What they get is the smelly, hard-core hippies I don't let in the door and the kind of j.d. high-school kids that think it's smart to hang around putzes like that. A lot of dope-pushing goes on. The cops don't like the place and the rousts draw professional troublemakers.

A real den of iniquity—I felt like I was walking onto a Casbah set. The last group had gone off and the Horsemen hadn't come on yet. So what you had was this crazy tent filled with hippies, half of them on acid or pot or amphetamine, or, for all I know, Ajax, high-school would-be hippies, also mostly stoned and getting ugly, and a few crazy schwartzes looking to fight cops. All of them standing around waiting for something to happen, and about ready to make it happen. I stood near the door, just in case. As they say, "The vibes were making me uptight."

All of a sudden the house lights go out and it's black as a network executive's heart. I hold my hand on my wallet—in this crowd, tell me there are no pickpockets. Just the pitch black and dead silence for what, ten beats, and then I start feeling something, I don't know, like something crawling along my bones, but I know it's some kind of subsonic effect and not my imagination, because all the hippies are standing still and you don't hear a sound.

Then from monster speakers so loud you feel it in your teeth, a heartbeat, but heavy, slow, half-time, like maybe a whale's heart. The thing crawling along my bones seems to be synchronized with the heartbeat and I feel almost like I am that big dumb heart beating there in the darkness.

Then a dark red spot—so faint it's almost infrared—hits the stage which they have wheeled out. On the stage are four uglies in crazy black robes—you know, like the Grim Reaper wears—with that ugly red light all over them like blood. Creepy. Boom-ba-boom. Boom-ba-boom. The heartbeat still going, still that subsonic bone-crawl, and the hippies are staring at the Four Horsemen like mesmerized chickens.

The bass player, a regular jungle bunny, picks up the rhythm of the heartbeat. Dum-da-dum. Dum-da-dum. The drummer beats it out with earsplitting rim shots. Then the electric guitar, tuned like a strangling cat, makes with horrible, heavy chords. Whang-ka-whang. Whang-ka-whang.

It's just awful, I feel it in my guts, my bones; my eardrums are just like some great big throbbing vein. Everybody is swaying to it; I'm swaying to it. Boom-ba-boom. Boom-ba-boom.

Then the guitarist starts to chant in rhythm with the heartbeat, in a hoarse, shrill voice like somebody dying: "*The* big *flash* . . . *the* big *flash* . . ."

And the guy at the visuals console diddles around and rings of light start to climb the walls of the tent, blue at the bottom becoming green as they get higher, then yellow, orange, and finally as they become a circle on the ceiling, eye-killing neon-red. Each circle takes exactly one heartbeat to climb the walls.

Boy, what an awful feeling! Like I was a tube of toothpaste being squeezed in rhythm till the top of my head felt like it was gonna squirt up with those circles of light through the ceiling.

And then they start to speed it up gradually. The same heartbeat, the same rim shots, same chords, same circles of light, same "*The* big *flash* . . . *the* big *flash* . . ." Same base, same subsonic bone-crawl, but just a little faster. . . . Then faster! Faster!

Thought I would die! Knew I would die! Heart beating like a lunatic. Rim shots like a machine gun. Circles of light sucking me up the walls, into that red neon hole.

Oy, incredible! Over and over, faster, faster, till the voice was a scream and the heartbeat a boom and the rim shots a whine and the guitar howled feedback and my bones were jumping out of my body—

Every spot in the place came on and I went blind from the sudden light—

An awful explosion sound came over every speaker, so loud it rocked me on my feet—

I felt myself squirting out of the top of my head and loved it.

Then:

The explosion became a rumble—

The light seemed to run together into a circle on the ceiling, leaving everything else black.

And the circle became a fireball.

The fireball became a slow-motion film of an atomic-bomb cloud as the rumbling died away. Then the picture faded into a moment of total darkness and the house lights came on.

What a number!

Gevalt, what an act!

So, after the show, when I got them alone and found out they had no manager, not even an option to the Mandala, I thought faster than I ever had in my life.

To make a long story short and sweet, I gave the network the royal screw. I signed the Horsemen to a contract that made me their manager and gave me twenty percent of their take. Then I booked them into the American Dream at ten thousand a week, wrote a check as proprietor of the American Dream, handed the check to myself as manager of the Four Horsemen, then resigned as a network flunky, leaving them with a ten-thousand-dollar bag and me with twenty percent of the hottest group since the Beatles.

What the hell, he who lives by the fine print shall perish by the fine print.

T minus 148 days . . . and counting. . . .

"You haven't seen the tape yet, have you, B.D.?" Jake said. He was nervous as hell. When you reach my level in the network structure, you're used to making subordinates nervous, but Jake Pitkin was head of network continuity, not some office boy, and certainly should be used to dealing with executives at my level. Was the rumor really true?

We were alone in the screening room. It was doubtful that the projectionist could hear us.

"No, I haven't seen it yet," I said. "But I've heard some strange stories."

Jake looked positively deathly. "About the tape?" he said.

"About you, Jake," I said, deprecating the rumor with an easy smile. "That you don't want to air the show."

"It's true, B.D.," Jake said quietly.

"Do you realize what you're saying? Whatever our personal tastes—and I personally think there's something unhealthy about them—the Four Horsemen are the hottest thing in the country right now and that dirty little thief Herm Gellman held us up for a quarter of a million for an hour show. It cost another two hundred thousand to make it. We've spent another hundred thousand on promotion. We're getting top dollar from the sponsors. There's over a million dollars one way or the other riding on that show. That's how much we blow if we don't air it."

"I know that, B.D.," Jake said. "I also know this could cost me my job. Think about that. Because knowing all that, I'm still against airing the tape. I'm going to run the closing segment for you. I'm sure enough that you'll agree with me to stake my job on it."

I had a terrible feeling in my stomach. I have superiors too and The Word was that "A Trip with the Four Horsemen" would be aired, period. No matter what. Something funny was going on. The price we were getting for commercial time was a precedent and the sponsor was a big aerospace company which had never bought network time before. What really bothered me was that Jake Pitkin had no reputation for courage; yet here he was laying his job on the line. He must be pretty sure I would come around to his way of thinking or he wouldn't dare. And though I couldn't tell Jake, I had no choice in the matter whatsoever.

"Okay, roll it," Jake said into the intercom mike. "What you're going to see," he said as the screening room lights went out, "is the last number."

On the screen: a shot of empty blue sky, with soft, lazy electric guitar chords behind it. The camera pans across a few clouds to an extremely long shot on the sun. As the sun, no more than a tiny circle of light, moves into the center of the screen, a sitar-drone comes in behind the guitar.

Very slowly, the camera begins to zoom in on

the sun. As the image of the sun expands, the sitar gets louder and the guitar begins to fade and a drum starts to give the sitar a beat. The sitar gets louder, the beat gets more pronounced and begins to speed up as the sun continues to expand. Finally, the whole screen is filled with unbearably bright light behind which the sitar and drum are in a frenzy.

Then over this, drowning out the sitar and drum, a voice like a sick thing in heat: "*Brighter . . . than a thousand suns . . .*"

The light dissolves into a closeup of a beautiful dark-haired girl with huge eyes and moist lips, and suddenly there is nothing on the sound track but soft guitar and voices crooning low: "*Brighter . . . oh, God, it's brighter . . . brighter . . . than a thousand suns . . .*"

The girl's face dissolves into a full shot of the Four Horsemen in their Grim Reaper robes and the same melody that had played behind the girl's face shifts into a minor key, picks up whining, reverberating electric guitar chords and a sitar-drone and becomes a dirge: "*Darker . . . the world grows darker . . .*"

And a series of cuts in time to the dirge:

A burning village in Asia strewn with bodies—

"*Darker . . . the world grows darker . . .*"

The corpse heap at Auschwitz—

"*Until it gets so dark . . .*"

A gigantic auto graveyard with gaunt Negro children dwarfed in the foreground—

"*I think I'll die . . .*"

A Washington ghetto in flames with the Capitol misty in the background—

"*. . . before the daylight comes . . .*"

A jump-cut to an extreme closeup on the lead

singer of the Horsemen, his face twisted into a mask of desperation and ecstasy. And the sitar is playing double-time, the guitar is wailing and he is screaming at the top of his lungs: "*But before I die, let me make that trip before the nothing comes . . .*"

The girl's face again, but transparent, with a blinding yellow light shining through it. The sitar beat gets faster and faster with the guitar whining behind it and the voice is working itself up into a howling frenzy: "*. . . the last big flash to light my sky . . .*"

Nothing but the blinding light now—

"*. . . and zap! the world is done . . .*"

An utterly black screen for a beat that becomes black, fading to blue at a horizon—

"*. . . but before we die let's dig that high that frees us from our binds . . . that blows all cool that ego-drool and burns us from our mind . . . the last big flash, mankind's last gas, the trip we can't take twice. . . .*"

Suddenly, the music stops dead for half a beat. Then:

The screen is lit up by an enormous fireball—

A shattering rumble—

The fireball coalesces into a mushroom-pillar cloud as the roar goes on. As the roar begins to die out, fire is visible inside the monstrous nuclear cloud. And the girl's face is faintly visible, superimposed over the cloud.

A soft voice, amplified over the roar, obscenely reverential now: "*Brighter . . . great God, it's brighter . . . brighter than a thousand suns. . . .*"

And the screen went blank and the lights came on.

I looked at Jake. Jake looked at me.

"That's sick," I said. "That's *really* sick."

"You don't want to run a thing like that, do you, B.D.?" Jake said softly.

I made some rapid mental calculations. The loathsome thing ran something under five minutes . . . it could be done. . . .

"You're right, Jake," I said. "We won't run a thing like that. We'll cut it out of the tape and squeeze in another commercial at each break. That should cover the time."

"You don't understand," Jake said. "The contract Herm rammed down our throats doesn't allow us to edit. The show's a package—all or nothing. Besides, the whole show's like that."

"All like that? What do you mean, all like that?"

Jake squirmed in his seat. "Those guys are . . . well, perverts, B.D.," he said.

"*Perverts?*"

"They're . . . well, they're in love with the atom bomb or something. Every number leads up to the same thing."

"You mean . . . they're *all* like that?"

"You got the picture, B.D.," Jake said. "We run an hour of *that*, or we run nothing at all."

"Jesus."

I knew what I wanted to say. Burn the tape and write off the million dollars. But I also knew it would cost me my job. And I knew that five minutes after I was out the door, they would have someone in my job who would see things their way. Even my superiors seemed to be just handing down The Word from higher up. I had no choice. There was no choice.

"I'm sorry, Jake," I said. "We run it."

"I resign," said Jake Pitkin, who had no reputation for courage.

T minus 10 days . . . and counting. . . .

"It's a clear violation of the Test-Ban Treaty," I said.

The Under Secretary looked as dazed as I felt. "We'll call it a peaceful use of atomic energy, and let the Russians scream," he said.

"It's insane."

"Perhaps," the Under Secretary said. "But you have your orders, General Carson, and I have mine. From higher up. At exactly eight-fifty-eight P.M. local time on July fourth, you will drop a fifty-kiloton atomic bomb on the designated ground zero at Yucca Flats."

"But the people . . . the television crews . . ."

"Will be at least two miles outside the danger zone. Surely, SAC can manage that kind of accuracy under 'laboratory conditions.'"

I stiffened. "I do not question the competence of any bomber crew under my command to perform this mission," I said. "I question the reason for the mission. I question the sanity of the orders."

The Under Secretary shrugged, and smiled wanly. "Welcome to the club."

"You mean you don't know what this is all about either?"

"All I know is what was transmitted to me by the Secretary of Defense, and I got the feeling he doesn't know everything, either. You know that the Pentagon has been screaming for the use of tactical nuclear weapons to end the war in Asia—you SAC boys have been screaming the loudest. Well, several months ago, the President conditionally approved a plan for the use of tactical nuclear weapons during the next monsoon season."

I whistled. The civilians were finally coming to their senses. Or were they?

"But what does that have to do with—?"

"Public opinion," the Under Secretary said. "It was conditional upon a drastic change in public opinion. At the time the plan was approved, the polls showed that seventy-eight point eight percent of the population opposed the use of tactical nuclear weapons, nine point eight percent favored their use and the rest were undecided or had no opinion. The President agreed to authorize the use of tactical nuclear weapons by a date, several months from now, which is still top secret, provided that by that date at least sixty-five percent of the population approved their use and no more than twenty percent actively opposed it."

"I see . . . just a ploy to keep the Joint Chiefs quiet."

"General Carson," the Under Secretary said, "apparently you are out of touch with the national mood. After the first Four Horsemen show, the polls showed that twenty-five percent of the population approved the use of nuclear weapons. After the second show, the figure was forty-one percent. It is now forty-eight percent. Only thirty-two percent are now actively opposed."

"You're trying to tell me that a rock group—"

"A rock group and the cult around it, General. It's become a national hysteria. There are imitators. Haven't you seen those buttons?"

"The ones with a mushroom cloud on them that say 'Do It'?"

The Under Secretary nodded. "Your guess is as good as mine whether the National Security Council just decided that the Horsemen hysteria could be used to mold public opinion, or whether the Four Horsemen were their creatures to begin with. But the results are the same either way—the Horsemen and the cult around them have won over precisely that element of the population which was most adamantly opposed to nuclear weapons: hippies, students, dropouts, draft-age youth. Demonstrations against the war and against nuclear weapons have died down. We're pretty close to that sixty-five percent. Someone—perhaps the President himself—has decided that one more big Four Horsemen show will put us over the top."

"The President is behind this?"

"No one else can authorize the detonation of an atomic bomb, after all," the Under Secretary said. "We're letting them do the show live from Yucca Flats. It's being sponsored by an aerospace company heavily dependent on defense contracts. We're letting them truck in a live audience. Of course the government is behind it."

"And SAC drops an A-bomb as the show-stopper?"

"Exactly."

"I saw one of those shows," I said. "My kids were watching it. I got the strangest feeling . . . I almost wanted that red telephone to ring. . . ."

"I know what you mean," the Under Secretary said. "Sometimes I get the feeling that whoever's behind this has gotten caught up in the hysteria themselves . . . that the Horsemen are now using whoever was using them . . . a closed circle. But I've been tired lately. The war's making us all so tired. If only we could get it all over with. . . ."

"We'd all like to get it over with one way or the other," I said.

T minus 60 minutes . . . and counting. . . .

I had orders to muster *Backfish's* crew for the live satellite relay on "The Four Horsemen's Fourth." Superficially, it might seem strange to order the whole Polaris fleet to watch a television show, but the morale factor involved was quite significant.

Polaris subs are frustrating duty. Only top sailors are chosen and a good sailor craves action. Yet if we are ever called upon to act, our mission will have been a failure. We spend most of our time honing skills that must never be used. Deterrence is a sound strategy but a terrible drain on the men of the deterrent forces—a drain exacerbated in the past by the negative attitude of our countrymen toward our mission. Men who, in the service of their country, polish their skills to a razor edge and then must refrain from exercising them have a right to resent being treated as pariahs.

Therefore the positive change in the public attitude toward us that seems to be associated with the Four Horsemen has made them mascots of a kind to the Polaris fleet. In their strange way they seem to speak for us and to us.

I chose to watch the show in the missile control center, where a full crew must always be ready to launch the missiles on five-minute notice. I have always felt a sense of communion with the duty watch in the missile control center that I cannot share with the other men under my command. Here we are not captain and crew, but mind and hand. Should the order come, the will to fire the missiles will be mine and the act will be theirs. At such a moment, it will be good not to feel alone.

All eyes were on the television set mounted above the main console as the show came on and . . .

The screen was filled with a whirling spiral pattern, metallic yellow on metallic blue. There was a droning sound that seemed part sitar and part electronic and I had the feeling that the sound was somehow coming from inside my head and the spiral seemed etched directly on my retinas. It hurt mildly, yet nothing in the world could have made me turn away.

Then came two voices, chanting against each other:

"Let it all come in . . ."

"Let it all come out . . ."

"In . . . *out* . . . in . . . *out* . . . in . . . *out* . . ."

My head seemed to be pulsing—in-*out*, in-*out*, in-*out*—and the spiral pattern began to pulse color changes with the words: yellow-on-blue (in) . . . green-on-red (*out*) . . . In-*out*-in-*out*-in-*out*-in-*out* . . .

In the screen . . . *out* my head . . . I seemed to be beating against some kind of invisible membrane between myself and the screen as if something were trying to embrace my mind and I were fighting it. . . . But why was I fighting it?

The pulsing, the chanting, got faster and faster till *in* could not be told from *out* and negative spiral after-images formed in my eyes faster than they could adjust to the changes, piled up on each other faster and faster till it seemed my head would explode—

The chanting and the droning broke and there were the Four Horsemen, in their robes, playing on some stage against a backdrop of clear blue sky. And a single voice, soothing now: "You are in . . ."

Then the view was directly above the Horsemen and I could see that they were on some kind of circular platform. The view moved slowly and smoothly up and away and I saw that the circular stage was atop a tall tower; around the tower and completely encircling it was a huge crowd seated on desert sands that stretched away to an empty infinity.

"And we are in and they are in . . ."

I was down among the crowd now; they seemed to melt and flow like plastic, pouring from the television screen to enfold me. . . .

"And we are all in here together. . . ."

A strange and beautiful feeling . . . the music got faster and wilder, ecstatic . . . the hull of the *Backfish* seemed unreal . . . the crowd was swaying to it around me . . . the distance between myself and the crowd seemed to dissolve . . . I was there . . . they were here. . . . We were transfixed . . .

"Oh, yeah, we are all in here together . . . together . . ."

T minus 45 minutes . . . and counting. . . .

Jeremy and I sat staring at the television screen, ignoring each other and everything around us. Even with the short watches and the short tours of duty, you can get to feeling pretty strange down here in a hole in the ground under tons of concrete, just you and the guy with the other key, with nothing to do but think dark thoughts and get on each other's nerves. We're all supposed to be as stable as men can be, or so they tell us, and they must be right because the world's still here. I mean, it wouldn't take much— just two guys on the same watch over the same three Minutemen flipping out at the same time, turning their keys in the dual lock, pressing the three buttons. . . . Pow! World War III!

A bad thought, the kind we're not supposd to think or I'll start watching Jeremy and he'll start watching me and we'll get a paranoia feedback going. . . . But that can't happen; we're too stable, too responsible. As long as we remember that it's healthy to feel a little spooky down here, we'll be all right.

But the television set is a good idea. It keeps us in contact with the outside world, keeps it real. It'd be too easy to start thinking that the missile control center down here is the only real world and that nothing that happens up there really matters. . . . Bad thought!

The Four Horsemen . . . somehow these guys help you get it all out. I mean that feeling that it might be better to release all that tension, get it all over with. Watching the Four Horsemen, you're able to go with it without doing any harm, let it wash over you and then through you. I suppose they are crazy; they're all the human craziness in ourselves that we've got to keep very careful watch over down here. Letting it all come out watching the Horsemen makes it surer that none of it will come out down here. I guess that's why a lot of us have taken to wearing those "Do It" buttons off duty. The brass doesn't mind; they seem to understand that it's the kind of inside sick joke we need to keep us functioning.

Now that spiral thing they had started the show with—and the droning—came back on. Zap! I was right back in the screen again, as if the commercial hadn't happened.

"We are all in here together . . ."

And then a closeup of the lead singer, looking straight at me, as close as Jeremy and somehow more real. A mean-looking guy with something behind his eyes that told me he knew where everything lousy and rotten was at.

A bass began to thrum behind him and some kind of electronic hum that set my teeth on edge. He began playing his guitar, mean and low-down. And singing in that kind of drop-dead tone of voice that starts brawls in bars:

"I stabbed my mother and I mugged my paw . . ."

A riff of heavy guitar chords echoed the words mockingly as a huge swastika (red-on-black, black-on-red) pulsed like a naked vein on the screen—

The face of the Horseman, leering—

"Nailed my sister to the toilet door . . ."

Guitar behind the pulsing swastika—

"Drowned a puppy in a ce-ment machine. . . . Burned a kitten just to hear it scream. . . ."

On the screen, just a big fire burning in slow-motion, and the voice became a slow, shrill, agonized wail:

"Oh, God, I've got this red-hot fire burning in the marrow of my brain. . . .

"Oh, yes, I got this fire burning . . . in the stinking marrow of my brain. . . .

"Gotta get me a blowtorch . . . and set some naked flesh on flame. . . ."

The fire dissolved into the face of a screaming Oriental woman, who ran through a burning village clawing at the napalm on her back.

"I got this message . . . boiling in the bubbles of my blood. . . . A man ain't nothing but a fire burning . . . in a dirty glob of mud. . . ."

A film clip of a Nuremberg rally: a revolving swastika of marching men waving torches—

Then the leader of the Horsemen superimposed over the twisted flaming cross:

"Don't you hate me baby, can't you feel somethin' screaming in your mind?

"Don't you hate me baby, feel me drowning you in slime!"

Just the face of the Horseman howling hate—

"Oh yes, I'm a monster, mother. . . ."

A long view of the crowd around the platform, on their feet, waving arms, screaming soundlessly. Then a quick zoom in and a kaleidoscope of faces, eyes feverish, mouths open and howling—

"Just call me–"

The face of the Horseman superimposed over the crazed faces of the crowd—

"Mankind!"

I looked at Jeremy. He was toying with the key on the chain around his neck. He was sweating. I suddenly realized that I was sweating, too, and that my own key was throbbing in my hand alive. . . .

T minus 13 minutes . . . and counting. . . .

A funny feeling, the captain watching the Four Horsemen here in the *Backfish's* missile control center with us. Sitting in front of my console watching the television set with the captain kind of breathing down my neck. I got the feeling he knew what was going through me and I couldn't know what was going through him . . . and it gave the fire inside me a kind of greasy feel I didn't like. . . .

Then the commercial was over and that spiral-thing came on again and—whoosh!—it sucked me right back into the television set and I stopped worrying about the captain or anything like that. . . .

Just the spiral going yellow-blue, red-green, and then starting to whirl and whirl, faster and faster, changing colors and whirling, whirling, whirling. . . . And the sound of a kind of Coney Island carousel tinkling behind it, faster and faster and faster, whirling and whirling and whirling, flashing red-green, yellow-blue, and whirling, whirling, whirling . . .

And this big hum filling my body and whirling, whirling, whirling . . . my muscles relaxing, going limp, whirling, whirling, whirling, all limp, whirling, whirling, whirling, oh so nice, just whirling, whirling . . .

And in the center of the flashing spiraling colors, a bright dot of colorless light, right at the center, not moving, not changing, while the whole world went whirling and whirling in colors around it, and the humming was coming from the dot the way the carousel music was coming from the spinning colors and the dot was humming its song to me. . . .

The dot was a light way down at the end of a long, whirling, whirling tunnel. The humming started to get a little louder. The bright dot started to get a little bigger. I was drifting down the tunnel toward it, whirling, whirling, whirling . . .

T minus 11 minutes . . . and counting. . . .

Whirling, whirling, whirling down a long, long tunnel of pulsing colors, whirling, whirling, toward the circle of light way down at the end of the tunnel. . . . How nice it would be to finally get there and soak up the beautiful hum filling my body and then I could forget that I was down here in this hole in the ground with a hard brass key in my hand, just Duke and me, down here in a cave under the ground that was a spiral of flashing colors, whirling, whirling toward the friendly light at the end of the tunnel, whirling, whirling . . .

T minus 10 minutes . . . and counting. . . .

The circle of light at the end of the whirling tunnel was getting bigger and bigger and the humming was getting louder and louder and I was feeling better and better and the *Backfish's* missile control center was getting dimmer and dimmer as the awful weight of command got lighter and lighter, whirling, whirling, and I felt so good I wanted to cry, whirling, whirling . . .

T minus 9 minutes . . . and counting. . . .

Whirling, whirling . . . I was whirling, Jeremy was whirling, the hole in the ground was whirling, and the circle of light at the end of the tunnel whirled closer and closer and—I was through! A place filled with yellow light. Pale metal-yellow light. Then pale metallic blue. Yellow. Blue. Yellow. Blue. Yellow-blue-yellow-blue-yellow-blue-yellow . . .

Pure light pulsing . . . and pure sound droning. And just the *feeling* of letters I couldn't read between the pulses—not-yellow and not-blue—too quick and too faint to be visible, but important, very important . . .

And then came a voice that seemed to be singing from inside my head, almost as if it were my own:

"*Oh, oh, oh . . . don't I really wanna know. . . . Oh, oh, oh . . . don't I really wanna know . . .*"

The world pulsing, flashing around those words I couldn't read, couldn't quite read, had to read, could *almost* read . . .

"*Oh, oh, oh . . . great God, I really wanna know. . . .*"

Strange amorphous shapes clouding the blue-yellow-blue flickering universe, hiding the words I had to read. . . . Damn it, why wouldn't they get out of the way so I could find out what I had to know!

"*Tell me tell me tell me tell me tell me. . . . Gotta know gotta know gotta know gotta know . . .*"

T minus 7 minutes . . . and counting. . . .

Couldn't read the words! Why wouldn't the captain let me read the words?

And that voice inside me: "*Gotta know . . . gotta know . . . gotta know why it hurts me so. . . .*" Why wouldn't it shut up and let me read the words? Why wouldn't it shut up and let me read the words? Why wouldn't the words hold still? Or just slow down a little? If they'd slow down a little, I could read them and then I'd know what I had to do. . . .

T minus 6 minutes . . . and counting. . . .

I felt the sweaty key in the palm of my hand . . . I saw Duke stroking his own key. Had to know! Now—through the pulsing blue-yellow-blue light and the unreadable words that were building up an awful pressure in the back of my brain—I could see the Four Horsemen. They were on their knees, crying, looking up at something and begging: "*Tell me tell me tell me tell me . . .*"

Then soft billows of rich red-and-orange fire filled the world and a huge voice was trying to speak. But it couldn't form the words. It stuttered and moaned—

The yellow-blue-yellow flashing around the words I couldn't read—the same words, I suddenly sensed, that the voice of the fire was trying so hard to form—and the Four Horsemen on their knees begging: "*Tell me tell me tell me . . .*"

The friendly warm fire trying so hard to speak—"*Tell me tell me tell me tell me. . . .*"

T minus 4 minutes . . . and counting. . . .

What were the words? What was the order? I could sense my men silently imploring me to tell them. After all, I was their captain, it was my duty to tell them. It was my duty to find out!

"Tell me tell me tell me . . ." the robed figures on their knees implored through the flickering pulse in my brain and I could almost make out the words . . . almost . . .

"Tell me tell me tell me . . ." I whispered to the warm orange fire that was trying so hard but couldn't quite form the words. The men were whispering it, too: "Tell me tell me . . ."

T minus 3 minutes . . . and counting. . . .

The question burning blue and yellow in my brain: What was the fire trying to tell me? What were the words I couldn't read?

Had to unlock the words! Had to find the key!

A key. . . . *The Key?* THE KEY! And there was the lock that imprisoned the words, right in front of me! Put the key in the lock. . . . I looked at Jeremy. Wasn't there some reason, long ago and far away, why Jeremy might try to stop me from putting the key in the lock?

But Jeremy didn't move as I fitted the key into the lock. . . .

T minus 2 minutes . . . and counting. . . .

Why wouldn't the captain tell me what the order was? The fire knew, but it couldn't tell. My head ached from the pulsing, but I couldn't read the words.

"Tell me tell me tell me . . ." I begged.

Then I realized that the captain was asking, too.

T minus 90 seconds . . . and counting. . . .

"Tell me tell me tell me . . ." the Horsemen begged. And the words I couldn't read were a fire in my brain.

Duke's key was in the lock in front of us. From very far away, he said: "We have to do it together."

Of course . . . our keys . . . our keys would unlock the words!

I put my key into the lock. One, two, three, we turned our keys together. A lid on the console popped open. Under the lid were three red buttons. Three signs on the console lit up in red letters: ARMED.

T minus 60 seconds . . . and counting. . . .

The men were waiting for me to give some order. I didn't know what the order was. A magnificent orange fire was trying to tell me but it couldn't get the words out. . . . Robed figures were praying to the fire. . . .

Then, through the yellow-blue flicker that hid the words I had to read, I saw a vast crowd encircling a tower. The crowd was on its feet begging silently—

The tower in the center of the crowd became the orange fire that was trying to tell me what the words were—

Became a great mushroom of billowing smoke and blinding orange-red glare. . . .

T minus 30 seconds . . . and counting. . . .

The huge pillar of fire was trying to tell Jeremy and me what the words were, what we had to do. The crowd was screaming at the cloud of flame. The yellow-blue flicker was getting faster and faster behind the mushroom cloud. I could almost read the words! I could see that there were two of them!

T minus 20 seconds . . . and counting. . . .

Why didn't the captain tell us? I could almost see the words!

Then I heard the crowd around the beautiful mushroom cloud shouting: "DO IT! DO IT! DO IT! DO IT! DO IT!"

T minus 10 seconds . . . and counting. . . .

"DO IT! DO IT! DO IT! DO IT! DO IT! DO IT! DO IT!"

What did they want me to do? Did Duke know?

9

The men were waiting! What was the order? They hunched over the firing controls, waiting. . . . The firing controls . . .?

"DO IT! DO IT! DO IT! DO IT! DO IT!"

8

"DO IT! DO IT! DO IT! DO IT! DO IT!": the crowd screaming.

"Jeremy!" I shouted. "I can read the words!"

7

My hands hovered over my bank of firing buttons. . . .

"DO IT! DO IT! DO IT! DO IT!" the words said.

Didn't the captain understand?

6

"What do they want us to do, Jeremy?"

5

Why didn't the mushroom cloud give the order? My men were waiting! A good sailor craves action.

Then a great voice spoke from the pillar of fire: "DO IT. . . DO IT. . . DO IT. . . ."

4

"There's only one thing we can do down here, Duke."

3

"The order, men! Action! Fire!"

2

Yes, yes, yes! Jeremy—

1

I reached for my bank of firing buttons. All along the console, the men reached for their buttons. But I was too fast for them! I would be the first!

0

THE BIG FLASH

Introduction to No Direction Home

A. J. Budrys, a critic I hold in high esteem, once complained of a short story collection of mine that the pieces showed no consistent overall style. I could see that he was right, but I still can't understand what he was complaining about.

It has always seemed self-evident to me that prose style and form should be determined by the requirement of any given material—by the style of the content, of the reality depicted, of the consciousness of the viewpoint character through whom the reader is experiencing the story at any given point. When a writer applies the same style to all the material he uses, you end up with stylization, mannerism, and ultimately self-parody.

Nevertheless, so puissant a critic is A. J. Budrys that the technical astuteness with which he pointed out exactly what I was doing was quite valuable to me, whether I found his viewpoint wrongheaded or not. I thought about this question of style and content more deeply.

Okay, my style from story to story was "incon-

sistent,'' and for what I at least thought was good reason. But why should it be consistent even within the same story?

After all, the multiplex reality we walk through all the time betrays no such stylistic consistency. Our brains are warped from one cartoon style to another with dizzying rapidity. We learn new ways of doing this to ourselves all the time. A lot of us even enjoy it. Most readers of science fiction certainly do. It's the essence of modern consciousness, it's where we are. . . .

As for where we're going. . . .

No Direction Home

How does it feel
To be on your own?
With no direction home.
Like a complete unknown.
Like a rolling stone.
—Bob Dylan,
from "Like a Rolling Stone"

"But I once *did* succeed in stuffing it all back in Pandora's box," Richarson said, taking another hit. "You remember Pandora Deutchman, don't you, Will? Everybody in the biochemistry department stuffed it all in Pandora's box at one time or another. I seem to vaguely remember one party when you did it yourself."

"Oh, you're a real comedian, Dave," Goldberg said, stubbing out his roach and jamming a cork into the glass vial which he had been filling from the petcock at the end of the apparatus's run. "Any day now I expect you to start slipping strychnine into the goods. That'd be pretty good for a yock, too."

"You know, I never thought of that before. Maybe you got something there. Let a few people go out with a smile, satisfaction guaranteed. Christ, Will, we could tell them exactly what it was and still sell some of the stuff."

"That's not funny, man," Goldberg said, handing the vial to Richarson, who carefully snugged it away with the others in the excelsior-packed box. "It's not funny because it's true."

"Hey, you're not getting an attack of morals, are you? Don't move, I'll be right back with some methalin—that oughta get your head straight."

"My head is straight already. Canabinolic acid, our own invention."

"*Canabinolic acid*? Where did you get that, in a drugstore? We haven't bothered with it for three years."

Goldberg placed another empty vial in the rack under the petcock and opened the valve. "Bought it on the street for kicks," he said. "Kids are brewing it in their bathtubs now." He shook his head, almost a random gesture. "Remember what a bitch the original synthesis was?"

"Science marches on!"

"Too bad we couldn't have patented the stuff," Goldberg said as he contemplated the thin stream of clear green liquid entering the open mouth of the glass vial. "We could've retired off the royalties by now."

"If we had the Mafia to collect for us."

"That might be arranged."

"Yeah, well, maybe I should look into it," Richarson said as Goldberg handed him another full vial. "We shouldn't be pigs about it, though. Just about ten percent off the top at the manufacturing end. I don't believe in stifling private enterprise."

"No, really, Dave," Goldberg said, "maybe we made a mistake in not trying to patent the stuff.

People *do* patent combo psychedelics, you know."

"You don't mean *people*, man, you mean outfits like American Marijuana and Psychedelics, Inc. They can afford the lawyers and grease. They can work the FDA's head. We can't."

Goldberg opened the petcock valve. "Yeah, well, at least it'll be six months or so before the dope industry or anyone else figures out how to synthesize this new crap, and by that time I think I'll have just about licked the decay problem in the cocanol extraction process. We should be one step ahead of the squares for at least another year."

"You know what I think, Will?" Richarson said, patting the side of the half-filled box of vials. "I think we got a holy mission, is what I think. I think we're servants of the evolutionary process. Every time we come up with a new psychedelic, we're advancing the evolution of human consciousness. We develop the stuff and make our bread off it for a while, and then the dope industry comes up with our synthesis and mass-produces it, and then we gotta come up with the next drug out so we can still set our tables in style. If it weren't for the dope industry and the way the drug laws are set up, we could stand still and become bloated plutocrats just by putting out the same old dope year after year. This way, we're doing some good in the world; we're doing something to further human evolution."

Goldberg handed him another full vial. "Screw human evolution," he said. "What has human evolution ever done for us?"

"As you know, Dr. Taller, we're having some unforeseen side effects with eucomorfamine," General Carlyle said, stuffing his favorite Dunhill with rough-cut burley. Taller took out a pack of Golds, extracted a joint, and lit it with a lighter bearing an air force, rather than a Psychedelics, Inc., insignia. Perhaps this had been a deliberate gesture, perhaps not.

"With a psychedelic as new as eucomorfamine, General," Taller said, "no side effects can quite be called 'unforeseen.' After all, even Project Groundhog itself is an experiment."

Carlyle lit his pipe and sucked in a mouthful of smoke, which was good and carcinogenic; the general believed that a good soldier should cultivate at least one foolhardy minor vice. "No word-games, please, doctor," he said. "Eucomorfamine is supposed to help our men in the Groundhog moonbase deal with the claustrophobic conditions; it is not supposed to promote faggotry in the ranks. The reports I've been getting indicate that the drug is doing both. The air force does not want it to do both. Therefore, by definition, eucomorfamine has an undesirable side effect. Therefore, your contract is up for review."

"General, General, psychedelics are not uniforms, after all. You can't expect us to tailor them to order. You asked for a drug that would combat claustrophobia without impairing alertness or the sleep cycle or attention span or initiative. You think this is easy? Eucomorfamine produces claustrophilia without any side effect but a raising of the level of sexual energy. As such, I consider it one of the minor miracles of psychedelic science."

"That's all very well, Taller, but surely you can see that we simply cannot tolerate violent homosexual behavior among our men in the moonbase."

Taller smiled, perhaps somewhat fatuously. "But you can't very well tolerate a high rate of claustrophobic breakdown, either," he said. "You have only four obvious alternatives, General Carlyle: continue to use eucomorfamine and accept a certain level of homosexual incidents, discontinue eucomorfamine and accept a very high level of claustrophobic breakdown, or cancel Project Groundhog. Or . . ."

It dawned upon the general that he had been the object of a rather sophisticated sales pitch. "Or go to a drug that would cancel out the side effect of eucomorfamine," he said. "Your company just wouldn't happen to have such a drug in the works, would it?"

Dr. Taller gave him a we're-all-men-of-the-world grin. "Psychedelics, Inc., *has* been working on a sexual suppressant," he admitted none too grudgingly. "Not an easy psychic spec to fill. The problem is that if you actually decrease sexual energy, you tend to get impaired performance in the higher cerebral centers, which is all very well in penal institutions, but hardly acceptable in Project Groundhog's case. The trick is to channel the excess energy elsewhere. We decided that the only viable alternative was to siphon it off into mystical fugue-states. Once we worked it out, the biochemistry became merely a matter of detail. We're about ready to bring the drug we've developed—trade name nadabrin—into the production stage."

The general's pipe had gone out. He did not bother to relight it. Instead, he took five milligrams of lebemil, which seemed more to the point at the moment. "This nadabrin," he said very deliberately, "it bleeds off the excess sexuality into *what*? Fugue-states? Trances? We certainly don't need a drug that makes our men psychotic."

"Of course not. About three hundred micrograms of nadabrin will give a man a mystical experience that lasts less than four hours. He won't be much good to you during that time, to be sure, but his sexual energy level will be severely depressed for about a week. Three hundred micrograms to each man on eucomorfamine, say every five days, to be on the safe side."

General Carlyle relit his pipe and ruminated. Things seemed to be looking up. "Sounds pretty good," he finally admitted. "But what about the content of the mystical experiences? Nothing that would impair devotion to duty?"

Taller snubbed out his roach. "I've taken nadabrin myself," he said. "No problems."

"What was it like?"

Taller once again put on his fatuous smile. "That's the best part of nadabrin," he said. "I don't remember what it was like. You don't retain any memories of what happens to you under nadabrin. Genuine fugue-state. So you can be sure the mystical experiences don't have any undesirable content, can't you? Or at any rate, you can be sure that the experience can't impair a man's military performance."

"What the men don't remember can't hurt them, eh?" Carlyle muttered into his pipestem.

"What was that, General?"

"I said I'd recommend that we give it a try."

They sat together in a corner booth back in the smoke, sizing each other up while the crowd in the joint yammered and swirled around them in some other reality, like Bavarian merry-go-round.

"What are you on?" he said, noticing that her hair seemed black and seamless like a beetle's carapace, a dark metal helmet framing her pale face in glory. Wow.

"Peyotadrene," she said, her lips moving like incredibly jeweled and articulated metal flower petals. "Been up for about three hours. What's your trip?"

"Canabinolic acid," he said, the distortion of his mouth's movement casting his face into an ideogramic pattern which was barely decipherable to her perception as a foreshadowing of energy release. Maybe they would make it.

"I haven't tried any of that stuff for months," she said. "I hardly remember what that reality feels like." Her skin luminesced from within, a translucent white china mask over a yellow candle-flame. She was a magnificent artifact, a creation of jaded and sophisticated gods.

"It feels good," he said, his eyebrows forming a set of curves which, when considered as part of a pattern containing the movement of his lips against his teeth, indicated a clear desire to donate energy to the filling of her void. They *would* make it. "Call me old-fashioned, maybe, but I still think canabinolic acid is groovy stuff."

"Do you think you could go on a sex trip behind

it?" she asked. The folds and wrinkles of her ears had been carved with microprecision out of pink ivory.

"Well, I suppose so, in a peculiar kind of way," he said, hunching his shoulders forward in a clear gesture of offering, an alignment with the pattern of her movement through space-time that he could clearly perceive as intersecting her trajectory. "I mean, if you want me to ball you, I think I can make it."

The tiny gold hairs on her face were a microscopic field of wheat shimmering in a shifting summer breeze as she said, "That's the most meaningful thing anyone has said to me in hours."

The convergence of every energy configuration in the entire universe toward complete identity with the standing wave pattern of its maximum ideal structure was brightly mirrored for the world to see in the angle between the curves of her lips as she spoke.

Cardinal McGavin took a peyotadrene-mescamil combo and five milligrams of metadrene an hour and a half before his meeting with Cardinal Rillo; he had decided to try to deal with Rome on a mystical rather than a political level, and that particular prescription made him feel most deeply Christian. And the Good Lord knew that it could become very difficult to feel deeply Christian when dealing with a representative of the Pope.

Cardinal Rillo arrived punctually at three, just as Cardinal McGavin was approaching his mystical peak; the man's punctuality was legend.

Cardinal McGavin felt pathos in that: the sadness of a Prince of the Church whose major impact on the souls of his fellows lay in his slavery to the hands of a clock. Because the ascetic-looking old man, with his colorless eyes and pencil-thin lips, was so thoroughly unlovable, Cardinal McGavin found himself cherishing the man for his very existential hopelessness. He sent forth a silent prayer that he, or if not he, then at least someone, might be chosen as an instrument through which this poor, cold creature might be granted a measure of Divine Grace.

Cardinal Rillo accepted the amenities with cold formality, and in the same spirit agreed to share some claret. Cardinal McGavin knew better than to offer a joint; Cardinal Rillo had been in the forefront of the opposition which had caused the Pope to delay his inevitable encyclical on marijuana for long, ludicrous years. That the Pope had chosen such an emissary in this matter was not a good sign.

Cardinal Rillo sipped at his wine in sour silence for long moments while Cardinal McGavin was nearly overcome with sorrow at the thought of the loneliness of the soul of this man, who could not even break the solemnity of his persona to share some Vatican gossip over a little wine with a fellow cardinal. Finally, the papal emissary cleared his throat—a dry, archaic gesture—and got right to the point.

"The Pontiff has instructed me to convey his concern at the addition of psychedelics to the composition of the communion host in the Archdiocese of New York," he said, the tone of his voice making it perfectly clear that he wished the

Holy Father had given him a much less cautious warning to deliver. But if the Pope had learned anything at all from the realities of this schismatic era, it was caution, especially when dealing with the American hierarchy, whose allegiance to Rome was based on nothing firmer than nostalgia and symbolic convenience. The Pope had been the last to be convinced of his own fallibility, but in the last few years events seemed to have finally brought the new refinement of Divine Truth home.

"I acknowledge and respect the Holy Father's concern," Cardinal McGavin said. "I shall pray for divine resolution of his doubt."

"I didn't say anything about doubt!" Cardinal Rillo snapped, his lips moving with the crispness of pincers. "How can you impute doubt to the Holy Father?"

Cardinal McGavin's spirit soared over a momentary spark of anger at the man's pigheadedness; he tried to give Cardinal Rillo's soul a portion of peace. "I stand corrected," he said. "I shall pray for the alleviation of the Holy Father's concern."

But Cardinal Rillo was implacable and inconsolable; his face was a membrane of control over a musculature of rage. "You can more easily relieve the Holy Father's concern by removing the peyotadrene from your hosts!" he said.

"Are those the words of the Holy Father?" Cardinal McGavin asked, knowing the answer.

"Those are *my* words, Cardinal McGavin," Cardinal Rillo said, "and you would do well to heed them. The fate of your immortal soul may be at stake."

A flash of insight, a sudden small satori, rippled through Cardinal McGavin: Rillo was sincere. For him, the question of a chemically augmented host was not a matter of Church politics, as it probably was to the Pope; it touched on an area of deep religious conviction. Cardinal Rillo was indeed concerned for the state of his soul and it behooved him, both as a cardinal and as a Catholic, to treat the matter seriously on that level. For, after all, chemically augmented communion was a matter of deep religious conviction for him as well. He and Cardinal Rillo faced each other across a gap of existentially meaningful theological disagreement.

"Perhaps the fate of yours as well, Cardinal Rillo," he said.

"I didn't come here all the way from Rome to seek spiritual guidance from a man who is skating on the edge of heresy, Cardinal McGavin. I came here to deliver the Holy Father's warning that an encyclical may be issued against your position. Need I remind you that if you disobey such an encyclical you may be excommunicated?"

"Would you be genuinely sorry to see that happen?" Cardinal McGavin asked, wondering how much of the threat was Rillo's wishful thinking, and how much the instructions of the Pope. "Or would you simply feel that the Church had defended itself properly?"

"Both," Cardinal Rillo said without hesitation.

"I like that answer," Cardinal McGavin said, tossing down the rest of his glass of claret. It was a good answer—sincere on both counts. Cardinal Rillo feared both for the Church and for the soul of the archbishop of New York, and there was no doubt that he quite properly put the Church first.

His sincerity was spiritually refreshing, even though he was thoroughly wrong all around. "But you see, part of the gift of grace that comes with a scientifically sound chemical augmentation of communion is a certainty that no one—not even the Pope—can do anything to cut you off from communion with God. In psychedelic communion, one experiences the love of God directly. It's always just a host away; faith is no longer even necessary."

Cardinal Rillo grew somber. "It is my duty to report that to the Pope," he said. "I trust you realize that."

"Who am I talking to, Cardinal Rillo, you or the Pope?"

"You are talking to the Catholic Church, Cardinal McGavin," Cardinal Rillo said. "I am an emissary of the Holy Father." Cardinal McGavin felt an instant pang of guilt: his sharpness had caused Cardinal Rillo to imply an untruth out of anger, for surely his papal mission was far more limited than he had tried to intimate. The Pope was too much of a realist to make the empty threat of excommunication against a Prince of the Church who believed that his power of excommunication was itself meaningless.

But, again, a sudden flash of insight illuminated the cardinal's mind with truth: in the eyes of Cardinal Rillo—in the eyes of an important segment of the Church hierarchy—the threat of excommunication still held real meaning. To accept their position on chemically augmented communion was to accept the notion that the word of the Pope could withdraw a man from Divine

Grace. To accept the sanctity and validity of psychedelic communion was to deny the validity of excommunication.

"You know, Cardinal Rillo," he said, "I firmly believe that if I am excommunicated by the Pope, it will threaten my soul not one iota."

"That's merely cheap blasphemy!"

"I'm sorry," Cardinal McGavin said sincerely. "I meant to be neither cheap nor blasphemous. All I was trying to do was explain that excommunication can hardly be meaningful when God through the psychedelic sciences has seen fit to grant us a means of direct experience of His countenance. I believe with all my heart that this is true. You believe with all your heart that it is not."

"I believe that what you experience in your psychedelic communion is nothing less than a masterstroke of Satan, Cardinal McGavin. Evil is infinitely subtle; might not it finally masquerade as the ultimate good? The Devil is not known as the Prince of Liars without reason. I believe that you are serving Satan in what you sincerely believe is the service of God. Is there any way that you can be sure that I am wrong?"

"Can you be sure that *I'm* not right?" Cardinal McGavin said. "If I am, you are attempting to stifle the will of God and willfully removing yourself from His Grace."

"We cannot both be right. . . ." Cardinal Rillo said.

And the burning glare of a terrible and dark mystical insight filled Cardinal McGavin's soul with terror, a harsh illumination of his existential relationship to the Church and to God: they both couldn't be right, but there was no reason why they both couldn't be wrong. Apart from both God and Satan existed the void.

Dr. Braden gave Johnny a pat-on-the-head smile and handed him a mango-flavored lollipop from the supply of goodies in his lower left desk drawer. Johnny took the lollipop, unwrapped it quickly, popped it into his mouth, leaned back in his chair, and began to suck the sweet avidly, oblivious to the rest of the world. It was a good sign—a preschooler with a proper reaction to a proper basic prescription should focus strongly and completely on the most interesting element in its environment; he should be fond of unusual flavors. In the first four years of its life, a child's sensorium should be tuned to accept the widest possible spectrum of sensual stimulation.

Braden turned his attention to the boy's mother, who sat rather nervously on the edge of her chair, smoking a joint. "Now, now, Mrs. Lindstrom, there's nothing to worry about," he said. "Johnny has been responding quite normally to his prescription. His attention span is suitably short for a child of his age; his sensual range slightly exceeds the optimum norm; his sleep pattern is regular and properly deep. And as you requested, he has been given a constant sense of universal love."

"But then why did the school doctor ask me to have his basic prescription changed, Dr. Braden? He said that Johnny's prescription was giving him the wrong personality pattern for a school-age child."

Dr. Braden was rather annoyed, though of course he would never betray it to the nervous young mother. He knew the sort of failed G.P. who usually occupied a school doctor's position; a faded old fool who knew about as much about psychedelic pediatrics as he did about brain surgery. What he did know was worse than nothing—a smattering of half-assed generalities and pure rubbish that was just enough to convince him that he was an expert—which entitled him to go around frightening the mothers of other people's patients, no doubt.

"I'm . . . ah, certain you misunderstood what the school doctor said, Mrs. Lindstrom," Dr. Braden said. "At least I hope you did, because if you didn't, then the man is mistaken. You see, modern psychedelic pediatrics recognizes that the child needs to have his consciousness focused in different areas at different stages of his development if he is to grow up to be a healthy, maximized individual. A child of Johnny's age is in a transitional stage. In order to prepare him for schooling, I'll simply have to alter his prescription so as to increase his attention span, lower his sensory intensity a shade, and increase his interest in abstractions. Then he'll do fine in school, Mrs. Lindstrom."

Dr. Braden gave the young woman a moderately stern admonishing frown. "You really should have brought Johnny in for a checkup *before* he started school, you know."

Mrs. Lindstrom puffed nervously on her joint while Johnny continued to suck happily on his lollipop. "Well . . . I was sort of afraid to, Dr. Braden," she admitted. "I know it sounds silly, but I was afraid that if you changed his prescription to what the school wanted, you'd stop the paxum. I didn't want that—I think it's more important for Johnny to continue to feel universal love than to increase his attention span or any of that stuff. You're not going to stop the paxum, are you?"

"Quite the contrary, Mrs. Lindstrom," Dr. Braden said. "I'm going to increase his dose slightly and give him ten milligrams of orodalamine daily. He'll submit to the necessary authority of his teachers with a sense of trust and love, rather than out of fear."

For the first time during the visit, Mrs. Lindstrom smiled. "Then it all really *is* all right, isn't it?" She radiated happiness born of relief.

Dr. Braden smiled back at her, basking in the sudden surge of good vibrations. This was his peak experience in pediatrics: feeling the genuine gratitude of a worried mother whose fears he had thoroughly relieved. This was what being a doctor was all about. She trusted him. She put the consciousness of her child in his hands, trusting that those hands would not falter or fail. He was proud and grateful to be a psychedelic pediatrician. He was maximizing human happiness.

"Yes, Mrs. Lindstrom," he said soothingly, "everything is going to be all right."

In the chair in the corner, Johnny Lindstrom sucked on his lollipop, his face transfigured with boyish bliss.

There were moments when Bill Watney got a soul-deep queasy feeling about psychedelic design, and lately he was getting those bad flashes more and more often. He was glad to have caught Spiegelman alone in the designers' lounge; if anyone could do anything for his head, Lennie was it. "I dunno," he said, washing down fifteen milligrams of lebemil with a stiff shot of bourbon, "I'm really thinking of getting out of this business."

Leonard Spiegelman lit a Gold with his fourteen-carat-gold lighter—nothing but the best for the best in the business—smiled across the coffee table at Watney, and said quite genially, "You're out of your mind, Bill."

Watney sat hunched slightly forward in his easy chair, studying Spiegelman, the best artist Psychedelics, Inc., had, and envying the older man—envying not only his talent, but his attitude toward his work. Lennie Spiegelman was not only certain that what he was doing was right, he enjoyed every minute of it. Watney wished he could be like Spiegelman. Spiegelman was happy; he radiated the contented aura of a man who really did have everything he wanted.

Spiegelman opened his arms in a gesture that seemed to make the whole designers' lounge his personal property. "We're the world's best-pampered artists," he said. "We come up with two or three viable drug designs a year, and we can live like kings. And we're practicing the world's ultimate art form: creating realities. We're the luckiest mothers alive! Why would anyone with your talent want out of psychedelic design?"

Watney found it difficult to put into words, which was ridiculous for a psychedelic designer, whose work it was to describe new possibilities in human consciousness well enough for the biochemists to develop psychedelics which would transform his specs into styles of reality. It was humiliating to be at a loss for words in front of Lennie Spiegelman, a man he both envied and admired. "I'm getting bad flashes lately," he finally said, "deep flashes that go through every style of consciousness that I try, flashes that tell me I should be ashamed and disgusted about what I'm doing."

Oh-oh, Lennie Spiegelman thought, the kid is coming up with his first case of designer's cafard. He's floundering around with that no-direction-home syndrome and he thinks it's the end of the world. "I know what's bothering you, Bill," he said. "It happens to all of us at one time or another. You feel that designing psychedelic specs is a solipsistic occupation, right? You think there's something morally wrong about designing new styles of consciousness for other people, that we're playing God, that continually altering people's consciousness in ways only we fully understand is a thing that mere mortals have no right to do, like hubris, eh?"

Watney flashed admiration for Spiegelman—his certainty *wasn't* based on a thick ignorance of the existential doubt of their situation. There was hope in that, too. "How can you understand all that, Lennie," he said, "and still dig psychedelic design the way you do?"

"Because it's a load of crap, that's why," Spiegelman said. "Look, kid, we're artists—commercial artists at that. We design psychedelics, styles of reality; we don't tell anyone what to think. If people like the realities we design for them, they buy the drugs, and if they don't like our art, they don't. People aren't going to buy food that tastes lousy, music that makes their ears hurt, or drugs that put them in bummer realities. *Somebody* is going to design styles of consciousness for the human race; if not artists like us, then a lot of crummy politicians and power freaks."

"But what makes us any better than them? Why do we have any more right to play games with the consciousness of the human race than they do?"

The kid is really dense, Spiegelman thought. But then he smiled, remembering that he had been on the same stupid trip when he was Watney's age. "Because we're artists, and they're not," he said. "We're not out to control people. We get our kicks from carving something beautiful out of the void. All we want to do is enrich people's lives. We're creating new styles of consciousness that we think are improved realities, but we're not shoving them down people's throats. We're just laying out our wares for the public—right doesn't enter into it. We have a compulsion to practice our art. Right and wrong are arbitrary concepts that vary with the style of consciousness, so how on earth can you talk about the right and wrong of psychedelic design? The only way you can judge is by an aesthetic criterion—are we producing good art or bad?"

"Yeah, but doesn't *that* vary with the style of consciousness, too? Who can judge in an absolute sense whether your stuff is artistically pleasing or not?"

"Jesus Christ, Bill, *I* can judge, can't I?" Spiegelman said. "I know when a set of psychedelic specs is a successful work of art. It either pleases me or it doesn't."

It finally dawned on Watney that that was precisely what was eating at him. A psychedelic designer altered his own reality with a wide spectrum of drugs and then designed other psychedelics to alter other people's realities. Where was anyone's anchor?

"But don't you see, Lennie?" he said. "We don't know what the hell we're doing. We're taking the human race on an evolutionary trip, but we don't know where we're going. We're flying blind."

Spiegelman took a big drag on his joint. The kid was starting to get to him; he was whining too much. Watney didn't want anything out of line—just certainty! "You want me to tell you there's a way you can know when a design is right or wrong in some absolute evolutionary framework, right?" he said. "Well, I'm sorry, Bill, there's nothing but us and the void and whatever we carve out of it. We're our own creations; our realities are our own works of art. We're out here all alone."

Watney was living through one of his flashes of dread, and he saw that Spiegelman's words described its content exactly. "But that's exactly what's eating at me!" he said. "Where in hell is our basic reality?"

"There is no basic reality. I thought they taught that in kindergarten these days."

"But what about the basic state? What about the way our reality was before the art of psychedelic design? What about the consciousness style that evolved naturally over millions of years? Damn it, that was the basic reality, and we've lost it!"

"The hell it was!" Spiegelman said. "Our pre-psychedelic consciousness evolved on a mindless random basis. What makes that reality superior to any other? Just because it was first? We may be flying blind, but natural evolution was worse—it was an idiot process without an ounce of consciousness behind it."

"Goddamn it, you're right all the way down the line, Lennie!" Watney cried in anguish. "But why do you feel so good about it while I feel so rotten? I want to be able to feel the way you do, but I can't."

"Of course you can, Bill," Spiegelman said. He abstractedly remembered that he had felt like Watney years ago, but there was no existential reality behind it. What more could a man want than a random universe that was anything he could make of it and nothing else? Who wouldn't rather have a style of consciousness created by an artist than one that was the result of a lot of stupid evolutionary accidents?

He says it with such certainty, Watney thought. Christ, how I want him to be right! How I'd like to face the uncertainty of it all, the void, with the courage of Lennie Spiegelman! Spiegelman had been in the business for fifteen years; maybe he *had* finally figured it all out.

"I wish I could believe that," Watney said.

Spiegelman smiled, remembering what a solemn jerk he himself had been ten years ago. "Ten years ago, I felt just like you feel now," he said. "But I got my head together and now here I am, fat and happy and digging what I'm doing."

"How, Lennie, for Christ's sake, *how?*"

"Fifty mikes of methalin, forty milligrams of lebemil and twenty milligrams of peyotadrene daily," Spiegelman said. "It made a new man out of me, and it'll make a new man out of you."

"How do you feel, man?" Kip said, taking the

joint out of his mouth and peering intently into Jonesy's eyes. Jonesy looked really weird—pale, manic, maybe a little crazed. Kip was starting to feel glad that Jonesy hadn't talked him into taking the trip with him.

"Oh, wow," Jonesy croaked, "I feel strange, I feel *really* strange, and it doesn't feel so good. . . ."

The sun was high in the cloudless blue sky, a golden fountain of radiant energy filling Kip's being. The wood and bark of the tree against which they sat was an organic reality connecting the skin of his back to the bowels of the earth in an unbroken circuit of protoplasmic electricity. He was a flower of his planet, rooted deep in the rich soil, basking in the cosmic nectar of the sunshine.

But behind Jonesy's eyes was some kind of awful gray vortex. Jonesy looked really bad. Jonesy was definitely floating on the edges of a bummer.

"I don't feel good at all," Jonesy said. "Man, you know, the ground is covered with all kinds of hard dead things and the grass is filled with mindless insects and the sun is hot, man. I think I'm burning."

"Take it easy, don't freak. You're on a trip, that's all," Kip said from some asshole superior viewpoint. He just didn't understand, he didn't understand how heavy this trip was, what it felt like to have your head raw and naked out here. Like cut off from every energy flow in the universe—a construction of fragile matter, protoplasmic ooze is all, isolated in an energy vacuum existing in relationship to nothing but empty void and horrible mindless matter.

"You don't understand, Kip," he said. "This is reality, the way it *really* is, and, man, it's horrible, just a great big ugly machine made up of lots of other machines; you're a machine. I'm a machine—it's all mechanical clockwork. We're just lumps of dead matter run by machinery, kept alive by chemical and electric processes."

Golden sunlight soaked through Kip's skin and turned the core of his being into a miniature stellar phoenix. The wind, through random blades of grass, made love to the bare soles of his feet. What was all this machinery crap? What the hell was Jonesy gibbering about? Man, who would want to put himself in a bummer reality like that?

"You're just on a bummer, Jonesy," he said. "Take it easy. You're not seeing the universe the way it really is, as if that meant anything. Reality is all in your head. You're just freaking out behind nothing."

"That's it, that's *exactly* it! I'm freaking out behind nothing. Like zero. Like cipher. Like the void. Nothing is where we're *really* at."

How could he explain it—that reality was really just a lot of empty vacuum that went on to infinity in space and time? The perfect nothingness had minor contaminations of dead matter here and there. A little of this matter had fallen together through a complex series of random accidents to contaminate the universal deadness with trace elements of life, protoplasmic slime, biochemical clockwork. Some of this clockwork was complicated enough to generate thought, consciousness. And that was all there ever was or would ever be anywhere in space and time. Clockwork mechanisms rapidly running down in the cold black void. Everything that wasn't dead matter already would end up that way sooner or later.

"This is the way it really is," Jonesy said. "People used to live in this bummer all the time. It's the way it is, and nothing we can do can change it."

"I can change it," Kip said, taking his pillbox out of his pocket. "Just say the word. Let me know when you've had enough and I'll bring you out of it. Lebemil, peyotadrene, mescamil, you name it."

"You don't understand, man, it's *real.* That's the trip I'm on. I haven't taken anything at all for twelve hours, remember? It's the natural state, it's reality itself, and, man, it's awful. It's a horrible bummer. Christ, why did I have to talk myself into this? I don't want to see the universe this way. Who needs it?"

Kip was starting to get pissed off—Jonesy was becoming a real bring-down. Why did he have to pick a beautiful day like this to take his stupid nothing-trip?

"Then *take* something already," he said, offering Jonesy the pillbox.

Shakily, Jonesy scooped out a cap of peyotadrene and a fifteen-milligram tab of lebemil and wolfed them down dry. "How did people *live* before psychedelics?" he said. "How could they stand it?"

"Who knows?" Kip said, closing his eyes and staring straight at the sun, diffusing his consciousness into the universe of golden orange light encompassed by his eyelids. "Maybe they had some way of not thinking about it."

PHASE THREE

Those Who Survive

Introduction

So here we come full circle round to a kind of condensed version of the magical mystery tour of the ruins of America that I decided I wasn't going to write. "Sierra Maestra," "A Thing of Beauty," and "The Lost Continent" all in their various ways depict futures in which America as we know or dream it—the pre-eminent nation of the world, the economic colossus, the leading edge of the human future—has fallen.

Science fiction, after all, is the literature of multiple futures, and we cannot gaze clear-eyed at our possible futures without admitting of the possibility of tragedy. Indeed even the most optimistic literature—and optimistic science fiction in particular—that doesn't ground its optimism in the acknowledgement of the possibility of tragedy rings as hollow as a television commercial for condominiums in tomorrow. In the moral universe of space adventure, the good, the true, and the brave always prevail. In the real world, however, the good guys can fuck up. Or even learn that they weren't the good guys after all.

Yet though these stories admit of the possibility

of tragedy, I don't think you can call them nihilistic or devoid of hope. Because, to our constant surprise, life goes on after tragedy. There are always those who will survive. Perhaps with their possibilities diminished, perhaps with their noble aspirations destroyed, perhaps tortured by the memory of the lost golden age of their ancestors, perhaps exercising their courages in a smaller arena. But still surviving with hopes and dreams of their own.

The Empire of the Pharaohs is dust, the Golden Age of Greece is a memory and a setting of rotting ruins, and the Glory that was Rome is now just the capital of Italy. But Egyptians and Greeks and Romans survive to brood on the past and contemplate the possibilities of the post-Imperial future.

Introduction to Sierra Maestra

For years the title "Sierra Maestra" rattled around my brain, linked to an image that haunted me. An aging revolutionary from the 1960s sitting high up on a mountaintop contemplating his imminent return to the world below in long-delayed triumph, like Fidel Castro about to make his final push on Batista after all those years up in the Sierra Maestra.

An image and a title do not a story make, and they didn't become one till one day in New York, staying in Charles Platt's vacant apartment with Dona Sadock in the middle of severe transcoastal staggers and hassles that kept us moving from one base camp in the city to another and made us feel like refugees.

A news break comes on the radio to the effect that Cass Elliot has died. She choked to death on a sandwich in the middle of a come-back tour.

I knew Mama Cass after the Mamas and the Papas broke up about the time a lot of people's 1960s California fantasies were evaporating in the sere sun of the 1970s. Like many, she was making the transition from being a culture star to taking care of business, getting her career in show biz order. What you'd expect, with IRS hassles and manager numbers and bookings and the usual stuff that goes with just being an entertainer instead of a myth riding in limousines.

But she was proving herself a survivor, rescuing herself from the debris of the countercultural collapse. And then she chokes to death on a sandwich.

I had known Mama Cass and Dona had known others in her karmic position and had had a little taste of it herself, and somehow this story was becoming archetypal for a generation.

Survivors ourselves in a certain sense, we identified with survivors, but Dona retained a certain Byronic sentiment for the myth of the fallen mighty. She reflected dourly on the number of faded countercultural heroes who had died recently in less than a blaze of glory. Jim Morrison, heart attack. Jimmy Hendrix, choked on his own puke. Janis Joplin, ODed. Phil Ochs, suicide. Brian Jones, drowned in his own swimming pool.

Mama Cass suffocated by a sandwich.

Is this the way the world ends, not with a bang but with a banana peel?

I'm not sure why, and I'm not sure what all that has to do with it, but that image in my head immediately came down from its own Sierra Maestra and became this story. I sat right down and wrote it.

Sierra Maestra

Sitting here on my mountaintop watching their world crumble, I feel, at this advanced age, neither elation nor remorse, only the entropic force of history following its inexorable course. Did Fidel Castro feel thus watching the Batista regime sagging into decay from its own weight from his remote stronghold in the Sierra Maestra? I doubt it, for Fidel was a much younger man and those were much younger days, when revolution was a word we all took seriously and literally. But de Gaulle, waiting in haughty isolation as the Fourth Republic slowly collapsed toward his inevitability, and Juan Peron, watching Argentina flounder in the vacuum of his long, long exile, I think, would both have appreciated the irony of what I feel as this night slowly falls.

Far below me, Central Park is an oblong island of darkness in the pattern of lights that still covers most of Manhattan, a foreflash of what is soon to come. Even now, I can see the blackout rolling up the West Side from 34th Street to 59th, and the searchlight beam of a police helicopter probing the dark and empty streets for the creatures of night. It is all too easy to fantasize guerrilla armies marshaling in the secret shrubbery of permanently blacked-out Central Park, battalions of legendary muggers imbued with revolutionary consciousness at last.

But such fantasies are for the police, peering down from their helicopters into the shadows. In truth, the muggers are long since gone from the Park for lack of victims mad enough to brave the blackout, deprived of prey by the power of their own mystique. It is even possible to sympathize with them; in the early days of the blackout there must have been a time when they lurked behind their bushes fondling their saps forlornly like Indians hopelessly awaiting the return of the buffalo.

Automatic weapons fire crackles and sparkles for a few moments over the mid-40s and helicopters begin to converge. Watching the beams of their searchlights and listening to the ominous whunk-whunk of their rotors from my penthouse balcony, I feel a surge of adrenaline course through my old arteries, and it is easy to imagine this as the opening rounds of long-awaited Armageddon. But the firing is over before this fantasy can even take shape—just a routine patrol taking pot-shots at suspected looters in the free-fire zone.

I take a last private toke from my joint, fling the still burning butt over the parapet, and watch the glowing ember fall thirty stories into the darkness. "Roaches," we used to call them in the old days when pot was illegal and the smoking of it therefore a sacrament, a tiny act of revolution. In that sense, perhaps, the legalization of marijuana may be seen as the last act of true political cunning of which our enemies were capable, the final co-option. Now, of course, they are no longer capable of even being our enemies—we all become allies of necessity against entropy in the end. How foolish it seems, to have waged such a protracted and debilitating struggle over the THC molecule. But then, haven't men fought longer and deadlier wars over pure symbols like the cross, or even the interpretation of random snatches of scripture, while the true enemy of us all cackles up there in the vacuum?

The burning ember, like its half-forgotten symbolic import, disappears into the arms of darkness, and I finally turn and walk back into my chambers to confront those who have gathered at my bidding. How spiderlike that thought seems as I think it. How spiderlike we have become in our long secret sojourn in the Sierra Maestra of the soul. Have we finally made ourselves unfit to wield power by the very process we have put ourselves through in order to ensnare it? I smile ruefully and feel more at peace as I encompass the reality of this moral doubt, for only when those who wield power maintain a healthy fear of being wielded by it may justice yet live.

As I walk into the plushness of my huge living room and see those who have gathered there, I am suddenly struck by the unpleasant realization that we all have become old and we all have become rich. In the old days, we feared the one and at least professed to eschew the other. But we chose long ago not merely to survive but to attempt to prevail. To accumulate power without spending it is to accumulate money, and to acquire wisdom and patience means accumulating years. So here we are, heirs and paladins of what began decades ago as a "youthful rebellion" about to come into our own as graybeards and elder statesmen. We believed in those days that no one our present age was to be trusted; hopefully this lesson has been deepened and enriched by irony, rather than unlearned. If we can be rulers who do not trust ourselves, America may yet be salvaged.

"Heavy thoughts?" Sandra says. Once, in Berkeley, in the flush of the '60s, we were lovers, and once again, longer and deeper, in the '80s. In the wrinkled parchment of her face, I can see the young girl inside her, and the full blossom of her beauty in middle years. I have loved them both and some part of me loves them still.

"We've become the people we warned ourselves about," I say, blunting the edge with slyness. "Old fogies conspiring to rule the world from a penthouse. Senators, Congresspeople, capitalists and media barons."

She laughs her bright changeless laugh as we walk across the room to the square of sofas where the others are waiting, and it drives the shadows from my mind. Long ago, she was with me when we so solemnly dedicated our lives to changing the world by next week, and later we were together once more when the Compact was made and we all went our long-term temporary ways to infiltrate by osmosis. Always that laughter made me sing inside, and now I suddenly decide that when the inevitable occurs, Sandra will be with me again, as my Vice-President. Thus do we decide high policy, and why not, it is part of what makes us who we are. We shall be a government not of laws but of living, feeling men and women, a government not of structures but of souls. Still, I cannot help but feel the shade of Juan Peron smirking knowingly over my shoulder in this moment.

As Sandra and I seat ourselves together, I feel the eyes of the others following my movements with a new and disquieting expectancy, as if I am already a figure in some historical diorama, and it seems as if I can already feel the leaden mantle of state falling upon me. Fear comes over me, a ghastly sort of loneliness, a pall of isolation descending. And I resolve that as President I will walk the streets and eat in the restaurants like an ordinary citizen. Better to risk assassins' bullets than this terrifying and certain distancing, this death-in-life. It will be called bravado. Only I will know that it is fear.

"*Mr. President,*" Bart Lorenzi says with gentle sarcasm, and the rest smile. This is as close to a vote as we are prone to come. We have known each other, our destinies and our trajectories, for so long that nothing beyond this is necessary. We are like a family, each with his role, each with his place.

"Aren't you being a bit premature?" I say archly, and at this we all laugh together, for the pattern that has brought us to this moment is decades old, built slowly and carefully like a stone cathedral, no hot-blooded coup d'etat.

As medieval architects drew up plans for cathedrals whose completion they would never live to see, so did we draw up the Compact and assign ourselves our eventual positions in the completed structure according to our inclinations and oportunities. Bart Lorenzi to become our banking baron, financier of industries and minor governments, intimate of the Gnomes of Zurich.

Eric Winshell to move slowly up in the hierarchy of the State Department into his present position. Warren Hinckly to build Ecomotors General. Ted Davies to ascend to the Joint Chiefs of Staff. Sandra, Lillian Margulies, Julian Clay, Fred Banyan, Roger Pulaski to cautiously, quietly, and carefully move upward through the conventional political processes until now we have a Chairman of the House Ways and Means Committee, Senators and Representatives of high seniority and Sandra as Speaker of the House.

All of us accumulating subordinates and allies personally loyal to us on our way up, secreting them into the interstices of government, finance, industry, and the military, furthering their careers discreetly as best we could, until now the score of people in this room represent the tip of an enormous iceberg. Not a conspiracy, but an infinitely subtle web of personal loyalties, shared consciousness, common goals, and yes, love.

And I too was chosen for my distant destiny long decades ago. In a sense, I have been running unsuccessfully for the Presidency for a quarter of a century—first almost as a national joke; then as a visionary from my secure Senate seat, accumulating weight and solidity; now, finally, as a remote elder statesman whose old prophecies have long since come to pass, whose far-out and impractical proposals are now seen by the millions as the right roads not taken in the easy clarity of failure's hindsight.

No, there is nothing like prematurity here.

Roger swirls his glass of bourbon, cubes of ice tinkling against the glass, talisman of long years cultivating friendships with southern Senators.

"Just got the word from the White House. The Vice-President's letter of resignation has arrived. Your appointment to succeed him will be announced tomorrow morning."

I nod. Even this endgame strategy has been planned for decades. The Agnew resignation and the Nixon resignation pointed the way back in the '70s. The Vice-President resigns or is removed, the choice of a new Vice-President is forced upon the President, he is confirmed by Congress, then the President resigns. Technically, all that is required is Congressional acquiescence to the choice of an incumbent President and the necessary leverage on two men. And Constitutionality is scrupulously maintained. In the beginning this did not seem important to us, but now the decades have taught us the wisdom of remaining within the Constitutional framework. Once the Constitution is successfully breached, the entire document is destroyed and we become a nation of tooth and claw. I shall not play Caesar to our republic.

"Do you expect any trouble in the Senate?" Sandra asks.

Roger shakes his head. "We've had the votes for a long time. Sanderman may try a filibuster, but I think we have the votes for a quick cloture too."

"Sanderman won't try it," Bart says authoritatively. "I've bought up his notes on that Coastal Island development and he's been made to understand his position."

"It's all in place," Julian says.

The words are like the final stone placed at the top of the last cathedral arch. The coup—and I might as well admit to myself that it *is* a coup d'etat, albeit a Constitutional coup—is but the mechanism for bringing about the technical transfer of power, for midwiving the inevitability we have engineered. For catching the ripe fruit dropping from the tree of history, if one prefers a more dialectical viewpoint.

I turn to Katherine Broxon, publisher of *Time* since Bart acquired it for us seven years ago, and cock an inquisitive eyebrow. "We're printing already. The cover story on the President hinting at his failing health. He'll be able to step aside gracefully."

"No problems with recognition," Eric says. "Even the Japanese will be relieved to have you in office. At least for the time being."

"The polls?"

"It'll be one big sigh of national relief," Katherine says. "The people don't want to wait till the next election. The mood is that they've waited too long already."

I relax against the plush piling of the couch. In addition to a Constitutional coup, we are going to have a democratically approved coup like the return of de Gaulle in '58 or that of Peron in '74. The people are bone-weary of economic depression, fading electrical power, unemployment, permanent inflation, protein starvation, and a government that can only throw up its hands and admit its helplessness. Like a hard granite boulder buried under geological layers of soft sandstone, we bided our time, content to merely endure until the inevitable forces of erosion ate away the strata around us. Until now we stand alone on the desolate plain, the only rock to cleave to. Until even our former enemies turn to us in despair.

I look slowly around the room, each face in turn, confronting each pair of eyes like tunnels through time, seeing beyond the gray hair, the tapestries of wrinkles, the succession of personas we have assumed down the decades, to the changeless essences within. Or changeless they seem from this strange perspective crosswise in time. Are we not the same beings whose eyes met in this same soul-to-soul contact so many years ago when the communal organism that we have become was given birth? In the long-gone terminology of the '60s, have we not remained forever young?

But why do I feel this blossoming of dread, this void unfolding the cold petals of its flower within me? Why do their eyes seem to recede down long stone corridors of perspective, why does my own living room seem like an immense cavern of millennial gloom rimed with the mineral accretions of ages?

I rise from the couch and I can feel the creakiness of my knees, the softness of my internal organs, and my head is like some great hollow globe tottering atop a fleshy structure grown too frail to support it.

"I think I'd like to be alone for a bit," I say, and the simple sentence sounds ridiculously theatrical as my mouth moves around the words; my movements seem exaggeratedly slow and fluid, pregnant with meaning, as I walk across the soft carpet toward the balcony. Images out of films and history books pile up in my mind as I walk—Mussolini stepping out on his balcony to bask in the cheering of the masses. Imperial Caesars accepting homage. John Kennedy walking down a lonely beach with head bowed, white smoke rising over the Vatican and a sepulchral voice intoning, "*Habemus Papum.*"

But when I emerge onto my balcony, there is no sudden ovation, no waiting crowd; nothing greets me but the night. The blackout has spread itself over Manhattan now, only rectilinear islands of light remain in a sparse checkerboard pattern, and to the south the giant buildings of midtown are a cruel and jagged cordillera of dark mountains against a sky in which faint stars shine like the dying lights of America's faded glory far below. Police helicopters whunk-whunk over the somnolent city like carrion flies buzzing around a bonepile, their white searchlight beams moving like ghostly fingers over the empty streets. It is a scene, a moment, of utter loneliness, unfit for the eye of man.

I light another joint, take a tiny puff, and let it glow between my fingers as a candle against the darkness. I force myself to think of the future, of the weeks and months to come, of the "steps that must be taken," as the news magazines will phrase it. Bart will announce the forgiveness of the government notes he has bought up by stealth, nearly a quarter of the National Debt, and that will give the dollar a stability it has not had in decades. But banks will fall like Southeast Asian dominoes and the financial community will scream in rage. The hundred percent tax on profits in excess of ten percent will move the GNP toward full employment stasis, but industrialists and stockholders will fly into a fury as the stock market plummets, perhaps into oblivion. The ban on even private electric cars will hit the ordinary citizen in his pocketbook and his psyche, even though their largest manufacturer, Ecomotors General, will patriotically urge support of the move in the national interest. The food export quotas will make America an object of loathing in Asia and Africa. It is going to get so much darker before the dawn.

I am going to be a hated man.

This first cold realization squeezes my heart like a fist. No souls will sing at the sound of my name, no voices will cheer my motorcade. The transformation will be a decade in the making; I have always known it, but now I feel it in the hollow places of my brittle bones. I will not see the lights come on again, I will not taste the freshened air. I will not see the food factories churning out their endless bounty. I will never bask in the love of the people. I will be cursed and reviled and assassins will mutter my name as they oil their guns in secret cellars. One day a bullet will burst in my brain, *sic semper tyrannis.*

I look out over the spectral city and doubt creeps into my soul. What if we were wrong? What if we have let too much history slip by as we waited in our Sierra Maestra for the day of vindication to arrive? What if it is too late; perhaps entropy has already won its final victory while we husbanded and conserved our lives and substances to no avail. Perhaps we should have risked all in hot-blooded revolution and died in fire rather than ice. We chose and we became that which we had chosen. Now as we come into our own, we have no choices left. I am one with the inevitability of history and I will never know whether for good or ill.

Nor will I be granted even the luxury of sharing my doubts, for now I must become a man of iron, a monument of stone, an icon of the certainty I can no longer feel. A current of wind whistles around my parapet. It is so cold and lonely up here on the mountaintop.

"Why is this night different from all other nights?" Sandra has come out onto the balcony beside me. I do not look at her. I do not have to, I can feel her presence with me; with me yet apart, for now even she will forever be distanced from me by the geometries of state. This is what we must share in this final phase, this is the dowry of our last affair.

I force a laugh, and an advertising jingle from the long-gone '60s. "We've come a long way, baby, to get where we're going today."

"A little afraid?" she says softly.

I nod. "And lonely." I suck on the joint and hand it to her. Let this cup pass from me, I think, knowing all too well that it will not. "This is as good a time as any to tell you," I say, grateful to move on to matters of state, already hiding myself in the machineries of power. "You're going to be my Vice-President." I allow her no choice, no pro forma gesture of refusal, as none has been allowed to me.

We turn to each other. She merely nods. There is no surprise, no false disclaimers, thank God. Our eyes meet over a distance that suddenly has widened. We take each other's hands and squeeze old warm flesh.

"It's getting chilly out here," she says, turning to face the lights of the living room where the others wait with questions of cabinet posts and policy with the eagerness of history waiting to be born.

I nod. "We've got to watch our health now," I say. "We're not as young as we used to be."

Hand in hand, our old bones creaking, we begin the march down from the Sierra Maestra, we descend from our mountain fastness to parade into the cities below.

Introduction to A Thing of Beauty

A funny thing happened while I was living in London.

In the depths of the bare-ass Arizona desert, a land developer was trying to move something called Lake Havasu City, a housing development in the grim and featureless wastes. The only geographic feature of notice at Lake Havasu City was the man-made lake constructed for it to be named after.

The British announce that they're demolishing London Bridge to build a new modern span across the Thames at the site and that London Bridge was therefore for sale to the highest bidder.

Well now, our good buddy in Arizona figures that London Bridge would look mighty impressive spanning Lake Havasu, that massive monumental stone work, those twin fortress-like towers that make it look like the drawbridge of a giant's castle, would give Lake Havasu an instant patina of English class and move those subdivi-

sions. Worth $5 million as the purchase of instant karma, right?

Which is what the turkey paid for his build-a-London-Bridge kit. Sight unseen, except for images on millions of picture postcards. The British crated the stones, labeled them like a paint-by-the-numbers set, cashed the check, and shipped the lot to Arizona, laughing their asses off all the while.

Why, you ask, were our British cousins laughing?

The land developer found out when he assembled what he had bought at Lake Havasu City.

London Bridge, right, certified genuine? As in "London Bridge is falling down?" Two great stone battlements outlined in medieval majesty against the desert sky? Class stuff, like Big Ben and the Tower of London, right?

Wrong.

That's not London Bridge, dummy!

That's Tower Bridge.

London Bridge is a flat featureless stone pontoon bridge, the medieval equivalent of a freeway span.

And that is what spans glorious Lake Havasu, shimmering in the heat waves as the spiritual ensign of fair Lake Havasu City.

A Thing of Beauty

"There's a gentleman by the name of Mr. Shiburo Ito to see you," my intercom said. "He is interested in the purchase of an historic artifact of some significance."

While I waited for him to enter my private office, I had computcentral display his specs on the screen discreetly built into the back of my desk. My Mr. Ito was none other than Ito of Ito Freight Boosters of Osaka; there was no need to purchase a readout from Dun & Bradstreet's private banks. If Shiburo Ito of Ito Boosters wrote a check for anything short of the national debt, it could be relied upon not to bounce.

The slight balding man who glided into my office wore a black silk kimono with a richly brocaded obi, Mendocino needlepoint by the look of it. No doubt, back in the miasmic smog of Osaka he bonged the peons with the latest skins from Saville Row. Everything about him was *just so;* he purchased confidently on that razor-edge between class and ostentation that only the Japanese can handle with such grace, and then only when they have millions of hard yen to back them up. Mr. Ito would be no sucker. He would want whatever he wanted for precise reasons all his own, and he would not be budgable from the center of his desires. The typical heavyweight Japanese businessman, a prime example of the breed that's pushed us out of the center of the international arena.

Mr. Ito bowed almost imperceptibly as he handed me his card. I countered by merely bobbing my head in his direction and remaining seated. These face and posture games may seem ridiculous, but you can't do business with the Japanese without playing them.

As he took a seat before me, Ito drew a black cylinder from the sleeve of his kimono and ceremoniously placed it on the desk before me.

"I have been given to understand that you are a connoisseur of Fillmore posters of the early-to-mid-1960s period, Mr. Harris," he said. "The repute of your collection has penetrated even to the environs of Osaka and Kyoto, where I make my habitation. Please permit me to make this minor addition. The thought that a contribution of mine may repose in such illustrious surroundings will afford me much pleasure and place me forever in your debt."

My hands trembled as I unwrapped the poster. With his financial resources, Ito's polite little gift could be almost anything but disappointing. My daddy loved to brag about the old expense-account days when American businessmen ran things, but you had to admit that the fringe benefits of business Japanese-style had plenty to recommend them.

But when I got the gift open, it took a real effort not to lose points by whistling out loud. For what I was holding was nothing less than a mint example of the very first Grateful Dead poster in subtle black and gray, a super-rare item, not available for any amount of sheer purchasing power. I dared not inquire as to how Mr. Ito had acquired it. We simply shared a long, silent moment contemplating the poster, its beauty and historicity transcending whatever questionable events might have transpired to bring us together in its presence.

How could I not like Mr. Ito now? Who can say that the Japanese occupy their present international position by economic might alone?

"I hope I may be afforded the opportunity to please your sensibilities as you have pleased mine, Mr. Ito," I finally said. That was the way to phrase it; you didn't thank them for a gift like this, and you brought them around to business as obliquely as possible.

Ito suddenly became obviously embarrassed, even furtive. "Forgive me my boldness, Mr. Harris, but I have hopes that you may be able to assist me in resolving a domestic matter of some delicacy."

"A domestic matter?"

"Just so. I realize that this is an embarrassing intrusion, but you are obviously a man of refinement and infinite discretion, so if you will forgive my forwardness . . ."

His composure seemed to totally evaporate, as if he was going to ask me to pimp for some disgusting perversion he had. I had the feeling that the power had suddenly taken a quantum jump in my direction, that a large financial opportunity was about to present itself.

"Please feel free, Mr. Ito . . ."

Ito smiled nervously. "My wife comes from a

family of extreme artistic attainment," he said. "In fact, both her parents have attained the exalted status of National Cultural Treasures, a distinction of which they never tire of reminding me. While I have achieved a large measure of financial success in the freight booster enterprise, they regard me as *nikulturi*, a mere merchant, severely lacking in aesthetic refinement as compared to their own illustrious selves. You understand the situation, Mr. Harris?"

I nodded as sympathetically as I could. These Japs certainly have a genius for making life difficult for themselves! Here was a major Japanese industrialist shrinking into low posture at the very thought of his sponging in-laws, who he could probably buy and sell out of petty cash. At the same time, he was obviously out to cream the sons-of-bitches in some crazy way that would only make sense to a Japanese. Seems to me the Japanese are better at running the world than they are at running their lives.

"Mr. Harris, I wish to acquire a major American artifact for the gardens of my Kyoto estate. Frankly, it must be of sufficient magnitude so as to remind the parents of my wife of my success in the material realm every time they should chance to gaze upon it, and I shall display it in a manner which will assure that they gaze upon it often. But, of course, it must be of sufficient beauty and historicity so as to prove to them that my taste is no less elevated than their own. Thus shall I gain respect in their eyes and reestablish tranquility in my household. I have been given to understand that you are a valued councilor in such matters, and I am eager to inspect whatever such objects you may deem appropriate."

So that was it! He wanted to buy something big enough to bong the minds of his artsy-fartsy relatives, but he really didn't trust his own taste; he wanted me to show him something he would want to see. And he was swimming like a goldfish in a sea of yen! I could hardly believe my good luck. How much could I take him for?

"Ah . . . what size artifact did you have in mind, Mr. Ito?" I asked as casually as I could.

"I wish to acquire a major piece of American monumental architecture so that I may convert the gardens of my estate into a shrine to its beauty and historicity. Therefore, a piece of classical proportions is required. Of course, it must be worthy of enshrinement; otherwise, an embarrassing loss of esteem will surely ensue."

"Of course."

This was not going to be just another Howard Johnson or gas-station sale; even something like an old Hilton or the Cooperstown Baseball Hall of Fame I unloaded last year was thinking too small. In his own way, Ito was telling me that price was no object—the sky was the limit. This was the dream of a lifetime! A sucker with a bottomless bank account placing himself trustingly in my tender hands!

"Should it please you, Mr. Ito," I said, "we can inspect several possibilities here in New York immediately. My jumper is on the roof."

"Most gracious of you to interrupt your most busy schedule on my behalf, Mr. Harris. I would be delighted."

I lifted the jumper off the roof, floated her to a thousand feet, then took a Mach one point five jump south over the decayed concrete jungles at the tip of Manhattan. The curve brought us back to float about a mile north of Bedloe's Island. I took her down to three hundred and brought her in toward the Statue of Liberty at a slow drift, losing altitude imperceptibly as we crept up on the Headless Lady, so that by the time we were just offshore we were right down on the deck. It was a nice touch to make the goods look more impressive—manipulating the perspectives so that the huge, green, headless statue, with its patina of firebomb soot, seemed to rise up out of the bay like a ruined colossus as we floated toward it.

Mr. Ito betrayed no sign of emotion. He stared straight ahead out of the bubble without so much as a word or a flicker of gesture.

"As you are no doubt aware, this is the famous Statue of Liberty," I said. "Like most such artifacts, it is available to any buyer who will display it with proper dignity. Of course, I would have no trouble convincing the Bureau of National Antiquities that your intentions are exemplary in this regard."

I set the autopilot to circle the island at fifty yards offshore so that Ito could get a fully rounded view and see how well the statue would look from any angle, how eminently suitable it was for enshrinement. But he still sat there with less expression on his face than the average C-grade servitor.

"You can see that nothing has been touched since the insurrectionists blew the statue's head off," I said, trying to drum up his interest with a pitch. "Thus the statue has picked up yet another level of historical significance to enhance its already formidable venerability. Originally a gift from France, it has historical significance as an emblem of kinship between the American and French revolutions. Situated as it is in the mouth of New York Harbor, it became a symbol of America itself to generations of immigrants. And the damage the insurrectionists did only serves as a reminder of how lucky we were to come through that mess as lightly as we did. Also, it adds a certain melancholy atmosphere, don't you think? Emotion, intrinsic beauty, and historicity combined in one elegant piece of monumental statuary. And the asking price is a good deal less than you might suppose."

Mr. Ito seemed embarrassed when he finally spoke. "I trust you will forgive my saying so, Mr. Harris, since the emotion is engendered by the highest regard for the noble past of your great nation, but I find this particular artifact somewhat depressing."

"How so, Mr. Ito?"

The jumper completed a circle of the Statue of Liberty and began another as Mr. Ito lowered his eyes and stared at the oily waters of the bay as he answered.

"The symbolism of this broken statue is quite saddening, representing as it does a decline from your nation's past greatness. For me to enshrine such an artifact in Kyoto would be an ignoble act, an insult to the memory of your nation's greatness. It would be a statement of overweening pride."

Can you beat that? *He* was offended because he felt that displaying the statue in Japan would be insulting the United States, and, therefore, I was implying he was *nikulturi* by offering it to him. All that the damned thing was to any American was one more piece of old junk left over from the glory days that the Japanese, who were nuts for such rubbish, might be persuaded to pay through the nose for the dubious privilege of carting away. These Japs could drive you crazy—who else could you offend by suggesting they do something that they thought would offend you, but you thought was just fine in the first place?

"I hope I haven't offended you, Mr. Ito," I blurted out. I could have bitten my tongue off the moment I said it, because it was exactly the wrong thing to say. I *had* offended him, and it was only further offense to put him in a position where politeness demanded that he deny it.

"I'm sure that could not have been further from your intention, Mr. Harris," Ito said with convincing sincerity, "A pang of sadness at the perishability of greatness, nothing more. In fact, as such, the experience might be said to be healthful to the soul. But making such an artifact a permanent part of one's surroundings would be more than I could bear."

Was this his true feeling, or just smooth Japanese politeness? Who could tell what these people really felt? Sometimes I think they don't even know what they feel themselves. But, at any rate, I had to show him something that would change his mood, and fast. Hmmmm. . . .

"Tell me, Mr. Ito, are you fond of baseball?"

His eyes lit up like satellite beacons and the heavy mood evaporated in the warm, almost childish, glow of his sudden smile. "Ah, yes!" he said. "I retain a box at Osaka Stadium, though I must confess I secretly retain a partiality for the Giants. How strange it is that this profound game has so declined in the country of its origin."

"Perhaps. But that very fact has placed something on the market which I'm sure you'll find most congenial. Shall we go?"

"By all means," Mr. Ito said. "I find our present environs somewhat overbearing."

I floated the jumper to five hundred feet and programmed a Mach two point five jump curve to the north that quickly put the great hunk of moldering, dirty copper far behind. It's amazing how much sickening emotion the Japanese are able to attach to almost any piece of old junk. *Our* old junk at that, as if Japan didn't have enough useless old clutter of its own. But I certainly shouldn't complain about it; it makes me a pretty good living. Everyone knows the old saying about a fool and his money.

* * *

The jumper's trajectory put us at float over the confluence of the Harlem and East rivers at a thousand feet. Without dropping any lower, I whipped the jumper northeast over the Bronx at three hundred miles per hour. This area had been covered by tenements before the insurrection, and had been thoroughly razed by firebombs, high explosives, and napalm. No one had ever found an economic reason for clearing away the miles of rubble, and now the scarred earth and ruined buildings were covered with tall grass, poison sumac, tangled scrub growth, and scattered thickets of trees which might merge to form a forest in another generation or two. Because of the crazy, jagged, overgrown topography, this land was utterly useless, and no one lived here except some pathetic remnants of old hippie tribes that kept to themselves and weren't worth hunting down. Their occasional huts and patchwork tents were the only signs of human habitation in the area. This was *really* depressing territory and I wanted to get Mr. Ito over it high and fast.

Fortunately, we didn't have far to go, and, in a couple of minutes, I had the jumper floating at five hundred feet over our objective, the only really intact structure in the area. Mr. Ito's stone face lit up with such boyish pleasure that I knew I had it made; I had figured right when I figured he couldn't resist something like this.

"So!" he cried in delight. "Yankee Stadium!"

The ancient ballpark had come through the insurrection with nothing worse than some atmospheric blackening and cratering of its concrete exterior walls. Everything around it had been pretty well demolished except for a short section of old elevated subway line which still stood beside it, a soft, rusty-red skeleton covered with vines and moss. The surrounding ruins were thoroughly overgrown, huge piles of rubble, truncated buildings, rusted-out tanks, forming tangled manmade jungled foothills around the high point of the stadium, which itself had creepers and vines growing all over it, partially blending it into the wild, overgrown landscape.

The Burea of National Antiquities had circled the stadium with a high, electrified, barbed-wire fence to keep out the hippies who roamed the badlands. A lone guard armed with a Japanese-made slicer patrolled the fence in endless circles at fifteen feet on a one-man skimmer. I brought the jumper down to fifty feet and orbited the stadium